Dear QPB Reader:

I am not the toughest Indian in the world, though I did indeed write this book of short stories titled *The Toughest Indian in the World*. Truthfully speaking, I'm somewhere in the fiftieth percentile when it comes to indigenous toughness, but know plenty of tough and real Indians and tried to create a series of tough and fictional Indians in these stories.

At their most basic level, these are love stories, though love, of course, is far from basic. These pages contain good and bad love, straight and gay love, inter- and intra-racial love, and a little sex, too. However, I'm the kind of guy who usually writes, "They went to bed," and then immediately cuts to a paragraph describing either the pleasurable afterglow or the nagging guilt, or both.

At their most original level, these are the tales of white-collar Indians, of Indian lawyers, teachers, and poets. After all, when did you last read a story about a high school English teacher who happens to be Native American? When did you last come across a story that shoved Shakespeare and Sitting Bull into the same sentence? I've never read such stories, so I decided to write a few of them. That's one of the great joys of being a writer: you can write about anything you want, though, of course, you have no control over the reaction to what you write. Of course, awaiting the unpredictable response is also one of the great joys of being a writer.

So, yes, I joyfully and fearfully await your reaction to my book. Please enjoy any magic contained herein and I beg you to forgive any mistakes.

Hey, to paraphrase the Rolling Stones, we Indians (and Indian writers) are interested in love and hope and sex and dreams, just like all of you tough (and not-so-tough) readers out there in the huge old world.

Best,

Sherman Alexie

Sherman Alexie

THE TOUGHEST
INDIAN
IN THE WORLD

▲▲▲▲▲▲▲▲▲▲▲▲▲▲▲▲▲▲▲▲▲▲▲▲▲▲▲▲▲▲▲▲▲▲▲▲▲▲

SHERMAN ALEXIE

ATLANTIC MONTHLY PRESS

NEW YORK

Copyright © 2000 by Sherman Alexie

The story "The Toughest Indian in the World" originally appeared, in slightly different form, in *The New Yorker*.

Published simultaneously in Canada
Printed in the United States of America

Library of Congress Cataloging-in-Publication Data
Alexie, Sherman, 1966–
    The toughest Indian in the world : stories / by Sherman Alexie.
      p. cm.
    Contents: Assimilation—The toughest Indian in the world—Class—South by southwest—The sin eaters—Indian country—Saint Junior—Dear John Wayne—One good man.
    ISBN 0-87113-801-8
    ISBN 0-87113-812-3 (Limited Edition)
    1. United States—Social life and customs—20th century—Fiction. 2. West (U.S.)—Social life and customs—Fiction. 3. Indians of North America—Fiction. I. Title.
PS3551.L35774 T68 2000
813'.54—dc21   99-086360

DESIGN BY LAURA HAMMOND HOUGH

Atlantic Monthly Press
841 Broadway
New York, NY 10003

00 01 02 03   10 9 8 7 6 5 4

FOR DIANE AND JOSEPH,

Indios de Norte Americanos

CONTENTS

▲▲▲▲▲▲▲▲▲▲▲▲▲▲▲▲▲▲▲▲▲▲▲▲▲▲▲▲▲▲▲▲▲▲▲▲▲▲▲

THE TOUGHEST INDIAN IN THE WORLD

ASSIMILATION

▲▲▲

Regarding love, marriage, and sex, both Shakespeare and Sitting Bull knew the only truth: treaties get broken. Therefore, Mary Lynn wanted to have sex with any man other than her husband. For the first time in her life, she wanted to go to bed with an Indian man only because he was Indian. She was a Coeur d'Alene Indian married to a white man; she was a wife who wanted to have sex with an indigenous stranger. She didn't care about the stranger's job or his hobbies, or whether he was due for a Cost of Living raise, or owned ten thousand miles of model railroad track. She didn't care if he was handsome or ugly, mostly because she wasn't sure exactly what those terms meant anymore and how much relevance they truly had when it came to choosing sexual partners. Oh, she'd married a very handsome man, there was no doubt about that, and she was still attracted to her husband, to his long, graceful fingers, to his arrogance and utter lack of fear in social situations—he'd say anything to anybody—but lately, she'd been forced to concentrate too hard when making love to him. If she didn't focus completely on him, on the smallest details of his body, then she would drift away from the bed and float around the room like a bored angel. Of course, all this made her feel like a failure, especially since it seemed

that her husband had yet to notice her growing disinterest. She wanted
to be a good lover, wife, and partner, but she'd obviously developed
some form of sexual dyslexia or had picked up a mutant, contagious,
and erotic strain of Attention Deficit Disorder. She felt baffled by the
complications of sex. She haunted the aisles of bookstores and desperately paged through every book in the self-help section and studied every diagram and chart in the human sensuality encyclopedias.
She wanted answers. She wanted to feel it again, whatever *it* was.

A few summers ago, during Crow Fair, Mary Lynn had been standing in a Montana supermarket, in the produce aisle, when a homely
white woman, her spiky blond hair still wet from a trailer-house
shower, walked by in a white T-shirt and blue jeans, and though Mary
Lynn was straight—having politely declined all three lesbian over-
tures thrown at her in her life—she'd felt a warm breeze pass through
her DNA in that ugly woman's wake, and had briefly wanted to knock
her to the linoleum and do beautiful things to her. Mary Lynn had
never before felt such lust—in Montana, of all places, for a white
woman who was functionally illiterate and underemployed!—and had
not since felt that sensually about any other woman or man.

Who could explain such things, these vagaries of love? There were
many people who would blame Mary Lynn's unhappiness, her dissat-
isfaction, on her ethnicity. God, she thought, how simple and earnest
was that particular bit of psychotherapy! Yes, she was most certainly a
Coeur d'Alene—she'd grown up on the rez, had been very happy during her time there, and had left without serious regrets or full-time
enemies—but that wasn't the only way to define her. She wished that
she could be called Coeur d'Alene as a description, rather than as an
excuse, reasons, prescription, placebo, prediction, or diminutive. She
only wanted to be understood as eccentric and complicated!

Her most cherished eccentricity: when she was feeling her most
lonely, she'd put one of the Big Mom Singers's powwow CDs on the

stereo (*I'm not afraid of death, hey, ya, hey, death is my cousin, hey, ya, ha, ha*) and read from Emily Dickinson's poetry (*Because I could not stop for Death— / He kindly stopped for me—*).

Her most important complication: she was a woman in a turbulent marriage that was threatening to go bad, or had gone bad and might get worse.

Yes, she was a Coeur d'Alene woman, passionately and dispassionately, who wanted to cheat on her white husband because he was white. She wanted to find an anonymous lover, an Indian man who would fade away into the crowd when she was done with him, a man whose face could appear on the back of her milk carton. She didn't care if he was the kind of man who knew the punch lines to everybody's dirty jokes, or if he was the kind of man who read Zane Grey before he went to sleep, or if he was both of those men simultaneously. She simply wanted to find the darkest Indian in Seattle—the man with the greatest amount of melanin—and get naked with him in a cheap motel room. Therefore, she walked up to a flabby Lummi Indian man in a coffee shop and asked him to make love to her.

"Now," she said. "Before I change my mind."

He hesitated for a brief moment, wondering why he was the chosen one, and then took her by the hand. He decided to believe he was a handsome man.

"Don't you want to know my name?" he asked before she put her hand over his mouth.

"Don't talk to me," she said. "Don't say one word. Just take me to the closest motel and fuck me."

The obscenity bothered her. It felt staged, forced, as if she were an actress in a three-in-the-morning cable-television movie. But she was acting, wasn't she? She was not an adulteress, was she?

Why exactly did she want to have sex with an Indian stranger? She told herself it was because of pessimism, existentialism, even nihilism, but those reasons—*those words*—were a function of her vocabulary and not of her motivations. If forced to admit the truth, or some version of the truth, she'd testify she was about to go to bed with an Indian stranger because she wanted to know how it would feel. After all, she'd slept with a white stranger in her life, so why not include a Native American? Why not practice a carnal form of affirmative action? By God, her infidelity was a political act! Rebellion, resistance, revolution!

In the motel room, Mary Lynn made the Indian take off his clothes first. Thirty pounds overweight, with purple scars crisscrossing his pale chest and belly, he trembled as he undressed. He wore a wedding ring on his right hand. She knew that some Europeans wore their wedding bands on the right hand—so maybe this Indian was married to a French woman—but Mary Lynn also knew that some divorced Americans wore rings on their right hands as symbols of pain, of mourning. Mary Lynn didn't care if he was married or not, or whether he shared custody of the sons and daughters, or whether he had any children at all. She was grateful that he was plain and desperate and lonely.

Mary Lynn stepped close to him, took his hand, and slid his thumb into her mouth. She sucked on it and felt ridiculous. His skin was salty and oily, the taste of a working man. She closed her eyes and thought about her husband, a professional who had his shirts laundered. In one hour, he was going to meet her at a new downtown restaurant.

She walked a slow, tight circle around the Indian. She stood behind him, reached around his thick waist, and held his erect penis. He moaned and she decided that she hated him. She decided to hate all men. Hate, hate, hate, she thought, and then let her hate go.

She was lovely and intelligent, and had grown up with Indian women who were more lovely and more intelligent, but who also had far less ambition and mendacity. She'd once read in a book, perhaps by Primo Levi or Elie Wiesel, that the survivors of the Nazi death camps were the Jews who lied, cheated, murdered, stole, and subverted. You must remember, said Levi or Wiesel, that the best of us did not survive the camps. Mary Lynn felt the same way about the reservation. Before she'd turned ten, she'd attended the funerals of seventeen good women—the best of the Coeur d'Alenes—and had read about the deaths of eighteen more good women since she'd left the rez. But what about the Coeur d'Alene men—those liars, cheats, and thieves—who'd survived, even thrived? Mary Lynn wanted nothing to do with them, then or now. As a teenager, she'd dated only white boys. As an adult, she'd only dated white men. God, she hated to admit it, but white men—her teachers, coaches, bosses, and lovers—had always been more dependable than the Indian men in her life. White men had rarely disappointed her, but they'd never surprised her either. White men were neutral, she thought, just like Belgium! And when has Belgium ever been sexy? When has Belgium caused a grown woman to shake with fear and guilt? She didn't want to feel Belgian; she wanted to feel dangerous.

In the cheap motel room, Mary Lynn breathed deeply. The Indian smelled of old sweat and a shirt worn twice before washing. She ran her finger along the ugly scars on his belly and chest. She wanted to know the scars' creation story—she hoped this Indian man was a warrior with a history of knife fighting—but she feared he was only carrying the transplanted heart and lungs of another man. She pushed him onto the bed, onto the scratchy comforter. She'd once read that scientists had examined a hotel-room comforter and discovered four hundred and thirty-two different samples of sperm. God, she thought, those scientists obviously had too much time on their hands and, in the end, had failed to ask the most important questions: Who left the samples? Spouses, strangers? Were these exchanges of money, tenderness, disease? Was there love?

"This has to be quick," she said to the stranger beside her.

▲

Jeremiah, her husband, was already angry when Mary Lynn arrived thirty minutes late at the restaurant and he nearly lost all of his self-control when they were asked to wait for the next available table. He often raged at strangers, though he was incredibly patient and kind with their four children. Mary Lynn had seen that kind of rage in other white men when their wishes and desires were ignored. At ball games, in parking lots, and especially in airports, white men demanded to receive the privileges whose very existence they denied. White men could be so predictable, thought Mary Lynn. She thought: O, Jeremiah! O, season ticket holder! O, monthly parker! O, frequent flyer! She dreamed of him out there, sitting in the airplane with eighty-seven other white men wearing their second-best suits, all of them traveling toward small rooms in the Ramadas, Radissons, and sometimes the Hyatts, where they all separately watched the same pay-per-view porno that showed everything except penetration. What's the point of porno without graphic penetration? Mary Lynn knew it only made these lonely men feel all that more lonely. And didn't they deserve better, these white salesmen and middle managers, these twenty-first century Willie Lomans, who only wanted to be better men than their fathers had been? Of course, thought Mary Lynn, these sons definitely deserved better—they were smarter and more tender and generous than all previous generations of white

American men—but they'd never receive their just rewards, and thus
their anger was justified and banal.

"Calm down," Mary Lynn said to her husband as he continued to
rage at the restaurant hostess.

Mary Lynn said those two words to him more often in their marriage than any other combination of words.

"It could be twenty, thirty minutes," said the hostess. "Maybe longer."

"We'll wait outside," said Jeremiah. He breathed deeply, remembering some mantra that his therapist had taught him.

Mary Lynn's mantra: I cheated on my husband, I cheated on my
husband.

"We'll call your name," said the hostess, a white woman who was
tired of men no matter what their color. "When."

Their backs pressed against the brick wall, their feet crossed on the
sidewalk, on a warm Seattle evening, Mary Lynn and Jeremiah smoked
faux cigarettes filled with some foul-tasting, overwhelmingly organic
herb substance. For years they had smoked unfiltered Camels, but had
quit after all four of their parents had simultaneously suffered through
at least one form of cancer. Mary Lynn had called them the Mormon Tabernacle Goddamn Cancer Choir, though none of them was
Mormon and all of them were altos. With and without grace, they
had all survived the radiation, chemotherapy, and in-hospital cable-
television bingo games, with their bodies reasonably intact, only to
resume their previously self-destructive habits. After so many nights
spent in hospital corridors, waiting rooms, and armchairs, Mary Lynn
and Jeremiah hated doctors, all doctors, even the ones on television,
especially the ones on television. United in their obsessive hatred,
Mary Lynn and Jeremiah resorted to taking vitamins, eating free-
range chicken, and smoking cigarettes rolled together and marketed
by six odoriferous white liberals in Northern California.

As they waited for a table, Mary Lynn and Jeremiah watched dozens of people arrive and get seated immediately.

"I bet they don't have reservations," he said.

"I hate these cigarettes," she said.

"Why do you keep buying them?"

"Because the cashier at the health-food store is cute."

"You're shallow."

"Like a mud puddle."

Mary Lynn hated going out on weeknights. She hated driving into the city. She hated waiting for a table. Standing outside the downtown restaurant, desperate to hear their names, she decided to hate Jeremiah for a few seconds. Hate, hate, hate, she thought, and then she let her hate go. She wondered if she smelled like sex, like indigenous sex, and if a white man could recognize the scent of an enemy. She'd showered, but the water pressure had been weak and the soap bar too small.

"Let's go someplace else," she said.

"No. Five seconds after we leave, they'll call our names."

"But we won't know they called our names."

"But I'll feel it."

"It must be difficult to be psychic and insecure."

"I knew you were going to say that."

Clad in leather jackets and black jeans, standing inches apart but never quite touching, both handsome to the point of distraction, smoking crappy cigarettes that appeared to be real cigarettes, they could have been the subjects of a Schultz photograph or a Runnette poem.

The title of the photograph: "Infidelity."

The title of the poem: "More Infidelity."

Jeremiah's virtue was reasonably intact, though he'd recently been involved in a flirtatious near-affair with a coworker. At the crucial moment, when the last button was about to be unbuttoned, when consummation was just a fingertip away, Jeremiah had pushed his potential lover away and said I can't, I just can't, I love my marriage. He didn't admit to love for his spouse, partner, wife. No, he confessed his love for marriage, for the blessed union, for the legal document, for the shared mortgage payments, and for their four children.

Mary Lynn wondered what would happen if she grew pregnant with the Lummi's baby. Would this full-blood baby look more Indian than her half-blood sons and daughters?

"Don't they know who I am?" she asked her husband as they waited outside the downtown restaurant. She wasn't pregnant; there would be no paternity tests, no revealing of great secrets. His secret: he was still in love with a white woman from high school he hadn't seen in decades. What Mary Lynn knew: he was truly in love with the idea of a white woman from a mythical high school, with a prom queen named If Only or a homecoming princess named My Life Could Have Been Different.

"I'm sure they know who you are," he said. "That's why we're on the wait list. Otherwise, we'd be heading for McDonald's or Denny's."

"Your kinds of places."

"Dependable. The Big Mac you eat in Hong Kong or Des Moines tastes just like the Big Mac in Seattle."

"Sounds like colonialism to me."

"Colonialism ain't all bad."

"Put that on a bumper sticker."

This place was called Tan Tan, though it would soon be trendy enough to go by a nickname: Tan's. Maybe Tan's would become T's, and then T's would be identified only by a slight turn of the head or a certain widening of the eyes. After that, the downhill slide in reputation would be inevitable, whether or not the culinary content and quality of the restaurant remained exactly the same or improved. As it was, Tan Tan was a pan-Asian restaurant whose ownership and chefs—head, sauce, and line—were white, though most of the wait staff appeared to be one form of Asian or another.

"Don't you hate it?" Jeremiah asked. "When they have Chinese waiters in sushi joints? Or Korean dishwashers in a Thai noodle house?"

"I hadn't really thought about it," she said.

"No, think about it, these restaurants, these Asian restaurants, they hire Asians indiscriminately because they think white people won't be able to tell the difference."

"White people can't tell the difference."

"I can."

"Hey, Geronimo, you've been hanging around Indians too long to be white."

"Fucking an Indian doesn't make me Indian."

"So, that's what we're doing now? Fucking?"

"You have a problem with fucking?"

"No, not with the act itself, but I do have a problem with your sexual thesaurus."

Mary Lynn and Jeremiah had met in college, when they were still called Mary and Jerry. After sleeping together for the first time, after her first orgasm and his third, Mary had turned to Jerry and said, with absolute seriousness: If this thing is going to last, we have to stop the end rhyme. She had majored in Milton and Blake. He'd been a chemical engineer since the age of seven, with the degree being only a matter of formality, so he'd had plenty of time to wonder how an Indian from the reservation could be so smart. He still wondered how it had happened, though he'd never had the courage to ask her.

Now, a little more than two decades after graduating with a useless degree, Mary Lynn worked at Microsoft for a man named Dickinson. Jeremiah didn't know his first name, though he hoped it wasn't Emery, and had never met the guy, and didn't care if he ever did. Mary Lynn's job title and responsibilities were vague, so vague that Jeremiah had never asked her to elaborate. She often worked sixty-hour weeks and he didn't want to reward that behavior by expressing an interest in what specific tasks she performed for Bill Gates.

Waiting outside Tan Tan, he and she could smell ginger, burned rice, beer.

"Are they ever going to seat us?" she asked.

"Yeah, don't they know who you are?"

"I hear this place discriminates against white people."

"Really?"

"Yeah, I heard once, these lawyers, bunch of white guys in Nordstrom's suits, had to wait, like, two hours for a table."

"Were those billable hours?"

"It's getting hard for a white guy to find a place to eat."

"Damn affirmative action is what it is."

Their first child had been an accident, the result of a broken condom and a missed birth control pill. They named her Antonya, Toni for short. The second and third children, Robert and Michael, had been on purpose, and the fourth, Ariel, came after Mary Lynn thought she could no longer get pregnant.

Toni was fourteen, immature for her age, quite beautiful and narcissistic, with her translucent skin, her long blond hair, and eight-ball eyes. Botticelli eyes, she bragged after taking an Introduction to Art class. She never bothered to tell anybody she was Indian, mostly because nobody asked.

Jeremiah was quite sure that his daughter, his Antonya, had lost her virginity to the pimply quarterback of the junior varsity football team. He found the thought of his daughter's adolescent sexuality both curious and disturbing. Above all else, he believed that she was far too special to sleep with a cliché, let alone a junior varsity cliché.

Three months out of every year, Robert and Michael were the same age. Currently, they were both eleven. Dark-skinned, with their mother's black hair, strong jawline, and endless nose, they looked Indian, very Indian. Robert, who had refused to be called anything other than Robert, was the smart boy, a math prodigy, while Mikey was the basketball player.

When Mary Lynn's parents called from the reservation, they always asked after the boys, always invited the boys out for the weekend, the holidays, and the summer, and always sent the boys more elaborate gifts than they sent the two girls.

When Jeremiah had pointed out this discrepancy to Mary Lynn, she had readily agreed, but had made it clear that his parents also paid more attention to the boys. Jeremiah never mentioned it again, but had silently vowed to love the girls a little more than he loved the boys.

As if love were a thing that could be quantified, he thought.

He asked himself: What if I love the girls more because they look more like me, because they look more white than the boys?

Towheaded Ariel was two, and the clay of her personality was just beginning to harden, but she was certainly petulant and funny as hell, with the ability to sleep in sixteen-hour marathons that made her parents very nervous. She seemed to exist in her own world, enough so that she was periodically monitored for incipient autism. She treated her siblings as if they somehow bored her, and was the kind of kid who could stay alone in her crib for hours, amusing herself with all sorts of personal games and imaginary friends.

Mary Lynn insisted that her youngest daughter was going to be an artist, but Jeremiah didn't understand the child, and despite the fact that he was her father and forty-three years older, he felt inferior to Ariel.

He wondered if his wife was ever going to leave him because he was white.

When Tan Tan's doors swung open, laughter and smoke rolled out together.

"You got another cigarette?" he asked.

"Quit calling them cigarettes. They're not cigarettes. They're more like rose bushes. Hell, they're more like the shit that rose bushes grow in."

"You think we're going to get a table?"

"By the time we get a table, this place is going to be very unpopular."

"Do you want to leave?"

"Do you?"

"If you do."

"We told the baby-sitter we'd be home by ten."

They both wished that Toni were responsible enough to baby-sit her siblings, rather than needing to be sat along with them.

"What time is it?" she asked.

"Nine."

"Let's go home."

Last Christmas, when the kids had been splayed out all over the living room, buried to their shoulders in wrapping paper and expensive toys, Mary Lynn had studied her children's features, had recognized most of her face in her sons' faces and very little of it in her daughters', and had decided, quite facetiously, that the genetic score was tied.

We should have another kid, she'd said to Jeremiah, so we'll know if this is a white family or an Indian family.

It's a family family, he'd said, without a trace of humor.

Only a white guy would say that, she'd said.

Well, he'd said, you married a white guy.

The space between them had grown very cold at that moment, in that silence, and perhaps one or both of them might have said some-

thing truly destructive, but Ariel had started crying then, for no obvious reason, relieving both parents of the responsibility of finishing
that particular conversation. During the course of their relationship,
Mary Lynn and Jeremiah had often discussed race as a concept, as a
foreign country they occasionally visited, or as an enemy that existed
outside their house, as a destructive force they could fight against as
a couple, as a family. But race was also a constant presence, a house-
guest and permanent tenant who crept around all the rooms in their
shared lives, opening drawers, stealing utensils and small articles of
clothing, changing the temperature.

Before he'd married Mary Lynn, Jeremiah had always believed
there was too much talk of race, that white people were all too willing to be racist and that brown people were just as willing and just as
racist. As a rational scientist, he'd known that race was primarily a
social construct, illusionary, but as the husband of an Indian woman
and the father of Indian children, he'd since learned that race, whatever its construction, was real. Now, there were plenty of white people
who wanted to eliminate the idea of race, to cast it aside as an un-
wanted invention, but it was far too late for that. If white people are
the mad scientists who created race, thought Jeremiah, than we created race so we could enslave black people and kill Indians, and now
race has become the Frankenstein monster that has grown beyond
our control. Though he'd once been willfully blind, Jeremiah had
learned how to recognize that monster in the faces of whites and
Indians and in their eyes.

Long ago, Jeremiah and Mary Lynn had both decided to challenge
those who stared by staring back, by flinging each other against walls
and tongue-kissing with pornographic élan.

Long ago, they'd both decided to respond to any questions of why,
how, what, who, or when by simply stating: Love is Love. They knew

it was romantic bullshit, a simpleminded answer only satisfying for simpleminded people, but it was the best available defense.

Listen, Mary Lynn had once said to Jeremiah, asking somebody why they fall in love is like asking somebody why they believe in God.

You start asking questions like that, she had added, and you're either going to start a war or you're going to hear folk music.

You think too much, Jeremiah had said, rolling over and falling asleep.

Then, in the dark, as Jeremiah slept, Mary Lynn had masturbated while fantasizing about an Indian man with sundance scars on his chest.

After they left Tan Tan, they drove a sensible and indigenous Ford Taurus over the 520 bridge, back toward their house in Kirkland, a five-bedroom rancher only ten blocks away from the Microsoft campus. Mary Lynn walked to work. That made her feel privileged. She estimated there were twenty-two American Indians who had ever felt even a moment of privilege.

"We still have to eat," she said as she drove across the bridge. She felt strange. She wondered if she was ever going to feel normal again.

"How about Taco Bell drive-thru?" he asked.

"You devil, you're trying to get into my pants, aren't you?"

Impulsively, he dropped his head into her lap and pressed his lips against her black-jeaned crotch. She yelped and pushed him away. She wondered if he could smell her, if he could smell the Lummi Indian. Maybe he could, but he seemed to interpret it as something different, as something meant for him, as he pushed his head into her lap again. What was she supposed to do? She decided to laugh, so she did laugh as she pushed his face against her pubic bone. She loved the man for reasons she could not always explain. She closed her eyes, drove in that darkness, and felt dangerous.

Halfway across the bridge, Mary Lynn slammed on the brakes, not because she'd seen anything—her eyes were still closed—but because she'd felt something. The car skidded to a stop just inches from the bumper of a truck that had just missed sliding into the row of cars stopped ahead of it.

"What the hell is going on?" Jeremiah asked as he lifted his head from her lap.

"Traffic jam."

"Jesus, we'll never make it home by ten. We better call."

"The cell phone is in the glove."

Jeremiah dialed the home number but received only a busy signal.

"Toni must be talking to her boyfriend," she said.

"I don't like him."

"He doesn't like you."

"What the hell is going on? Why aren't we moving?"

"I don't know. Why don't you go check?"

Jeremiah climbed out of the car.

"I was kidding," she said as he closed the door behind him.

He walked up to the window of the truck ahead of him.

"You know what's going on?" Jeremiah asked the truck driver.

"Nope."

Jeremiah walked farther down the bridge. He wondered if there was a disabled car ahead, what the radio liked to call a "blocking accident." There was also the more serious "injury accident" and the deadly "accident with fatality involved." He had to drive this bridge ten times a week. The commute. White men had invented the commute, had deepened its meaning, had diversified its complications, and now spent most of the time trying to shorten it, reduce it, lessen it.

In the car, Mary Lynn wondered why Jeremiah always found it necessary to insert himself into every situation. He continually moved from the passive to the active. The man was kinetic. She wondered if it was a white thing. Possibly. But more likely, it was a Jeremiah thing. She remembered Mikey's third-grade-class's school play, an edited version of Hamlet. Jeremiah had walked onto the stage to help his son drag the unconscious Polonius, who had merely been clubbed over the head rather than stabbed to death, from the stage. Mortally embarrassed, Mikey had cried himself to sleep that night, positive that he was going to be an elementary-school pariah, while Jeremiah vainly tried to explain to the rest of the family why he had acted so impulsively.

I was just trying to be a good father, he had said.

Mary Lynn watched Jeremiah walk farther down the bridge. He was just a shadow, a silhouette. She was slapped by the brief, irrational fear that he would never return.

Husband, come back to me, she thought, and I will confess.

Impatient drivers honked their horns. Mary Lynn joined them. She hoped Jeremiah would recognize the specific sound of their horn and return to the car.

Listen to me, listen to me, listen to me, she thought as she pounded the steering wheel.

Jeremiah heard their car horn, but only as one note in the symphony of noise playing on the bridge. He walked through that noise, through an ever-increasing amount of noise, until he pushed through a sudden crowd of people and found himself witnessing a suicide.

Illuminated by headlights, the jumper was a white woman, pretty, wearing a sundress and good shoes. Jeremiah could see that much as she stood on the bridge railing, forty feet above the cold water.

He could hear sirens approaching from both sides of the bridge, but they would never make it through the traffic in time to save this woman.

The jumper was screaming somebody's name.

Jeremiah stepped closer, wanting to hear the name, wanting to have that information so that he could use it later. To what use, he didn't know, but he knew that name had value, importance. That name, the owner of that name, was the reason why the jumper stood on the bridge.

"Aaron," she said. The jumper screamed, "Aaron."

In the car, Mary Lynn could not see either Jeremiah or the jumper, but she could see dozens of drivers leaving their cars and running ahead.

She was suddenly and impossibly sure that her husband was the reason for this commotion, this emergency. He's dying, thought Mary Lynn, he's dead. This is not what I wanted, she thought, this is not why I cheated on him, this is not what was supposed to happen.

As more drivers left their cars and ran ahead, Mary Lynn dialed 911 on the cell phone and received only a busy signal.

She opened her door and stepped out, placed one foot on the pavement, and stopped.

The jumper did not stop. She turned to look at the crowd watching her. She looked into the anonymous faces, into the maw, and then looked back down at the black water.

Then she jumped.

Jeremiah rushed forward, along with a few others, and peered over the edge of the bridge. One brave man leapt off the bridge in a vain rescue attempt. Jeremiah stopped a redheaded young man from jumping.

"No," said Jeremiah. "It's too cold. You'll die too."

Jeremiah stared down into the black water, looking for the woman who'd jumped and the man who'd jumped after her.

In the car, or rather with one foot still in the car and one foot placed on the pavement outside of the car, Mary Lynn wept. Oh, God, she loved him, sometimes because he was white and often despite his whiteness. In her fear, she found the one truth Sitting Bull never knew: there was at least one white man who could be trusted.

The black water was silent.

Jeremiah stared down into that silence.

"Jesus, Jesus," said a lovely woman next to him. "Who was she? Who was she?"

"I'm never leaving," Jeremiah said.

"What?" asked the lovely woman, quite confused.

"My wife," said Jeremiah, strangely joyous. "I'm never leaving her." Ever the scientist and mathematician, Jeremiah knew that his wife was a constant. In his relief, he found the one truth Shakespeare never knew: gravity is overrated.

Jeremiah looked up through the crossbeams above him, as he stared at the black sky, at the clouds that he could not see but knew were there, the invisible clouds that covered the stars. He shouted out his wife's name, shouted it so loud that he could not speak in the morning.

In the car, Mary Lynn pounded the steering wheel. With one foot in the car and one foot out, she honked and honked the horn. She wondered if this was how the world was supposed to end, with everybody trapped on a bridge, with the black water pushing against their foundations.

Out on the bridge, four paramedics arrived far too late. Out of breath, exhausted from running across the bridge with medical gear and stretchers, the paramedics could only join the onlookers at the railing.

A boat, a small boat, a miracle, floated through the black water. They found the man, the would-be rescuer, who had jumped into the water after the young woman, but they could not find her.

Jeremiah pushed through the crowd, as he ran away from the place where the woman had jumped. Jeremiah ran across the bridge until he could see Mary Lynn. She and he loved each other across the distance.

THE TOUGHEST INDIAN
IN THE WORLD

▲▲▲▲▲▲▲▲▲▲▲▲▲▲▲▲▲▲▲▲▲▲▲▲▲▲▲▲▲▲▲▲▲▲▲▲▲▲▲

Being a Spokane Indian, I only pick up Indian hitchhikers. I learned this particular ceremony from my father, a Coeur d'Alene, who always stopped for those twentieth-century aboriginal nomads who refused to believe the salmon were gone. I don't know what they believed in exactly, but they wore hope like a bright shirt.

My father never taught me about hope. Instead, he continually told me that our salmon—our hope—would never come back, and though such lessons may seem cruel, I know enough to cover my heart in any crowd of white people.

"They'll kill you if they get the chance," my father said. "Love you or hate you, white people will shoot you in the heart. Even after all these years, they'll still smell the salmon on you, the dead salmon, and that will make white people dangerous."

All of us, Indian and white, are haunted by salmon.

When I was a boy, I leaned over the edge of one dam or another—perhaps Long Lake or Little Falls or the great gray dragon known as the Grand Coulee—and watched the ghosts of the salmon rise from the water to the sky and become constellations.

For most Indians, stars are nothing more than white tombstones scattered across a dark graveyard.

But the Indian hitchhikers my father picked up refused to admit the existence of sky, let alone the possibility that salmon might be stars. They were common people who believed only in the thumb and the foot. My father envied those simple Indian hitchhikers. He wanted to change their minds about salmon; he wanted to break open their hearts and see the future in their blood. He loved them.

▲

In 1975 or '76 or '77, driving along one highway or another, my father would point out a hitchhiker standing beside the road a mile or two in the distance.

"Indian," he said if it was an Indian, and he was never wrong, though I could never tell if the distant figure was male or female, let alone Indian or not.

If a distant figure happened to be white, my father would drive by without comment.

That was how I learned to be silent in the presence of white people.

The silence is not about hate or pain or fear. Indians just like to believe that white people will vanish, perhaps explode into smoke, if they are ignored enough times. Perhaps a thousand white families are still waiting for their sons and daughters to return home, and can't recognize them when they float back as morning fog.

"We better stop," my mother said from the passenger seat. She was one of those Spokane women who always wore a purple bandanna tied tightly around her head.

These days, her bandanna is usually red. There are reasons, motives, traditions behind the choice of color, but my mother keeps them secret.

"Make room," my father said to my siblings and me as we sat on the floor in the cavernous passenger area of our blue van. We sat on carpet samples because my father had torn out the seats in a sober rage not long after he bought the van from a crazy white man.

I have three brothers and three sisters now. Back then, I had four of each. I missed one of the funerals and cried myself sick during the other one.

"Make room," my father said again—he said everything twice—and only then did we scramble to make space for the Indian hitchhiker.

Of course, it was easy enough to make room for one hitchhiker, but Indians usually travel in packs. Once or twice, we picked up entire all-Indian basketball teams, along with their coaches, girlfriends, and cousins. Fifteen, twenty Indian strangers squeezed into the back of a blue van with nine wide-eyed Indian kids.

Back in those days, I loved the smell of Indians, and of Indian hitchhikers in particular. They were usually in some stage of drunkenness, often in need of soap and a towel, and always ready to sing.

Oh, the songs! Indian blues bellowed at the highest volumes. We called them "49s," those cross-cultural songs that combined Indian lyrics and rhythms with country-and-western and blues melodies. It seemed that every Indian knew all the lyrics to every Hank Williams song ever recorded. Hank was our Jesus, Patsy Cline was our Virgin Mary, and Freddy Fender, George Jones, Conway Twitty, Loretta Lynn, Tammy Wynette, Charley Pride, Ronnie Milsap, Tanya Tucker, Marty Robbins, Johnny Horton, Donna Fargo, and Charlie Rich were our disciples.

We all know that nostalgia is dangerous, but I remember those days with a clear conscience. Of course, we live in different days now, and there aren't as many Indian hitchhikers as there used to be.

▲

Now, I drive my own car, a 1998 Toyota Camry, the best-selling automobile in the United States, and therefore the one most often stolen. *Consumer Reports* has named it the most reliable family sedan for
sixteen years running, and I believe it.

In my Camry, I pick up three or four Indian hitchhikers a week.
Mostly men. They're usually headed home, back to their reservations
or somewhere close to their reservations. Indians hardly ever travel
in a straight line, so a Crow Indian might hitchhike west when his
reservation is back east in Montana. He has some people to see in
Seattle, he might explain if I ever asked him. But I never ask Indians
their reasons for hitchhiking. All that matters is this: They are Indians walking, raising their thumbs, and I am there to pick them up.

At the newspaper where I work, my fellow reporters think I'm crazy
to pick up hitchhikers. They're all white and never stop to pick up
anybody, let alone an Indian. After all, we're the ones who write
the stories and headlines: HITCHHIKER KILLS HUSBAND AND WIFE,
MISSING GIRL'S BODY FOUND, RAPIST STRIKES AGAIN. If I really tried,
maybe I could explain to them why I pick up any Indian, but who wants
to try? Instead, if they ask I just give them a smile and turn back to my
computer. My coworkers smile back and laugh loudly. They're always
laughing loudly at me, at one another, at themselves, at goofy typos in
the newspapers, at the idea of hitchhikers.

I dated one of them for a few months. Cindy. She covered the local
courts: speeding tickets and divorces, drunk driving and embezzle-
ment. Cindy firmly believed in the who-what-where-when-why-and-
how of journalism. In daily conversation, she talked like she was
writing the lead of her latest story. Hell, she talked like that in bed.

"How does that feel?" I asked, quite possibly the only Indian man
who has ever asked that question.

"I love it when you touch me there," she answered. "But it would help if you rubbed it about thirty percent lighter and with your thumb instead of your middle finger. And could you maybe turn the radio to a different station? KYZY would be good. I feel like soft jazz will work better for me right now. A minor chord, a C or G-flat, or something like that. Okay, honey?"

During lovemaking, I would get so exhausted by the size of her erotic vocabulary that I would fall asleep before my orgasm, continue pumping away as if I were awake, and then regain consciousness with a sudden start when I finally did come, more out of reflex than passion.

Don't get me wrong. Cindy is a good one, cute and smart, funny as hell, a good catch no matter how you define it, but she was also one of those white women who date only brown-skinned guys. Indians like me, black dudes, Mexicans, even a few Iranians. I started to feel like a trophy, or like one of those entries in a personal ad. I asked Cindy why she never dated pale boys.

"White guys bore me," she said. "All they want to talk about is their fathers."

"What do brown guys talk about?" I asked her.

"Their mothers," she said and laughed, then promptly left me for a public defender who was half Japanese and half African, a combination that left Cindy dizzy with the interracial possibilities.

Since Cindy, I haven't dated anyone. I live in my studio apartment with the ghosts of two dogs, Felix and Oscar, and a laptop computer stuffed with bad poems, the aborted halves of three novels, and some three-paragraph personality pieces I wrote for the newspaper.

I'm a features writer, and an Indian at that, so I get all the shit jobs. Not the dangerous shit jobs or the monotonous shit jobs. No. I get to write the articles designed to please the eye, ear, and heart. And there is no journalism more soul-endangering to write than journalism that aims to please.

So it was with reluctance that I climbed into my car last week and
headed down Highway 2 to write some damn pleasant story about
some damn pleasant people. Then I saw the Indian hitchhiker standing beside the road. He looked the way Indian hitchhikers usually
look. Long, straggly black hair. Brown eyes and skin. Missing a couple
of teeth. A bad complexion that used to be much worse. Crooked nose
that had been broken more than once. Big, misshapen ears. A few
whiskers masquerading as a mustache. Even before he climbed into
my car I could tell he was tough. He had some serious muscles that
threatened to rip through his blue jeans and denim jacket. When he
was in the car, I could see his hands up close, and they told his whole
story. His fingers were twisted into weird, permanent shapes, and his
knuckles were covered with layers of scar tissue.

"Jeez," I said. "You're a fighter, enit?"

I threw in the "enit," a reservation colloquialism, because I wanted
the fighter to know that I had grown up on the rez, in the woods, with
every Indian in the world.

The hitchhiker looked down at his hands, flexed them into fists. I
could tell it hurt him to do that.

"Yeah," he said. "I'm a fighter."

I pulled back onto the highway, looking over my shoulder to check
my blind spot.

"What tribe are you?" I asked him, inverting the last two words in
order to sound as aboriginal as possible.

"Lummi," he said. "What about you?"

"Spokane."

"I know some Spokanes. Haven't seen them in a long time."

He clutched his backpack in his lap like he didn't want to let it go
for anything. He reached inside a pocket and pulled out a piece of
deer jerky. I recognized it by the smell.

"Want some?" he asked.

"Sure."

It had been a long time since I'd eaten jerky. The salt, the gamy taste. I felt as Indian as Indian gets, driving down the road in a fast car, chewing on jerky, talking to an indigenous fighter.

"Where you headed?" I asked.

"Home. Back to the rez."

I nodded my head as I passed a big truck. The driver gave us a smile as we went by. I tooted the horn.

"Big truck," said the fighter.

▲

I haven't lived on my reservation for twelve years. But I live in Spokane, which is only an hour's drive from the rez. Still, I hardly ever go home. I don't know why not. I don't think about it much, I guess, but my mom and dad still live in the same house where I grew up. My brothers and sisters, too. The ghosts of my two dead siblings share an apartment in the converted high school. It's just a local call from Spokane to the rez, so I talk to all of them once or twice a week. Smoke signals courtesy of U.S. West Communications. Sometimes they call me up to talk about the stories they've seen that I've written for the newspaper. Pet pigs and support groups and science fairs. Once in a while, I used to fill in for the obituaries writer when she was sick. Then she died, and I had to write her obituary.

"How far are you going?" asked the fighter, meaning how much closer was he going to get to his reservation than he was now.

"Up to Wenatchee," I said. "I've got some people to interview there."

"Interview? What for?"

"I'm a reporter. I work for the newspaper."

"No," said the fighter, looking at me like I was stupid for thinking he was stupid. "I mean, what's the story about?"

"Oh, not much. There's two sets of twins who work for the fire department. Human-interest stuff, you know?"

"Two sets of twins, enit? That's weird."

He offered me more deer jerky, but I was too thirsty from the salty meat, so I offered him a Pepsi instead.

"Don't mind if I do," he said.

"They're in a cooler on the backseat," I said. "Grab me one, too."

He maneuvered his backpack carefully and found room enough to reach into the backseat for the soda pop. He opened my can first and handed it to me. A friendly gesture for a stranger. I took a big mouthful and hiccupped loudly.

"That always happens to me when I drink cold things," he said.

We sipped slowly after that. I kept my eyes on the road while he stared out the window into the wheat fields. We were quiet for many miles.

"Who do you fight?" I asked as we passed through another anonymous small town.

"Mostly Indians," he said. "Money fights, you know? I go from rez to rez, fighting the best they have. Winner takes all."

"Jeez, I never heard of that."

"Yeah, I guess it's illegal."

He rubbed his hands together. I could see fresh wounds.

"Man," I said. "Those fights must be rough."

The fighter stared out the window. I watched him for a little too long and almost drove off the road. Car horns sounded all around us.

"Jeez," the fighter said. "Close one, enit?"

"Close enough," I said.

He hugged his backpack more tightly, using it as a barrier between his chest and the dashboard. An Indian hitchhiker's version of a passenger-side air bag.

"Who'd you fight last?" I asked, trying to concentrate on the road.

"Some Flathead," he said. "In Arlee. He was supposed to be the toughest Indian in the world."

"Was he?"

"Nah, no way. Wasn't even close. Wasn't even tougher than me."

He told me how big the Flathead kid was, way over six feet tall and two hundred and some pounds. Big buck Indian. Had hands as big as this and arms as big as that. Had a chin like a damn buffalo. The fighter told me that he hit the Flathead kid harder than he ever hit anybody before.

"I hit him like he was a white man," the fighter said. "I hit him like he was two or three white men rolled into one."

But the Flathead kid would not go down, even though his face swelled up so bad that he looked like the Elephant Man. There were no referees, no judge, no bells to signal the end of the round. The winner was the Indian still standing. Punch after punch, man, and the kid would not go down.

"I was so tired after a while," said the fighter, "that I just took a step back and watched the kid. He stood there with his arms down, swaying from side to side like some toy, you know? Head bobbing on his neck like there was no bone at all. You couldn't even see his eyes no more. He was all messed up."

"What'd you do?" I asked.

"Ah, hell, I couldn't fight him no more. That kid was planning to die before he ever went down. So I just sat on the ground while they counted me out. Dumb Flathead kid didn't even know what was happening. I just sat on the ground while they raised his hand. While all the winners collected their money and all the losers cussed me out. I just sat there, man."

"Jeez," I said. "What happened next?"

"Not much. I sat there until everybody was gone. Then I stood up and decided to head for home. I'm tired of this shit. I just want to go home for a while. I got enough money to last me a long time. I'm a rich Indian, you hear? I'm a rich Indian."

The fighter finished his Pepsi, rolled down his window, and pitched the can out. I almost protested, but decided against it. I kept my empty can wedged between my legs.

"That's a hell of a story," I said.

"Ain't no story," he said. "It's what happened."

"Jeez," I said. "You would've been a warrior in the old days, enit? You would've been a killer. You would have stolen everybody's goddamn horses. That would've been you. You would've been it."

I was excited. I wanted the fighter to know how much I thought of him. He didn't even look at me.

"A killer," he said. "Sure."

▲

We didn't talk much after that. I pulled into Wenatchee just before sundown, and the fighter seemed happy to be leaving me.

"Thanks for the ride, cousin," he said as he climbed out. Indians always call each other cousin, especially if they're strangers.

"Wait," I said.

He looked at me, waiting impatiently.

I wanted to know if he had a place to sleep that night. It was supposed to get cold. There was a mountain range between Wenatchee and his reservation. Big mountains that were dormant volcanoes, but that could all blow up at any time. We wrote about it once in the newspaper. Things can change so quickly. So many emergencies and disasters that we can barely keep track. I wanted to tell him how much I cared about my job, even if I had to write about small-town firemen. I wanted to tell the fighter that I pick up all Indian hitchhikers, young and old, men and women, and get them a little closer to home, even if I can't get them all the way. I wanted to tell him that the night sky was a graveyard. I wanted to know if he was the toughest Indian in the world.

"It's late," I finally said. "You can crash with me, if you want."

He studied my face and then looked down the long road toward his reservation.

"Okay," he said. "That sounds good."

We got a room at the Pony Soldier Motel, and both of us laughed at the irony of it all. Inside the room, in a generic watercolor hanging above the bed, the U.S. Cavalry was kicking the crap out of a band of renegade Indians.

"What tribe you think they are?" I asked the fighter.

"All of them," he said.

The fighter crashed on the floor while I curled up in the uncomfortable bed. I couldn't sleep for the longest time. I listened to the fighter talk in his sleep. I stared up at the water-stained ceiling. I don't know what time it was when I finally drifted off, and I don't know what time it was when the fighter got into bed with me. He was naked and his penis was hard. I felt it press against my back as he snuggled up close to me, reached inside my underwear, and took my penis in his hand. Neither of us said a word. He continued to stroke me as he rubbed himself against my back. That went on for a long time. I had never been that close to another man, but the fighter's callused fingers felt better than I would have imagined if I had ever allowed myself to imagine such things.

"This isn't working," he whispered. "I can't come."

Without thinking, I reached around and took the fighter's penis in my hand. He was surprisingly small.

"No," he said. "I want to be inside you."

"I don't know," I said. "I've never done this before."

"It's okay," he said. "I'll be careful. I have rubbers."

Without waiting for my answer, he released me and got up from the bed. I turned to look at him. He was beautiful and scarred. So much brown skin marked with bruises, badly healed wounds, and tattoos. His long black hair was unbraided and hung down to his thin waist. My slacks and dress shirt were folded and draped over the chair near the window. My shoes were sitting on the table. Blue light filled the room. The fighter bent down to his pack and searched for his condoms. For reasons I could not explain then and cannot explain now, I kicked off my underwear and rolled over on my stomach. I could not see him, but I could hear him breathing heavily as he found the condoms, tore open a package, and rolled one over his penis. He crawled onto the bed, between my legs, and slid a pillow beneath my belly.

"Are you ready?" he asked.

"I'm not gay," I said.

"Sure," he said as he pushed himself into me. He was small but it hurt more than I expected, and I knew that I would be sore for days afterward. But I wanted him to save me. He didn't say anything. He just pumped into me for a few minutes, came with a loud sigh, and then pulled out. I quickly rolled off the bed and went into the bathroom. I locked the door behind me and stood there in the dark. I smelled like salmon.

"Hey," the fighter said through the door. "Are you okay?"

"Yes," I said. "I'm fine."

A long silence.

"Hey," he said. "Would you mind if I slept in the bed with you?"

I had no answer to that.

"Listen," I said. "That Flathead boy you fought? You know, the one you really beat up? The one who wouldn't fall down?"

In my mind, I could see the fighter pummeling that boy. Punch after punch. The boy too beaten to fight back, but too strong to fall down.

"Yeah, what about him?" asked the fighter.

"What was his name?"

"His name?"

"Yeah, his name."

"Elmer something or other."

"Did he have an Indian name?"

"I have no idea. How the hell would I know that?"

I stood there in the dark for a long time. I was chilled. I wanted to get into bed and fall asleep.

"Hey," I said. "I think, I think maybe—well, I think you should leave now."

"Yeah," said the fighter, not surprised. I heard him softly singing as he dressed and stuffed all of his belongings into his pack. I wanted to know what he was singing, so I opened the bathroom door just as he was opening the door to leave. He stopped, looked at me, and smiled.

"Hey, tough guy," he said. "You were good."

The fighter walked out the door, left it open, and walked away. I stood in the doorway and watched him continue his walk down the highway, past the city limits. I watched him rise from earth to sky and become a new constellation. I closed the door and wondered what was going to happen next. Feeling uncomfortable and cold, I went back into the bathroom. I ran the shower with the hottest water possible. I stared at myself in the mirror. Steam quickly filled the room. I threw a few shadow punches. Feeling stronger, I stepped into the shower and searched my body for changes. A middle-aged man needs to look for tumors. I dried myself with a towel too small for the job. Then I crawled naked into bed. I wondered if I was a warrior in this life and if I had been a warrior in a previous life. Lonely and laughing, I fell asleep. I didn't dream at all, not one bit. Or perhaps I dreamed but remembered none of it. Instead, I woke early the next

morning, before sunrise, and went out into the world. I walked past
my car. I stepped onto the pavement, still warm from the previous
day's sun. I started walking. In bare feet, I traveled upriver toward the
place where I was born and will someday die. At that moment, if you
had broken open my heart you could have looked inside and seen the
thin white skeletons of one thousand salmon.

CLASS

▲▲

She wanted to know if I was Catholic.

I was completely unprepared to respond with any degree of clarity to such a dangerous question. After all, we had been talking about the shrimp appetizers (which were covered with an ambitious pesto sauce) and where they fit, in terms of quality, in our very separate histories of shrimp appetizers in particular and seafood appetizers in general. I'd just been describing to her how cayenne and lobster seemed to be mortal enemies, one of the more secular and inane culinary observations I'd ever made, when she'd focused her blue eyes on me, really looked at me for the first time in the one minute and thirty-five seconds we'd known each other, and asked me if I was Catholic.

How do you answer a question like that, especially when you've just met the woman at one of those house parties where you'd expected to know everybody in attendance but had gradually come to realize that you knew only the host couple, and then only well enough to ask about the welfare of the two kids (a boy and a girl or two boys) you thought they parented? As far as I could tell, there were no priests, ministers, or pastors milling about, so I had no easy visual aids in guessing at the dominant denomination in the room. If there'd been a Jesuit priest, Hasidic rabbi, or Tibetan monk drinking a pale ale over by the saltwater aquarium, I might have known the best response, the clever, scintillating answer that would have compelled her to take me home with her for a long night of safe and casual sex.

"Well," she asked again, with a musical lilt in her voice. "Are you Catholic?"

Her left eye was a significantly darker blue than the right.

"Your eyes," I said, trying to change the subject. "They're different."

"I'm blind in this one," she said, pointing to the left eye.

"Oh, I'm sorry," I said, mortified by my lack of decorum.

"Why? It was my big brother who stabbed me with the pencil. He didn't mean it, though."

She told the story as if she'd only skinned a knee or received a slight concussion, as if the injury had been temporary.

"He was aiming for my little sister's eye," she added. "But she ducked. She was always more athletic than me."

"Where's your sister now?"

"She's dead. Car wreck. Bang, bang, bang."

So much pain for such a white woman. I wondered how often a man can say the wrong thing during the course of a particular conversation.

"What about your brother?" I asked, praying that he had not been driving the car that killed her sister.

"He's right over there," she said and pointed at a handsome man, taller than everybody else in the room, who was sitting on the carpeted stairs with a woman whose red hair I'd been admiring all evening. Though engaged in what appeared to be a passionate conversation, the brother sensed his sister's attention and looked up. Both of his eyes were the same shade of blue as her good eye.

"He's the one who did it," she said and tapped her blind eye.

In response, the brother smiled and tapped his left eye. He could see perfectly.

"You cruel bastard," she mouthed at him, though she made it sound like an affectionate nickname, like a tender legacy from childhood.

"You cruel bastard," she repeated. Her brother could obviously read her lips because he laughed again, loud enough for me to hear him over the din of the party, and hugged the redhead in a tender but formal way that indicated they'd made love only three or four times in their young relationship.

"Your brother," I said, trying to compliment her by complimenting the family genetics. "He's good-looking."

"He's okay," she said.

"He's got your eyes."

"Only one of them, remember," she said and moved one step closer to me. "Now, quit trying to change the subject. Tell me. Are you Catholic or are you not Catholic?"

"Baptized," I said. "But not confirmed."

"That's very ambiguous."

"I read somewhere that many women think ambiguity is sexy."

"Not me. I like men who are very specific."

"You don't like mystery?"

"I always know who did it," she said and moved so close that I could smell the red wine and dinner mints on her breath.

I took a step back.

"Don't be afraid," she said. "I'm not drunk. And I just chewed on a few Altoids because I thought I might be kissing somebody very soon."

She could read minds. She was also drunk enough that her brother had already pocketed the keys to her Lexus.

"Who is this somebody you're going to be kissing?" I asked. "And why just somebody? That sounds very ambiguous to me."

"And very sexy," she said and touched my hand. Blond, maybe thirty-five, and taller than me, she was the tenth most attractive white woman in the room. I always approached the tenth most attractive white woman at any gathering. I didn't have enough looks, charm, intelligence, or money to approach anybody more attractive than that, and I didn't have enough character to approach the less attractive. Crassly speaking, I'd always made sure to play ball only with my equals.

"You're Indian," she said, stretching the word into three syllables and nearly a fourth.

"Do you like that?"

"I like your hair," she said, touching the black braids that hung down past my chest. I'd been growing the braids since I'd graduated from law school. My hair impressed jurors but irritated judges. Perfect.

"I like your hair, too," I said and brushed a pale strand away from her forehead. I counted three blemishes and one mole on her face. I wanted to kiss the tips of her fingers. Women expected kisses on the parts of their bodies hidden by clothes, the private places, but were often surprised when I paid more attention to their public features: hands, hairline, the soft skin around their eyes.

"You're beautiful," I said.

"No, I'm not," she said. "I'm just pretty. But pretty is good enough."

I still didn't know her name, but I could have guessed at it. Her generation of white women usually carried two-syllable names, like Becky, Erin, and Wendy, or monosyllabic nicknames that lacked any adornment. Peg, Deb, or Sam. Efficient names, quick-in-the-shower names, just-brush-it-and-go names. Her mother and her mother's friends would be known by more ornate monikers, and if she had daughters, they would be named after their grandmothers. The country was filling up with little white girls named Rebecca, Elizabeth, and Willamena.

"Sara," I guessed. "Your name is Sara."

"With or without an *h*?" she asked.

"Without," I said, pleased with my psychic ability.

"Actually, it's neither. My name is Susan. Susan McDermott. Without the *h*."

"I'm Edgar Eagle Runner," I said, though my driver's license still read Edgar Joseph.

"Eagle Runner," she repeated, feeling the shape of my name fill her mouth, then roll past her tongue, teeth, and lips.

"Susan," I said.

"Eagle Runner," she whispered. "What kind of Indian are you?"

"Spokane."

"Never heard of it."

"We're a small tribe. Salmon people."

"The salmon are disappearing," she said.

"Yes," I said. "Yes, they are."

Susan McDermott and I were married in a small ceremony seven months later in St. Therese Catholic Church in Madrona, a gentrified neighborhood ten minutes from downtown Seattle. She'd been baptized at St. Therese as a toddler by a Jesuit who many years later went hiking on Mount Rainier and vanished. Father David or Joseph or Father Something Biblical. She didn't remember anything about him, neither the color of his hair nor the exact shape of his theology, but she thought that his disappearance was a metaphor for her love life.

"One day, many years ago," she said, "my heart walked into the snow and vanished. But then you found it and gave it heat."

"Is that a simile or a metaphor?" I asked.

"It might be an analogy," she said.

Our vows were witnessed by three dozen of Susan's best friends, along with most of her coworkers at the architecture firm, but Susan's handsome brother and parents stayed away as a protest against my pigmentation.

"I can understand fucking him," her brother had said upon hearing the news of our engagement. "But why do you want to share a checking account?"

He was so practical.

Half of the partners and all of my fellow associates from the law firm showed up to watch me tie the knot.

Velma, my dark-skinned mother, was overjoyed by my choice of mate. She'd always wanted me to marry a white woman and beget half-breed children who would marry white people who would beget quarter-bloods, and so on and so on, until simple mathematics killed the Indian in us.

When asked, my mother told white people she was Spanish, not Mexican, not Hispanic, not Chicana, and certainly not Spokane Indian with a little bit of Aztec thrown in for spice, even though she was all of these things.

As for me, I'd told any number of white women that I was part Aztec and I'd told a few that I was completely Aztec. That gave me some mystery, some ethnic weight, a history of glorious color and mass executions. Strangely enough, there were aphrodisiacal benefits to claiming to be descended from ritual cannibals. In any event, pretending to be an Aztec warrior was a lot more impressive than revealing I was just some bright kid who'd fought his way off the Spokane Indian Reservation in Washington State and was now a corporate lawyer in Seattle who pretended to have a lot more money that he did.

I'd emptied my meager savings account to pay for the wedding and reception, refusing to allow Susan to help, though she made twice what I did. I was living paycheck to paycheck, a bizarre circumstance for a man whose monthly wage exceeded his mother's yearly income as a social worker in the small city of Spokane, Washington.

My mother was an Indian woman who taught drunk white people not to drink, stoned whites not to smoke, and abusive whites not to throw the punch. A simple and honorable job. She was very good at it and I loved her. She wore a black dress to the wedding, nearly funeral wear, but brightened it with a salmon-colored scarf and matching shoes.

I counted seventeen white women at the wedding. On an average day, Susan would have been the fourth or fifth most attractive. On this, her wedding day, dressed in an ivory gown with plunging neckline, she was easily the most beautiful white woman in the chapel; she was more serene, sexy, and spiritual than the wooden Mary hanging on the west wall or the stained-glassed Mary filling up one of the windows.

Susan's niece, an eighteen-year-old, served as her maid of honor. She modeled teen wear for Nordstrom's. I tried not to stare at her. My best man was one of the partners in the law firm where I worked.

"Hey, Runner," he had said just before the ceremony began. "I love you, man."

I'd hugged him, feeling guilty. My friendship with him was strictly professional.

During the ceremony, he cried. I couldn't believe it. I'm not one of those men who believe tears are a sign of weakness. On the contrary, I believe it's entirely appropriate, even attractive, for a man to cry under certain circumstances, but my wedding was not tear-worthy. In fact, there was a decided lack of emotion during the ceremony, mostly due to the absence of Susan's immediate family.

My mother was the only member of my family sitting in the pews, but that didn't bother or surprise me. She was the only one I had invited.

The ceremony itself was short and simple, because Susan believed brevity was always more elegant, and more sexy, than excess. I agreed with her.

"I will," she said.

"I will," I said.

We did.

▲

During the first two years of our marriage, we attended thirty-seven cocktail parties, eighteen weddings, one divorce, seven Christmas parties, two New Year's Eve parties, three New Year's Day parties, nine birthday parties—only one of them for a child under the age of eighteen—six opera performances, nine literary readings, twelve museum openings, one museum closing, three ballets, including a revival of *Swan Lake* in New York City, one spouse-swapping party we left before we took off our coats, and thirty-two films, including most of those nominated for Oscars and two or three that had screened at the Sundance Film Festival.

I attended business lunches Monday through Friday, and occasionally on Saturdays, while Susan kept her Friday lunches free so she could carry on an affair with an architect named Harry. She'd begun the affair a few days after our first anniversary and it had gone on for seven months before she'd voluntarily quit him, never having known that I'd known about the tryst, that I'd discovered his love letters hidden in a shoe box at the bottom of her walk-in closet.

I hadn't been snooping on her when I'd found the letters and I didn't bother to read any of them past the salutation that began each. "My love, my love, my love," they'd read, three times, always three times, like a chant, like a prayer. Brokenhearted, betrayed, I'd kept the letters sacred by carefully placing them back, intact and unread, in the shoe box and sliding the box back into its hiding place.

I suppose I could have exacted revenge on her by sleeping with one or more of her friends or coworkers. I'd received any number of subtle offers to do such a thing, but I didn't want to embarrass her. Personal pain should never be made public. Instead, in quiet retaliation, I patronized prostitutes whenever I traveled out of town. Miami, Los Angeles, Boston. Chicago, Minneapolis, Houston.

In San Francisco for a deposition hearing, I called the first service
listed in the Yellow Pages.

"A-1 Escorts," said the woman. A husky voice, somehow menac-
ing. I'm sure her children hated the sound of it, even as I found myself aroused by its timbre.

"A-1 Escorts," she said again when I did not speak.

"Oh," I said. "Hi. Hello. Uh, I'm looking for some company this
evening."

"Where you at?"

"The Prescott."

"Nice place."

"Yeah, they have whirlpool bathtubs."

"Water sports will cost you extra."

"Oh, no, no, no. I'm, uh, rather traditional."

"Okay, Mr. Traditional, what are you looking for?"

I'd slept with seventeen prostitutes, all of them blond and blue-
eyed. Twelve of them had been busty while the other five had been
small-breasted. Eight of them had claimed to be college students; one
of them even had a chemistry textbook in her backpack.

"Do you employ any Indian women?" I asked.

"Indian? Like with the dot in the forehead?"

"No, no, that's East Indian. From India. I'm looking for American
Indian. You know, like Tonto."

"We don't have any boys."

"Oh, no, I mean, I want an Indian woman."

There was a long silence on the other end. Was she looking through
some kind of catalogue? Searching her inventory for the perfect
woman for me? Was she calling other escort companies, looking for
a referral? I wanted to hang up the phone. I'd never had intercourse
with an Indian woman.

"Yeah, we got somebody. She's a pro."

"What do you mean by pro?"

"She used to work pornos."

"Pornos?"

"Dirty movies? X-rated? You got them right there on the pay-per-view in your room, buddy."

"What's her name?"

"She calls herself Tawny Feather."

"You're kidding."

"I never kid."

I wondered what kind of Indian woman would call herself Tawny Feather. Sexually speaking, Indian women and men are simultaneously promiscuous and modest. That's a contradiction, but it also happens to be the truth. I just couldn't imagine an Indian woman who would star in pornographic movies.

"Well, you want a date or not?" asked the husky-voiced woman.

"How much?"

"How much you got?"

"How much you want?"

"Two hundred."

"Sold," I said.

"What room?"

"1216."

"Who should she ask for?"

"Geronimo."

"Ha, ha," she said and hung up the phone.

Less than an hour later, there was a knock on the door. I peered through the peephole and saw her.

Tawny Feather.

She wore a conservative tan suit and a string of fake pearls. Dream-catcher earrings, turquoise rings, a stainless-steel eagle pinned to her lapel. Good camouflage. Professional but eccentric. She looked like a woman on her way to or from a meeting. She looked like a woman with an Individualized Retirement Account.

She was also a white woman wearing a black wig over her short blond hair.

"You're not Indian," I said when I opened the door.

She looked me up and down.

"No, I'm not," she said. "But you are."

"Mostly."

"Well," she said as she stepped into the room and kissed my neck. "Then you can mostly pretend I'm Indian."

She stayed all night, which cost me another five hundred dollars, and ordered eggs and toast for breakfast, which cost me another twenty.

"You're the last one," I said as she prepared to leave.

"The last what?"

"My last prostitute."

"The last one today?" she asked. "Or the last one this month? What kind of time period are we talking about here?"

She swore she was an English major.

"The last one forever," I said.

She smiled, convinced that I was lying and/or fooling myself, having heard these same words from any number of customers. She knew that she and her coworkers were drugs for men like me.

"Sure I am," she said.

"No, really," I said. "I promise."

She laughed.

"Son," she said, though she was ten years younger than me. "You don't have to make me any damn promises."

She took off her black wig and handed it to me.

"You keep it," she said and gave me a free good-bye kiss.

▲

Exactly three years after our wedding, Susan gave birth to our first child, a boy. He weighed eight pounds, seven ounces, and was twenty-two inches long. A big baby. His hair was black and his eyes were a strange gray. He died ten minutes after leaving Susan's body.

▲

After our child died, Susan and I quit having sex. Or rather, she stopped wanting to have sex. I just want to tell the whole story. For months I pressured, coerced, seduced, and emotionally blackmailed her into sleeping with me. At first, I assumed she'd been engaged in another affair with another architect named Harry, but my private detective found only evidence of her grief: crying jags in public rest rooms, aimless wandering in the children's departments of Nordstrom's and the Bon Marche, and visits to a therapist I'd never heard about.

She wasn't touching anybody else but me. Our lives moved on.

After a year of reluctant sex, I believed her orgasms were mostly due to my refusal to quit touching her until she did come, the arduous culmination of my physical endeavors rather than the result of any emotional investment she might have had in fulfillment. And then, one night, while I was still inside her, moving my hips in rhythm with hers, I looked into her eyes, her blue eyes, and saw that her good eye held no more light in it than her dead eye. She wasn't literally blind, of course. She'd just stopped seeing me. I was startled by the sudden epiphany that she'd been faking her orgasms all along, certainly since our child had died, and probably since the first time we'd made love.

"What?" she asked, a huge question to ask and answer at any time in our lives. Her hands never left their usual place at the small of my back.

"I'm sorry," I told her, and I was sorry, and left her naked and alone in bed while I quickly dressed and went out for a drink.

I don't drink alcohol, never have, mostly because I don't want to maintain and confirm any of my ethnic stereotypes, let alone the most prevalent one, but also because my long-lost father, a half-breed, is still missing somewhere in the bottom of a tequila bottle. I had always wondered if he was a drunk because he was Indian or because he was white or because he was both.

Personally, I like bottled water, with gas, as the Europeans like to say. If I drink enough of that bubbly water in the right environment, I can get drunk. After a long night of Perrier or Pellegrino, I can still wake up with a vicious hangover. Obviously, I place entirely too much faith in the power of metaphor.

When I went out carousing with my fellow lawyers, I ended up in fancy hotel lounges, private clubs, and golf course cigar rooms, the places where the alcoholics adhere to a rigid dress code, but after leaving my marriage bed I wanted to drink in a place free from lawyers and their dress codes, from emotional obligations and beautiful white women, even the kind of white woman who might be the tenth most attractive in any room in the world.

I chose Chuck's, a dive near the corner of Virginia and First.

I'd driven by the place any number of times, had seen the Indians who loitered outside. I assumed it was an Indian bar, one of those establishments where the clientele, through chance and design, is mostly indigenous. I'd heard about these kinds of places. They are supposed to exist in every city.

"What can I get you?" asked the bartender when I sat on the stool closest to the door. She was an Indian woman with scars on her face and knuckles. A fighter. She was a woman who had once been pretty but had grown up in a place where pretty was punished. Now, twenty pounds overweight, on her way to forty pounds more, she was most likely saving money for a complete move to a city yet to be determined.

"Hey, handsome," she asked again as I stared blankly at her oft-broken nose. I decided that her face resembled most of the furniture in the bar: dark, stained by unknown insults, and in a continual state of repair. "What the fuck would you like to drink?"

"Water," I said, surprised that the word "fuck" could sound so friendly.

"Water?"

"Yeah, water."

She filled a glass from the tap behind her and plunked it down in front of me.

"A dollar," she said.

"For tap water?"

"For space rental."

I handed her a five-dollar bill.

"Keep the change," I said and took a big drink.

"Cool. Next time, you get a clean glass," she said and waited for my reaction.

I swallowed hard, kept my dinner down, and smiled.

"I don't need to know what's coming next," I said. "I like mysteries."

"What kind of mysteries?"

"Hard-boiled. The kind where the dog gets run over, the hero gets punched in the head, and the bad guy gets eaten by sharks."

"Not me," she said. "I got too much blood in my life already. I like romances."

I wondered if she wanted to sleep with me.

"You want something else," she said, "just shout it out. I'll hear you."

She moved to the other end of the bar where an old Indian man sipped at a cup of coffee. They talked and laughed. Surprisingly jealous of their camaraderie, I turned away and looked around the bar. It was a small place, maybe fifty feet long by twenty feet wide, with one pinball machine, one pool table, and two bathrooms. I supposed the place would be packed on a weekend.

As it was, on a cold Thursday, there were only five Indians in the bar, other than the bartender, her old friend, and me.

Two obese Indian women shared a table in the back, an Indian couple danced in front of a broken jukebox, and one large and muscular Indian guy played pool by himself. In his white T-shirt, blue-jean jacket, tight jeans, and cowboy boots, he looked like Chief Broom from *One Flew Over the Cuckoo's Nest*. I decided he could have killed me with a flick of one finger.

He looked up from his pool cue when he felt my eyes on him.

"What the fuck are you looking at?" he asked. His eyes were darker than the eight ball. I had no idea that "fuck" could be such a dangerous word.

"Nothing," I said.

Still holding his cue stick, he walked a few paces closer to me. I was afraid, very afraid.

"Nothing?" he asked. "Do I look like nothing to you?"

"No, no, that's not what I meant. I mean, I was just watching you play pool. That's all."

He stared at me, studied me like an owl might study a field mouse.

"You just keep your eyes to yourself," he said and turned back to his game.

I thought I was safe. I looked down to the bartender, who was shaking her head at me.

"Because I just, I just want to know," sputtered the big Indian. "I just want to know who the hell you think you are."

Furious, he shouted, a primal sort of noise, as he threw the cue stick against the wall. He rushed at me and lifted me by the collar.

"Who are you?" he shouted. "Who the fuck are you?"

"I'm nobody," I said, wet with fear. "Nobody. Nobody."

"Put him down, Junior," said the bartender.

Junior and I both turned to look at her. She held a pistol down by her hip, not as a threat, but more like a promise. Junior studied the bartender's face, estimated the level of her commitment, and dropped me back onto the stool.

He took a few steps back, pointed at me.

"I'm sick of little shits like you," he said. "Fucking urban Indians in your fancy fucking clothes. Fuck you. Fuck you."

I looked down and saw my denim jacket and polo shirt, the khakis and brown leather loafers. I looked like a Gap ad.

"I ever see you again," Junior said. "I'm going to dislocate your hips."

I flinched. Junior obviously had some working knowledge of human anatomy and the most effective means of creating pain therein. He saw my fear, examined its corners and edges, and decided it was large enough.

"Jesus," he said. "I don't know why I'm even talking to you. What are you going to do? You fucking wimp. You're not worth my time. Why don't you get the fuck out of here? Why don't you just get in your BMW, that's what you drive, enit? Why don't you get in your fucking BMW and get out of here before I change my mind, before I pop out one of your eyes with a fucking spoon, all right?"

I didn't drive a BMW; I drove a Saab.

"Yeah, fuck you," Junior said, thoroughly enjoying himself now. "Just drive back to your fucking mansion on Mercer Island or Edmonds or whatever white fucking neighborhood you live in. Drive back to your white wife. She's white, enit? Yeah, blond and blue-eyed, I bet. White, white. I bet her pussy hair is blond, too. Isn't it? Isn't it?"

I wanted to hate him.

"Go back to your mansion and read some fucking Teletubbies to your white fucking kids."

"What?" I asked.

"I said, go home to your white fucking kids."

"Fuck you," I said and completely surprised Junior. Good thing. He hesitated for a brief moment before he rushed at me again. His hesitation gave the bartender enough time to vault the bar and step in between Junior and me. I couldn't believe how fast she was.

She pressed the pistol tightly against Junior's forehead.

"Let it go, Junior," said the bartender.

"Why are you protecting him?" Junior asked.

"I don't give a shit about him," she said. "But I do care about you. You get into trouble again and you're going to jail forever. You know that."

Junior smiled.

"Sissy," he said to the bartender. "In another world, you and I are Romeo and Juliet."

"But we live in this world, Junior."

"Okay," said Sissy. "This is what's going to happen, Junior. You're going to walk over behind the bar, get yourself another Diet Pepsi, and mellow out. And Mr. Tap Water here is going to walk out the front door and never return. How does that sound to the both of you?"

"Make it two Pepsis," said Junior.

"Deal," said Sissy. "How about you, Polo?"

"Fuck him," I said.

Junior didn't move anything except his mouth.

"Sissy," he said. "How can you expect me to remain calm, how can you expect me to stay reasonable, when this guy so obviously wants to die?"

"I'll fight you," I said.

"What?" asked Sissy and Junior, both amazed.

"I'll fight you," I said again.

"All right, that's what I want to hear," said Junior. "Maybe you do have some balls. There's an alley out back."

"You don't want to do this," Sissy said to me.

"I'll meet you out there, Junior," I said.

Junior laughed and shook his head.

"Listen up, Tommy Hilfiger," he said. "I'm not stupid. I go out the back door and you're going to run out the front door. You don't have to make things so complicated. You want to leave, I'll let you leave. Just do it now, man."

"He's giving you a chance," Sissy said to me. "You better take it."

"No," I said. "I want to fight. I'll meet you out there. I promise."

Junior studied my eyes.

"You don't lie, do you?"

"I lie all the time," I said. "Most of the time. But I'm not lying now. I want to fight."

"All right, then, bring your best," he said and walked out the back door.

"Are you out of your mind?" Sissy asked. "Have you ever been in a fight?"

"I boxed a little in college."

"You boxed a little in college? You boxed a little in college? I can't believe this. Do you have any idea who Junior is?"

"No, why should I?"

"He's a pro."

"What? You mean, like a professional boxer?"

"No, man. A professional street fighter. No judges, no ring, no rules. The loser is the guy who don't get up."

"Isn't that illegal?"

"Illegal? Illegal? What, you think you're a lawyer now?"

"Actually, I am a lawyer."

Sissy laughed until tears ran down her face.

"Sweetheart," she said after she'd finally calmed down. "You need to leave. Please. Junior's got a wicked temper but he'll calm down soon enough. Hell, you come in a week from now and he'll probably buy you some water."

"Really?"

"No, not at all. I'm lying. You come in a week from now and Junior will break your thumbs."

She laughed again, laughed until she had to lean against the bar for support.

"Stop it," I said.

She kept laughing.

"Stop it," I shouted.

She kept laughing.

"Sweetheart," she said, trying to catch her breath. "I could kick your ass."

I shrugged off my denim jacket and marched for the back door. Sissy tried to stop me, but I pulled away from her and stepped into the alley.

Junior was surprised to see me. I felt a strange sense of pride. Without another word, I rushed at Junior, swinging at him with a wide right hook, with dreams of connecting with his jaw and knocking him out with one punch.

Deep in the heart of the heart of every Indian man's heart, he believes he is Crazy Horse.

My half-closed right hand whizzed over Junior's head as he expertly ducked under my wild punch and then rose, surely and accurately,

with a left uppercut that carried with it the moon and half of every
star in the universe.

▲

I woke up with my head in Sissy's lap. She was washing my face
with a cold towel.

"Where are we?" I asked.

"In the storeroom," she said.

"Where is he?"

"Gone."

My face hurt.

"Am I missing any teeth?"

"No," said Sissy. "But your nose is broken."

"Are you sure?"

"Trust me."

I looked up at her. I decided she was still pretty and pretty was good
enough. I grabbed her breast.

"Shit," she said and shoved me away.

I sprawled on the floor while she scrambled to her feet.

"What's wrong with you?" she asked. "What is wrong with you?"

"What do you mean? What?"

"Did you think, did you somehow get it into your crazy head that I
was going to fuck you back here? On the goddamn floor in the goddamn
dirt?"

I didn't know what to say.

"Jesus Christ, you really thought I was going to fuck you, didn't
you?"

"Well, I mean, I just . . ."

"You just thought because I'm an ugly woman that I'd be easy."

"You're not ugly," I said.

"Do you think I'm impressed by this fighting bullshit? Do you think it makes you some kind of warrior or something?"

She could read minds.

"You did, didn't you? All of you Indian guys think you're Crazy Horse."

I struggled to my feet and walked over to the sink. I looked in the mirror and saw a bloody mess. I also noticed that one of my braids was missing.

"Junior cut it off," said Sissy. "And took it with him. You're lucky he liked you. Otherwise, he would have taken a toe. He's done that before."

I couldn't imagine what that would have meant to my life.

"Look at you," she said. "Do you think that's attractive? Is that who you want to be?"

I carefully washed my face. My nose was most certainly broken.

"I just want to know, man. What are you doing here? Why'd you come here?"

My left eye was swelling shut. I wouldn't be able to see out of it in the morning.

"I wanted to be with my people," I said.

"Your people?" asked Sissy. "Your people? We're not your people."

"We're Indians."

"Yeah, we're Indians. You, me, Junior. But we live in this world and you live in your world."

"I don't like my world."

"You pathetic bastard," she said, her eyes swelling with tears that had nothing to do with laughter. "You sorry, sorry piece of shit. Do you know how much I want to live in your world? Do you know how much Junior wants to live in your world?"

Of course I knew. For most of my life, I'd dreamed about the world where I currently resided.

"Junior and me," she said. "We have to worry about having enough to eat. What do you have to worry about? That you're lonely? That you have a mortgage? That your wife doesn't love you? Fuck you, fuck you. *I have to worry about having enough to eat.*"

She stormed out of the room, leaving me alone.

I stood there in the dark for a long time. When I walked out, the bar was nearly empty. Another bartender was cleaning glasses. He didn't look at me. Sissy was gone. The front door was wide open. I stepped into the street and saw her sitting at the bus stop.

"I'm sorry," I said.

"Whatever."

"Can I give you a ride somewhere?"

"Do you really want to do that?" she asked.

"No," I said.

"Finally, you're being honest."

I stared at her. I wanted to say the exact right thing.

"Go home," she said. "Just go home."

I walked away, stopped halfway down the block.

"Do you have any kids?" I shouted back at her.

"Three," she said.

▲

Without changing my clothes, I crawled back into bed with Susan. Her skin was warm to the touch. The house ticked, ticked, ticked. In the morning, my pillow would be soaked with my blood.

"Where did you go?" Susan asked me.

"I was gone," I said. "But now I'm back."

SOUTH BY SOUTHWEST

▲▲

Seymour didn't want money—he wanted love—so he stole a pistol from the hot-plate old man living in the next apartment, then drove over to the International House of Pancakes, the one on Third, and ordered everybody to lie down on the floor.

The lunch-hour crowd did exactly as they were told. This was the International House of Pancakes and its patrons were used to such things.

In control, and because he wanted to be charming and memorable, Seymour kicked open the door to the kitchen and told the cooks to keep flipping the pancakes and pressing the waffles, to make sure the bacon and eggs didn't burn, and keep the coffee fresh.

This was Spokane, Washington, and he wanted the local newspaper to give him a name. Seymour wanted to be the Gentleman Bandit. He wanted to be the Man With Scotch Tape Wrapped Around His Broken Heart.

He was a white man and, therefore, he was allowed to be romantic.

This ain't going to take long, Seymour said to the cooks, and when it does end, everybody is still going to be hungry.

Seymour stood on top of a table. All of his life, he'd dreamed about standing on a table in the International House of Pancakes. He wondered if he would be remembered.

He wanted to be potentially dangerous.

Put your faces down, shouted Seymour to the diners, whose faces were already down. He said, I want you to put your lips on the floor and tell me what it tastes like.

He felt like he was capable of anything, like he might have to buy some bullets for his stolen pistol.

The money's in the safe, the money's in the safe, shouted one of the waitresses, but Seymour didn't need his life to become more difficult than it already was. He didn't want a thousand dollars or even a million dollars.

All I want is one dollar from each of you, said Seymour. He said, I know how hard it is to live in these depressed times, I just want a little bit of your hard-earned money.

He wanted to be kind.

From the floor, everybody held up a George Washington. On top of those human stems, the green bills bloomed and blossomed.

Good, good, said Seymour as he walked through the garden of money and collected forty-two dollars. Now, what I need, he said, what I need is somebody to run with me.

Where are you going? asked one of the cooks, a man who brought his own favorite spatula to work and carried it back home at the end of every shift.

Arizona, said Seymour, and the crowd oohed and aahed. He knew that everybody loves Arizona because Arizona is potentially dangerous. A man could strap a pistol to his hip and walk unmolested through the streets of Phoenix.

But I need somebody to go with me, said Seymour. He said, I aim to go on a nonviolent killing spree and I need somebody who will fall in love with me along the way.

From the floor, a fat Indian man raised his hand. He wore black sweatpants and a white T-shirt embossed with a photograph of Geronimo.

I'll go with you, said the fat Indian.

Are you gay? asked Seymour. I'm not gay. Are you gay?

No, sir, I am not homosexual, said the fat Indian, but I do believe in love.

Seymour thought about that for five seconds. And then he asked, You're an Indian, ain't you?

Yes, I am, yes, I am. Do you have a problem with that?

Only if you're one of those buffalo hunters. I can't have a nomad in my car. You just can't trust a nomad.

I come from a salmon tribe, said the fat Indian, and therefore I am a dependable man.

Well, then, you're going with me.

Seymour jumped down from the table and helped the fat Indian to his feet. They stood together in the half-light of the International House of Pancakes.

This place smells like smoke, said the fat Indian.

Salmon Boy, said Seymour, giving the fat Indian a brand-new name, in this cruel world, we're always going to smell like smoke.

Listen, said Seymour to the patrons still lying on the floor. He said, thank you for your kindness, tell them the Gentleman Bandit was here. Tell them it was the Man Who Was Looking For Love.

Seymour and Salmon Boy raced out of the restaurant and drove off in Seymour's car, a 1965 Chevrolet Malibu that carried more than two hundred thousand miles on the odometer.

You ever been to Arizona? Seymour asked Salmon Boy.

Once, when I was a boy. I went to a powwow in Flagstaff and lost my moccasins in the river there. My auntie spanked me until I cried like ten Indians.

I am sorry for your pain, said Seymour.

They drove the speed limit down Third Avenue, past four ham-
burger joints and a liquor store. They stopped at a red light.

Do you think the police are following us? asked Salmon Boy.

If they're not now, said Seymour, they soon will be.

Well, then, said Salmon Boy. He asked, Do you think we should
kiss now?

It seems like the right time, don't it? asked Seymour. He licked
his lips.

Yes, it does, said Salmon Boy. He wished he had a mint.

They kissed, keeping their tongues far away from each other, and
then told each other secrets.

Seymour said, When I was eleven years old, I made a dog lick
my balls.

Did you like it? asked Salmon Boy.

No, I threw up all over that mutt, said Seymour, and then it ran
away.

That's what happens when you get too far into love.

That's what happens.

When I was fifteen, said Salmon Boy, I stole eighty dollars from
my grandma. My mom and dad never knew. But my grandma must
have, she had to have, because she never talked to me again.

And then she died, said Salmon Boy.

Then the light was green and Seymour and Salmon Boy found
themselves traveling south along a back road near Enterprise, Oregon.
They had not slept in twenty-two hours.

They stopped when they saw a dead coyote nailed to a fence post.

That's a bad sign, ain't it? asked Seymour.

Yes, it is, said Salmon Boy.

What does it mean? asked the white man.

I have no idea, said the Indian.

They climbed out of the car and walked through the knee-deep snow to get to them: the fence post and the coyote.

They stared at the coyote the way the last two disciples stared at the resurrected Jesus.

The coyote had been there a long time, maybe for weeks, frozen stiff now, but certainly it had been freezing and unthawing, freezing and unthawing, during that unpredictable winter.

Seymour remembered the time, in the winter of 1966 or '67, when he walked into his parents' bedroom and caught them making love. Still naked, his father had jumped out of bed, taken Seymour by the hand, and led him down the hall. The hardwood floor was cold against Seymour's bare feet. Back in his own little bedroom, Seymour listened as his naked father explained why he was naked and why he'd been doing that strange and wonderful thing to his wife, to Seymour's mother.

See-See, his father had said to him, I'm doing it the best I can, so that your mother, your beautiful mother, will love me forever.

Salmon Boy, said Seymour as they studied the dead coyote, as they noticed one of his paws was missing, cut off and tucked into somebody's hatband maybe, or rolling around in some wild dog's belly perhaps.

Seymour said, My father had ambitions.

Salmon Boy smiled.

Like a good Indian, he knew when to talk and when to remain silent. Like a good Indian, he knew there was never a good time to talk.

We need to find a farmhouse, said Seymour, and we need to terrorize an old man and his wife. That is, he added, if we're going to do this nonviolent killing spree thing the right way.

Salmon Boy pointed out over the dead coyote's head. He pointed at the horizon where a red farmhouse sat like an apple on the white snow.

There it is, said Seymour, and Salmon Boy agreed.

Are we supposed to kiss now? asked Seymour, and Salmon Boy shrugged his shoulders.

I'm not sure I want to kiss you again, said Seymour. He said, But I will kiss you if you want it, because I don't want to hurt your feelings.

My feelings are my feelings, said Salmon Boy, they belong to me, and you don't have to worry about them at all.

All right then, we won't kiss no more. At least, not until we're sure about it.

Salmon Boy said, I believe in love.

Seymour and Salmon Boy climbed back into the car and drove down the plowed road toward the farmhouse. On both sides of them, the snowbanks rose high into the blue sky until it felt like they were driving down a tunnel.

Salmon Boy remembered the time his father won a free trip to Disneyland. They got half of the prize money and the whole family jumped into their blue van and headed for California. They were supposed to get the other half once they got to Disneyland, but something went wrong. There was nobody there to greet them and nobody answered the telephone back home. Salmon Boy and his whole family walked up to the gates of the Magic Kingdom and peered through the bars.

Inside, white people were having more fun than any Indians had ever had.

Salmon Boy remembered how all his family members counted up all the money in their pockets and discovered they carried enough coins for one loaf of bread and a package of cheese, and maybe, just maybe, enough gas to get them back home.

For twenty-six straight hours, Salmon Boy's father drove through the night and day, drove through a tunnel of sun, drove through a

tunnel of stars, and laughed like crazy when he drove over that
bridge that marked the entrance to the reservation.

My father loved me, Salmon Boy said to Seymour.

Well, then, said Seymour, that's a good thing to tell the police
when they finally catch us. It will explain everything.

You think they're still after us? asked Salmon Boy.

The police are always, always minutes behind us.

They knocked on the front door of the farmhouse. Seymour held
his unloaded pistol in his front pocket. He felt like somebody might
know how to save him.

An old white woman soon stood on the other side of the open door.

Who are you? she asked.

We are two desperate men on a nonviolent killing spree, said
Seymour.

And we're doing our best to fall in love, said Salmon Boy.

With who? asked the old woman.

With each other, said Seymour.

Well, then, she said, you better come in and get yourself something
to eat and drink. You're talking about some hard, hard work.

Seymour and Salmon Boy sat at her table while she made them
lemonade and ham sandwiches. Her husband had been dead for ten
long years, years that hung like lace in the attic, like an old quilt on
the bedroom wall, like a coyote nailed to a fence post.

My husband, she said, he's buried out there, back behind the barn.
You can't see his grave right now, but it's there, right there beneath
the snow.

The lemonade was sweet and the ham was salty and everything
was near-right with the world.

We only had one child, she said, a son, and he stood up one day,
walked out that door right there, and has never returned.

The old woman's eyes filled with tears. She asked, Didn't you go to high school with my son John?

Which one of us are you speaking to? asked Seymour.

I'm talking to both of you, she said.

Well, then, I have to say, said Seymour, that I don't remember anybody named John. I didn't even go to high school.

How about the Indian? asked the old woman.

His name is Salmon Boy.

Surely, you didn't go to school with my son, she said, because I would have remembered a crazy name like that.

She walked around on old legs and set an old coffeepot down over a blue flame.

My real name ain't Salmon Boy.

Real or not, my son didn't go to school with any Indians, she said. She stirred her coffee. All three of them stared down into its blackness.

Anyway, she said, I think I recognize everybody who visits me. I spend whole days with my visitors, thinking I know them, thinking I have to be a good hostess. They show up in the mornings mostly, and I feed them breakfast. I feed them lunch and dinner. Sometimes, at night, I get a bed ready for them, pillows and sheets and blankets, before I realize they aren't real.

She looked at the men.

Are you real? she asked.

Seymour and Salmon Boy looked at each other. They weren't sure.

But listen to me, she said, an old woman telling old stories. How about you boys? And this killing spree of yours, where are you heading to?

It's a nonviolent killing spree, said Seymour, and we're heading to Arizona.

So, she said, it's a north-south killing spree. That's a lot different than an east-west killing spree.

What's the difference?

More killing when you're moving west. More policemen when you're moving south. East-west takes a lot more discipline, more preparation. North-south, you just got to have enough passion. Passion is all you need. Do you boys have passion?

Seymour remembered his second wife, how she had fallen in love with her gynecologist and run away to Ames, Iowa, taking all of their children with her, so Seymour had dialed up 411, found his first wife's phone number, called her up at three in the morning, and had asked her to remarry him now, right now.

You're crazy, she said, that's why I never stopped loving you.

Then you'll marry me? he asked. Again? he asked.

Oh, I love you, she said, her voice breaking apart like glass. Then she said, I shouldn't have married you the first time, and then she hung up the phone.

It was five after three in the morning, so Seymour ran down the hallway with a twenty-dollar bill in his hand, and slid it beneath the door of the red-headed prostitute who lived in Apartment 7. He didn't want sex—he wanted redemption—so he ran back to his room, climbed into bed, and cried until the sun rose and slapped him across the eyes.

Do you boys have passion? asked the farmhouse old woman. She placed her wrinkled hand on Seymour's hand.

Salmon Boy was jealous.

The Indian remembered when he told his cousin she was more beautiful than any white girl he had ever seen. She'd taken off her shirt and bra to show him what she'd been hiding beneath. Small breasts, like birds with opened wings, sat down on her brown chest.

He loved her. He thought she was beautiful and young and would grow up to be beautiful and old.

Salmon Boy looked at the old white woman, saw her blue, blue eyes, and wondered if she'd been beautiful when she was a girl. He wondered if she had any Indian blood.

My husband was a soldier, said the old woman. She said, He was a reluctant soldier. He shot a dozen men, a dozen of those Japs, on some island in 1943. He shot twelve of them, shot six of them in the head, four of them in the heart, and two of them in the belly. He shot twelve of them without thinking, didn't stop to wonder what it meant, but then number thirteen came running over the hill, over the grassy hill.

What color was the grass? asked Seymour.

What do you mean? asked the old woman. She asked, What do you mean what color was the grass? The grass is always green. Don't you know that? Don't you know the grass is always green.

But it was a different part of the world, said Seymour, I thought maybe the grass is a different color in a different part of the world.

The grass is green in every part of the world, said the old woman. She said, On Mars, the grass is green.

The grass is green on my reservation, said Salmon Boy. He was telling the truth.

There you go, said the old woman, there you go. Even the Indian knows the grass is green. What's wrong with you? Didn't you learn anything when you went to high school? My son went to that same high school and he learned a few things before he disappeared forever. You bet he learned a few things.

But what about your husband? asked Seymour. He was trying to change the subject.

What about my husband? Did you know my husband? He was a hero during the Good War. He was a hero, even though he was a reluctant soldier. He shot twelve Japs, shot them all dead, but there was thirteen of them running, and that last one came over the hill, running through the green grass, and my husband tried to shoot him, but he couldn't pull the trigger, and that Jap ran a bayonet through my husband's heart, right through the middle of his heart. And they buried him right there on the beach, right there in the sand.

But I thought, said Seymour. He said, I thought your husband was buried behind the barn.

You're damn right, said the old woman. He's buried. He's buried in the snow out there, he's buried in the sand over there, there are pieces of my husband buried everywhere.

Salmon Boy stared down into his coffee. In that darkness, he saw a white man with a rifle.

He was a hero, said the old woman. My husband shot twelve Japs on the island. Twelve of them! Can you imagine that? All by himself. My husband, he always said he would whisper in my ear in the middle of the night, he always said most men can kill eleven people, but only a few can kill twelve, and only the best, the very best, can kill thirteen.

She put her head down on the cold table.

My husband, she said, he was never the best. He was a good man, but he was never a great man.

With her head down, she breathed deep. With her head down, she fell asleep like somebody had flipped a switch.

Seymour placed his left hand on her gray hair. He held it there.

Salmon Boy was jealous. He closed his eyes and sipped at his coffee. It was bitter and instant and when the Indian opened his eyes, he was sitting in the car right at the edge of the Grand Canyon.

Through the windshield, Salmon Boy watched as Seymour pointed the gun at a tourist family. Mother, father, son, daughter.

Here, here, said the father, you can have all my money.

I don't want your money, said Seymour, I want to know how you met, I want to know how you fell in love.

But that's our story, said the father, you can't steal it.

Tell me, tell me, shouted Seymour as he grabbed one of the children, the son, and held the empty pistol against his temple.

Please, please, said the mother, my husband was somebody else's husband when we met. But I waited for him. I didn't want to break up his marriage. I never told him I loved him. I just loved him and hoped that was enough. And it was and it was. They divorced and he called me three days later and asked me to marry him. We'd never been on a date, but he asked me to marry him. We'd never done anything but talk in the copy room, but he asked me to marry him. And I knew it was crazy but I married him and we've been married for fifteen years.

How does that happen? Seymour asked. He pushed the son back toward his parents, back toward his sister.

It happens all the time, said the father, you just never hear about it.

No, no, no, said Seymour, people don't love each other anymore. Not anymore like that. Not anymore.

Seymour turned toward the Grand Canyon, ran toward the void.

In the car, Salmon Boy held his breath because he was positive that Seymour was going to jump. Salmon Boy's blood climbed the ladder over his heart. But Seymour stopped just short of the chasm and threw the pistol down, down, down.

The pistol fell then and is still falling now.

Oh, said Salmon Boy as Seymour turned to face him.

How do you love a man? Seymour asked the sky, but the sky didn't answer.

Salmon Boy closed his eyes and when he opened them again he was lying in a motel room in Flagstaff, Arizona.

Seymour quietly slept on the other side of the bed, or perhaps he wasn't asleep at all.

Salmon Boy watched the television, watched a black-and-white movie where the people didn't make any sense.

Salmon Boy remembered another time, when he was a child, when his father was driving the family back from some powwow or another, when Salmon Boy had picked up the newspaper to discover that the *Batman* movie was playing on local television. The old-time Batman, the Adam-West-as-Batman Batman.

Can you drive faster? Salmon Boy asked his father. He wanted to watch the movie.

We'll never make it in time, said his father. But he loved his son and so he drove as fast as he could, through the tunnel of his son's dreams, through a tunnel crowded with all of his son's dreams.

They drove by a coyote nailed to a speed-limit sign.

They drove by a coyote howling from an overpass.

They drove by a coyote drinking a cup of coffee in a truck-stop diner.

When they reached the motel, Salmon Boy rushed into the room and switched on the television, expecting to see *Batman*, but saw only the last few moments of some other movie.

In that movie, a pretty white boy stares out a window into the falling snow, into a dark courtyard where the snow falls on a man riding a bicycle in circles, into the courtyard where a handsome man rides a bicycle around a statue of a broken heart, or perhaps it wasn't a broken heart at all, but Salmon Boy remembers it that way.

He remembers it now as he stares at the black-and-white movie where the characters don't make any sense, as Seymour sleeps on the other side of the bed, or pretends to be asleep.

Seymour, said Salmon Boy.

Yes, said Seymour.

I am the most lonely I have ever been.

I know.

Will you hold me close?

Yes, yes, I will.

Salmon Boy pushed himself into Seymour's arms. They both wore only their boxer shorts. Seymour's blue shorts contrasted with his pale skin while Salmon Boy's white boxers glowed in the dark.

I don't want to have sex, said Salmon Boy.

I don't either.

But how will we fall in love if we don't have sex?

I don't know.

They held each other tighter and tighter. They were afraid.

I am happy in your arms, said Seymour.

And I am happy in yours.

Is this what it feels like?

What?

To be loved, to be held, to be intimate without the fear of penetration?

I think so.

Yes, I think so, too. I think this is what women have wanted from men for all of our lives. I think they want to be held in our arms and fall asleep in the absence of body fluids.

I think you may be right.

They held each other tighter and tighter. They were not aroused. They were warm and safe.

Can we be like this forever? asked Salmon Boy.

I don't think that's possible.

Together, they watched the black-and-white movie where nothing made sense. They watched it until they fell asleep together and when they woke up they were sitting in a McDonald's in Tucson, Arizona.

They wore identical Grand Canyon T-shirts.

How much money do we have left? asked Seymour.

Counting the money the old woman gave us?

Of course.

Ten dollars.

That means we're in some definite financial trouble.

Appears that way.

And we've just about run out of Arizona, too.

And almost all of the south this country has.

And most of the southwest, as well.

Seymour looked around the McDonald's. He saw an Indian woman arguing with an Indian man. They spoke in some strange language.

What's that they're talking? asked Seymour.

Navajo, I think, said Salmon Boy. He'd always believed the Navajo were the most beautiful people on the planet. The man and woman arguing by the window were no exceptions. Their hair and skin were so dark that they looked purple, especially in the white light streaming through the glass.

Do you know what they're saying? asked Seymour.

I don't speak Navajo.

But you're Indian.

But I'm not Navajo.

Seymour didn't like to argue. He stared at the arguing Navajos until they sensed his attention, looked over, and flipped him off.

Seymour smiled and waved.

I don't think that was Navajo, he said. Seymour said, They look like aliens.

Some people think the Navajos are aliens, said Salmon Boy, like they came down in spaceships ten thousand years ago and took over.

Seymour kept staring until the Navajo couple gathered up their belongings and left the restaurant. He felt an ache in his heart. He wondered if that coyote was still nailed to the fence post. He wondered what Navajos looked like when they were naked and in love.

Do you think they love each other? he asked.

If they do, said Salmon Boy, then it's alien love. And I don't know anything about alien love.

Steven Spielberg knows.

That's because he's an alien, said Salmon Boy. The Jews and the Navajos came down in the same ships, he said. Salmon Boy asked, Didn't you know that Moses was a Navajo? He asked, Haven't you heard of the lost tribes?

Everybody is lost, said Seymour.

Salmon Boy wondered how much farther they could go on ten dollars. He wondered how much south, how much southwest, could fit into the world. He remembered that he'd left the television on when he walked over to the International House of Pancakes. He remembered thinking, I'm just going to be a few minutes. He wondered if the television was still playing, if the woman who lived in the apartment next door was pounding on the wall, screaming at him to turn it down, turn it down, turn it down.

Salmon Boy wondered why he was homesick for a place where he had lived alone.

Seymour sipped at his coffee. He remembered the story of a woman who dropped McDonald's coffee into her lap, burned herself to bits, and won a billion dollars in the lawsuit. He wondered if he should drop coffee into his lap, but then he realized his coffee was only lukewarm. If he dropped it into his lap, he might win fifty bucks for coffee-staining his blue jeans.

Seymour wondered if the world was a cruel place.

Are you learning how to love me? asked Seymour.

Salmon Boy sipped at his own coffee. He didn't know how to answer that question.

I took you to the Grand Canyon, said Seymour.

Seymour said, I have made you promises and I have kept them.

The silence smelled like smoke.

It's a difficult thing, Salmon Boy said after a long time. Salmon Boy whispered, It's a difficult thing for one man to love another man, whether they kiss each other or not.

We've only kissed once, said Seymour. Maybe we'll fall in love if we kiss a little more.

Do you think there's a number? asked Salmon Boy. Do you think there's a magic number written on every heart? Do you think you can kiss right up to some magic number and make a person love you?

Seymour looked around the Tucson McDonald's. There were white people and Navajos; there were people who preferred their Quarter Pounders with cheese and those who didn't care for cheese at all; and there were those who desperately wished that McDonald's would introduce onion rings to its menu.

Oh, Seymour thought, there are so many possibilities.

Do you think? he asked. Do you think there's somebody in here who might love me, who I might love?

I don't know, said Salmon Boy, but you are my friend, and I believe in love.

Salmon Boy remembered the reservation Indian girl who drowned in three feet of water, wrapped up in knots of seaweed, while three other Indian girls tried to pull her free. Salmon Boy believed that the life of that one drowned girl was worth the lives of every person in Arizona.

Salmon Boy placed his left hand over his heart to protect it.

How much money do we have? Seymour asked again. He wanted to be sure.

Ten dollars.

Then we're going to need more.

Yes, yes, we are.

Seymour leapt to his feet, stood on a table in McDonald's.

Excuse me, shouted Seymour, but we are here to take your money, not all of it, but enough to continue, enough to keep moving south.

Seymour did not have the pistol, but he held his hand in the shape of a pistol. He clung tightly to the idea of a pistol.

Click, click, click on the empty chambers.

Seymour wanted to be kind and he wanted to be romantic. He wanted to be the Man Who Saved the Indian. He wanted to be the Coyote Nailed to a Fence Post. He wanted to be the Man Who Could Shoot Thirteen People.

He was a white man, and therefore he could dream.

Seymour ordered everybody to lie down on the floor. He ordered them to give up all the money they could spare. Salmon Boy stared down into his coffee cup. In that blackness, he saw the headlights of a fast car.

Please, please, give us your money, said Seymour. Just a dollar or two, he said.

The people in McDonald's gave up their money like an offering. They filled the plate. They moved that much closer to God.

Hurry, hurry, Seymour shouted. The police are right behind us, they're right behind us.

Salmon Boy stared down into his coffee cup and saw a blue man with a gun.

Oh, said Salmon Boy. He said, Oh, as he rose to his feet and stood on the table beside Seymour. They were men in love with the idea of being in love.

Please, he said. He said, Please.

Seymour took all the money his victims could spare, and then he took Salmon Boy's hand, and they ran outside into all the south and southwest that remained in the world.

THE SIN EATERS

▲▲▲

I dreamed about war on the night before the war began, and though nobody officially called it a war until years later, I woke that next morning with the sure knowledge that the war, or whatever they wanted to call it, was about to begin and that I would be a soldier in a small shirt.

On that morning, the sun rose and bloomed like blood in a glass syringe. The entire Spokane Indian Reservation and all of its people and places were clean and scrubbed. The Spokane River rose up from its bed like a man who had been healed and joyously wept all the way down to its confluence with the Columbia River. There was water everywhere: a thousand streams interrupted by makeshift waterfalls; small ponds hidden beneath a mask of thick fronds and anonymous blossoms; blankets of dew draped over the shoulders of isolated knolls. An entire civilization of insects lived in the mud puddle formed by one truck tire and a recent rainstorm. The blades of grass, the narrow pine needles, and the stalks of roadside wheat were as sharp and bright as surgical tools.

Those were the days before the first color televisions were smuggled onto the reservation, but after a man with blue eyes had dropped two symmetrical slices of the sun on Japan. All of it happened before a handsome Catholic was assassinated in Dallas, leaving a bright red mark on the tape measure of time, but after the men with blue eyes had carried dark-eyed children into the ovens and made them ash.

I was a dark-eyed Indian boy who leaned against pine trees and broke them in half. I was twelve years old and strong, with fluid skin that was the same color as Chimacum Creek in April, May, when the mud and water were indistinguishable from each other.

Those were the days of the old stories, and in many of those stories I was the Indian boy who was capable of anything.

In one of those stories, I lifted a grown man, Edgar Horse, draped him over my shoulder like an old quilt, and carried him for two miles from the gnarled pine tree in front of the tribal high school all the way down to the trading post in downtown Wellpinit. I carried Edgar, as many others had carried Edgar, because we were living in the days before Indians discovered wheelchairs and the idea of wheelchairs.

In another of those stories, I was the maker of songs. Widowed grandmothers gave me dollar bills and I invented songs about their long-dead husbands. Often, as I sang, the grandmothers would weep tears that I collected into tin cups and fed to the huckleberry bushes growing on the low hills of the reservation. All these years later, those huckleberries still taste like grief, and a cellar filled with preserved huckleberries is a graveyard stacked high with glass tombstones.

Because I was the maker of songs, young men gave me small gifts, a blank piece of linen paper, a stick of gum, an envelope decorated with a beautiful, canceled stamp, and in return I taught them love songs. I taught those young men the love songs that transformed scraps of newspaper into thin birds. In the middle of a city, in the middle of a strong wind, a thousand paper birds rattled and sang. I taught those young men the love songs that forced horses to bow their heads and kneel in the fields, the love songs that revealed the secrets of fire, the love songs that healed, the love songs that precipitated wars.

In another of those stories, in one of many stories about me, about the reservation where I was born, I was the small soldier who lived with his Spokane Indian mother and his Coeur d'Alene Indian father in a two-bedroom house in a valley near the Spokane River.

I slept alone in one bedroom while my parents shared the second. The living room was small, with just enough space for an end table, console radio, and tattered couch. The kitchen was the largest room in the house. We spent most of our waking hours there at the table that my father had carved from a fallen pine tree. My father had built almost every piece of furniture in the house, but he was not a good carpenter. The chairs rocked though they were not rocking chairs. We had to place one of my father's old work shirts under one short leg of the dining table to prevent food from sliding into our laps. The radio and all of its bright and mysterious internal organs sat inside a series of homemade wooden boxes that had to be replaced every few months because of small electrical fires.

When those fires burned, my father would laugh and dance. He would pick up the flames with his bare hands and hold them close to his chest.

Indians will love anything if given the chance.

I loved our house. I cried whenever I left it. I never wanted to leave it. I wanted to grow old in that house. I wanted to become the crazy elder who'd lived in the same house for all of his life. When I died there, I wanted to have ninety years of stories hanging in the closets.

Beside the house, a pine tree bent its back like an old Indian woman walking in a strong wind. A forest of old women marched from horizon to horizon. Two crows, looking for rodents and songbirds, floated in the morning sky. A mile above the crows, clumsy airplanes left behind thick veins of smoke. Miles and miles above the airplanes, seven sibling planets kept track of our secrets.

On that morning and inside that house, I pulled back the covers of my dream of war and the covers of my bed, and stepped onto the cold, uneven floor. Our house leaned in whatever direction the wind happened to be blowing. I walked into the kitchen. The wind was blowing from east to west.

"Mother, there's going to be a war," I said to the woman with brown skin and black hair. She was sitting at the table with a cup of coffee. The coffee was thick with grounds. The blue china cup was chipped at its edges. She had purchased it, as is, at a secondhand store in the city of Spokane. My mother's eyes were as dark as the eyes of a salmon who has just returned to the place where it was spawned.

"Jonah," she said to me and laughed. My mother had named me after a man who'd survived a miracle. Because of that, she seemed to regard every action of mine, no matter how ordinary, as a miracle of its own. That morning, as I stepped into her kitchen, fresh from a dream of war, my mother pointed at the miracle of my fevered face and mussed hair. She set her cup on the table and took me into her arms. She said my name again and laughed, as if I had truly just emerged from the belly of a whale, and not from the belly of a dream where the enemy soldiers wore surgical gloves and white smocks.

"The soldiers are coming," I said to my mother. "We have to hide."

"Where are we going to hide?" she asked. She thought we were playing a game. She covered my face and eyes with the thick curtain of her hair.

"I can't see," I said.

"Of course," she said. "If you can't see the soldiers, they can't see you."

She was wrong. I could have seen those soldiers if I had been blind from birth. Flames rose from their footprints.

"We can hide between the walls," I said. "Or beneath the floor."

"Like Anne Frank," said my mother.

"No," I said. "She didn't hide good enough."

I knew the long history of children who had been forced to hide in clumsy places and were subsequently discovered.

"Hush, hush," said my mother.

"We're going to die," I said.

"Don't say that," said my mother. "Don't ever say that."

I looked up into the salt seas of her eyes. She was my mother, my priest, my chair in the confessional. I sat in her lap and whispered in her ear.

"Please," I said. "Believe me."

My mother was supposed to be stronger than I would ever be. She was supposed to convince me that my dream was not real. She was supposed to tell me that the enemy soldiers were marching only through the killing fields of my imagination. She was supposed to heal me. All of my life, she had healed me whenever I was ill.

"Jonah," she said, using my name as she might have used aspirin or penicillin. "It was a dream."

"There was so much blood," I said. "A whole river of blood. And the Indians were trying to swim through it. Trying to swim for home. But the soldiers kept pulling us out of the water. They skinned us and hung us up to dry. Then they ate us up. They ate every one of us. And they ate every part of us. Except our skins. They fed our skins to the dogs. And the dogs were fighting over our skins. Just growling and fighting. It's true."

"Oh, Jonah," said my mother. "It was just a nightmare."

"It's real," I said and wept. "I know it's real."

"Oh, Jonah," said my mother as she wept with me.

We were still weeping together at the kitchen table when my father returned from the night shift at the mine. He stared at us with dark eyes. His black hair was cut close to his scalp. His face was a relief map:

rivers of scars, the desert floor of skin, and the badlands of wrinkles. With tremendous power and grace, he strode across the kitchen toward us. He was a huge man whose clothes never seemed to fit him correctly. My father placed his left hand on my mother's shoulder and his right hand on my head.

Though my father was a bad carpenter, he had always been a clever magician. I knew he could conjure up different spells with each hand. His left hand made my mother's back arch in the night. His right hand pulled down ripe apples from the surprised pine trees. His left hand made the sky open up and rain. His right hand started fires when he snapped his fingers. When he clasped his hands together in prayer, or slapped them together in applause, the distance between the earth and moon changed.

On that morning, when my father set his left hand on my mother's shoulder and his right on my head, I knew he was trying to stop our crying. I wanted him to stop the war from coming. But my mother and I continued to weep, and I knew the enemy soldiers continued to march toward us.

"What's wrong?" asked my father, feeling powerless.

"He had a nightmare," said my mother. "He thinks a war is coming."

"Then why are you crying?" he asked her.

"He's scaring me."

My father wrapped his huge arms around his wife and son. He had no magic left in his hands. Bright tears fell from my father's eyes and burned the kitchen table. He raised his face toward the ceiling and the sky beyond it, and opened his mouth to sing or scream. He was afraid too, for reasons he did not understand.

My dream of war filled the room like oxygen. The three of us breathed it in and choked on it. We tasted it. It tasted like salt; it tasted like blood.

I don't know how long the three of us wept together. Minutes or hours could have passed. I burrowed into my mother and father. I wanted to hide between the walls of their ribs or beneath the floors of their hearts.

"Wait," my father said after a long time. "Listen."

My mother and I listened. We heard a storm approaching.

"Thunder," said my mother.

"Lightning," said my father.

"War," I said.

"Rain," said my mother.

"Dark clouds," said my father.

"War," I said.

"Floods," said my mother.

"Famine," said my father.

"War," I said.

Together, my parents and I stepped into our front yard and stared up into the sky. We saw the big planes roar noisily through the rough air above the reservation. We saw the soldiers step from the bellies of those planes and drop toward the earth. We saw a thousand parachutes open into a thousand green blossoms. All over the Spokane Indian Reservation, all over every reservation in the country, those green blossoms fell onto empty fields, onto powwow grounds, and onto the roofs of tribal schools and health clinics. Those green blossoms fell between pine trees, beside deep and shallow rivers, and among the sacred and utilitarian headstones of our dead.

My parents and I watched one green blossom float down into our front yard. Then one more, and another, and a fourth. A fifth and sixth. The seventh landed in the back of our wagon.

A garden of parachutes.

With rifles raised, the soldiers advanced on us. I saw four white faces, two black faces, and a face that looked like mine.

"Step away from the house!" shouted the soldier-who-looked-like-me. "And lie facedown on the ground!"

My parents and I did as we were told. As I was lying on the grass, I watched an ant carry the dead body of another ant.

I was afraid.

I knew that other soldiers, white ones, black ones, and ones who looked like me, were parachuting onto every reservation in the country.

I could hear one million Indians holding their breath.

On our reservation, other soldiers soon arrived and swarmed into the house. I didn't know what they were looking for.

"Your names!" a black soldier shouted at our backs as he stood above us. I couldn't tell if he was making a statement or asking a question.

"What are your names?" asked the black soldier.

"We're the Lots," said my father. Still on the ground, I turned my head to look at my father's face, but his head was turned the other way. I turned back to look at my mother's face and saw that her eyes were closed tight. I wondered if she was praying.

"Joseph, Sarah, and Jonah Lot?" asked the black soldier. He knew our names.

"What are your names?" I asked.

"Quiet," said the black soldier. I could hear the fear in his voice. He was afraid of us, or perhaps he was afraid of what was happening to the world, to him. He was the kind of soldier who had always followed orders, who had never questioned them, and who now did not know how to change at the moment when he desired, more than anything, to change.

Rifle shots in the distance. The earth trembled because somebody beautiful was running. Then more rifle shots. The wind shrieked because somebody beautiful was falling. Then more rifle shots. The earth trembled because somebody beautiful had fallen into dust. Then silence for twelve seconds. I counted them. One second, I inhaled. Two seconds, I exhaled. Six seconds, I inhaled. Seven seconds, I exhaled. Eleven seconds, I inhaled. Twelve seconds, I exhaled. Then one final rifle shot.

"What is your name?" I asked the black soldier. He ignored me.

"Are you Joseph, Sarah, and Jonah Lot?" asked the soldier. Tears were running down his face.

"Yes," said my father.

"Joseph is full-blood Coeur d'Alene, Sarah is full-blood Spokane," the black soldier said to a white soldier. "The Coeur d'Alene and Spokane are both Interior Salish tribes, so there should be no problem of contamination with the child."

I heard the word *contamination* and cried out. I thought of disease, of deadly viruses floating invisibly through the air.

"Are there any other children?" asked the white soldier.

"No," said the black soldier. "The child was supposed to be a twin, but the other baby was stillborn."

My mother gasped. I wondered if her body had remembered the pain of my birth, and the greater pain of giving birth to my dead brother.

"What is this about?" asked my father. I could hear the fear in his voice. He tried to disguise it as anger. He turned his head to look at me. I could see the fear in his face. I'd never been more afraid of the fear in any man's eyes.

"Quiet," said a white soldier as he kicked my father in the ribs.

"Careful," said the soldier-who-looked-like-me. "Don't draw blood."

Contamination.

A white soldier suddenly pulled me to my feet and looked me in the eyes. His eyes were an impossible green.

"Don't hurt my baby," begged my mother.

"What was your brother's name?"

"His name was Joseph," I said. "Same as my dad."

The white soldier nodded his head as if he'd known it all along.

"Leave him alone!" shouted my father as he tried to rise from the ground. A white soldier smashed him back down with the butt of his rifle. My father bled into the dirt.

"Damn it," said the soldier-who-looked-like-me. "I told you. No blood."

Contamination.

The red glow poured from my father's nose and mouth. My mother clawed at the dirt as if she thought she could escape by digging a tunnel.

"Jonah," said the white soldier. "We don't mean to hurt you. Or your parents."

"Yes, you do," I said. "You're going to eat us. You're going to drink our blood."

The white soldier's face grew harder. Marble, granite, quartz.

"Jonah," he said. "We've come to take you away from here. We need you."

"I knew you were coming," I said.

My father tried to breathe through his shattered nose and mouth. My mother pressed her face into the ground and wore it like a mask.

I bit deeply into my palm.

"I surrender," I said to the white soldier as I offered my bloodied hand to him.

▲

War is a church.

In my church, my mother and father were frozen in the stained-glass window above the altar. The red glass of my father's bloody face was cradled by the blue glass of my mother's dress.

Memory is a church on fire.

In my church, a soldier dropped a lighted match at the wooden feet of a crucified Jesus and watched the fire wrap around the savior like a shroud. Flames lifted away from Jesus' body like angels and blessed the parched pews, threadbare curtains, and brittle hymnal books. Two rows of flames sang in the choir box. Flames climbed up the altar and walls to embrace my stained-glass parents.

The glass darkened with smoke.

The glass melted in the fire.

The glass exploded in the heat.

My parents' faces fell to pieces in my mind only moments after those soldiers landed in our front yard. I began to forget pieces of my parents' faces only moments after I was taken from them. By the time I was loaded into a school bus with twenty other kids from the reservation, I could remember only the dark of my mother's eyes and the curve of my father's jaw. By the time our bus crossed the border of the reservation, taking us away from what we had known and into what we could never have predicted, I had forgotten almost every piece of my parents' faces. I touched my face, remembering that its features owed their shapes to the shapes of my parents' faces, but I felt nothing familiar. I was strange and foreign.

Outside the bus, the landscape was familiar. With my parents, in our horse-drawn wagon, I had often traveled along that highway from the Spokane Indian Reservation into the city of Spokane. The black-top road split the wheat fields into halves. On one side, irrigation equipment stepped like giant insects across the field. On the other side, a white farmer sat in a still tractor. He watched our bus slowly pass from left to right across his horizon. Farther along, a tribe of starlings perched in one pine tree. I raised my hand to wave a greeting to them and one thousand birds lifted simultaneously into flight. The grain silos were painted with the names of ghost towns. Those silos could have been the tombstones of giants. Red lights blinked at the tops of radio antenna towers. An orphaned stretch of barbed-wire fence was partially submerged in a roadside pond.

Suddenly, everything looked dangerous. Sharp stars ripped through the fabric of the morning sky. Morning dew boiled and cooked green leaves. Sun dogs snarled and snapped at one another. The vanishing point was the tip of a needle.

Inside the bus, a dozen soldiers stood in the aisle between the seats. Another soldier drove the bus. I counted them again and again. There were ten white soldiers, two black soldiers, and the soldier-who-looked-like-me. I sat a few seats behind the black soldier who was driving the bus. In the back, Arlene and Kim, the Cox twins, hugged each other and wailed. Farther forward, the five Juniors, four boys and one girl, pushed their faces against the windows. There were two boys named James—one who went by Jimmy and one who went by Jamie—and three Johns. Jimmy was the chess player and Jamie was dyslexic. The three Johns hated one another. Randy Peone, the green-eyed Spokane, was shouting curses in English and Salish, the languages of our tribe. A white soldier quickly pinned Randy to his seat, tied his arms behind his back, and covered his mouth with duct tape. There were three Kateris, all named after the Mohawk woman who was canonized when her smallpox scars disappeared. Two of the Kateris prayed quietly, while the third had long ago discarded her faith and was now trying to pry a spring loose from her seat to use as a weapon. Teddy, who had a white father, sat with his half-brother, Tyrone, who had a black father. Billy the Retard was smiling. I wondered if this new world was the world he'd been living in all along and if he was now happy that the rest of the Indian kids had finally joined him. Sam the Indian, who was really white, trembled in the seat across the aisle from me.

"Jonah, is it real?" asked Sam the Indian. He was a small boy, the subject of a thousand reservation schoolyard taunts, but none of that mattered in the bus. At that moment, as we all traveled together down the longest highway in tribal history, Sam the Indian was instantly loved and beloved by all of the Indians on that bus. Sam the Indian was a white child who loved Indians, who had come to live among us, and who had never been allowed to learn any of our secrets. As we Indians cowered in our seats, we all made silent apologies to Sam. We all said silent prayers for his safety because we had all, collectively and unconsciously, just decided that Sam's pale skin contained some kind of magic. We thought the white soldiers would notice Sam's white skin and call him brother. We thought they'd lift Sam to their shoulders in celebration, in some kind of strange and raucous cere-mony, and carry him away while all of us Indian children made our escape. We all thought Sam could save us, but I was the only one who spoke to him.

"Help us," I said to Sam.

Sam did not understand.

"Jonah," he said. "Is this real?"

"It's real," I said.

"Quiet," said the white soldier standing between us.

Sam the Indian looked from me to the soldier and back to me.

"Why is it real?" asked Sam the Indian.

"Quiet," said the white soldier again without looking at us. I was happy I didn't have to answer Sam's question. I'm not sure what I would have said. And if I had told the truth, if I had given Sam an answer that was close to the truth, I might have lost all hope and faith. I might have closed my eyes and never opened them again.

"Why is it real?" asked Sam again.

"Shut up," said the white soldier. He swallowed hard. I wondered if he hated us. I couldn't see any obvious hate in his blue eyes. I studied the eyes of all of the soldiers. Five of the white soldiers had blue eyes, one had green, one had hazel, and the other had brown. One of the black soldiers had light brown eyes but I couldn't see the eyes of the other black soldier, who was driving the bus.

I studied the face of the soldier-who-looked-like-me. He was the tallest soldier. He had a cross tattooed on the back of his right hand. He couldn't have been older than eighteen or nineteen. He had brown eyes and skin. His hair was blacker than mine. He had a thin purple scar that arced from the corner of his left eye back toward his ear. His eyes passed over me as he scanned the faces of his prisoners. It was not enough. I wanted him to study my face as carefully as I was studying his face. I wanted him to tell me why he was a soldier holding a rifle instead of a fellow prisoner sitting in the seat beside me. I wanted to know the story of his scar.

"Where are you taking us?" I asked as I stood in my seat.

"Quiet," said that white soldier for the third time as he pushed me back down.

I rose again.

"Where are you taking us?" I asked.

That white soldier wrapped his left hand around my throat and squeezed.

"You get to breathe," said the soldier. "Or you get to ask questions. You make the choice."

"Release that boy," said another white soldier.

That white soldier gave my throat one last squeeze and dropped me to the floor. I coughed and gagged.

The bus was quiet. I lay on the floor and heard the *hum-hum-hum* of the bus wheels. I closed my eyes and pressed my hands flat against the floor. As the bus traveled, I could feel every pebble and irregularity in the road.

We traveled for twenty-two miles. I lay on the floor and counted each mile, counted each and every part of a mile, until the bus pulled into the small town of Wright. From my place on the floor, I could hear the loud murmurs of a gathered crowd. I climbed into my seat and looked out the window. Other soldiers were marching in neat rows beside the bus. The citizens of Wright were lined up on both sides of the road. I could see the smiles on some of their white faces. Others were clapping and singing. A few waved as the bus passed them by. One or two were laughing. Fathers lifted sons onto shoulders for a better view. Mothers kneeled next to daughters and made justifications. White teenagers stood on the hoods of cars. Some silently pumped their fists into the sky in celebration, while others screamed unintelligibly and threw obscene gestures at us.

A blood parade.

I could also see the pain and terror in other white faces. Pale hands pressed to open mouths. Mothers dragged their daughters away. Young white women wept and screamed. Strong men broke through the crowds and stood in front of the bus, trying to stop it, but the soldiers beat them and dragged them away. A Jesuit priest stood on the roof of the bank and shouted prayers for everybody on the bus. The Presbyterian minister attempted to stop the bus by ramming it with her ancient automobile. The bus barely slowed as it crushed her. Parishioners pulled her body from the wreck and wept. Neighbor scuffled with neighbor. One son fainted in the street after he saw the hate in his father's eyes.

The crowd, friendly and not, surged toward the bus.

Outside the bus, the soldiers panicked and fired indiscriminately, while inside the bus, the soldiers pushed us down into our seats and covered us with their bodies.

Outside, a burning tire rolled past a little girl in a yellow dress.

Inside, the high-pitched screams of Indian children could have been the high-pitched wails of Indian singers.

Outside, the hands that pounded on the bus could have been the same hands that pounded drums.

That music sounded exactly the same as all of the music I had ever heard before.

One singing bullet passed through the front window of a blue house, through the living room and narrow kitchen, and out the back window where it lodged in the thick bark of an oak tree.

The clouds of smoke were shaped like horses.

Inside, I struggled against the white soldier who covered me. I punched and kicked at him, but he did not respond. At first, I thought he was immune to pain, but then I looked up at his face and saw the dark bullet hole between his eyes. With all of my strength, I pushed his body to the floor. He was a young man, barely older than me, and I mourned his death as I had been taught to mourn, briefly and powerfully.

"I'm sorry," I said to him. I kneeled beside him, touched his face, and closed his blue eyes.

I prayed for him, the enemy, and wondered if he had prayed for me the night before, or the week before, when he had first been told, when he had first been given the orders, the battle plan, when he first discovered that he would be coming to my reservation to steal me away from my mother and father. I wondered if he had mourned for me.

Looking at him, his slight body and small hands, purple and yellow with bruises, I knew he had prayed for me. I knew he had wrapped those pale hands so tightly into prayer fists that he'd bruised his skin.

Prayer is painful.

Using a vocabulary I did not understand, the other soldiers were screaming orders at one another.

War and the idea of war.

I stood as the bus rolled past the last few protesters standing at the edge of the town and gained speed. Still standing, I looked back and saw one small white boy sitting in his wheelchair in the middle of the road. He was as bald and translucent as a newborn. As the town rioted behind him, that white boy weakly raised his arm. He grew smaller and smaller as the bus accelerated. Soon that pale boy was a shadow rising just above the horizon, then he was a part of the horizon, and then he was nothing at all.

On the bus, the soldiers cursed and wept angry tears. One green-eyed white soldier touched the face of the white soldier who had been shot in the head.

"He's dead," that green-eyed white soldier whispered to me.

"I know," I said. "He covered me."

I had been saved.

"Okay, okay, grunts," shouted the soldier-who-looked-like-me. "Let's get it together. Let's get our shit together."

The soldiers stood and straightened as one body. I was made instantly jealous by their obvious tribal bond. The soldiers pushed all of us back into our seats. Most of us sat with our backs straight, as we had been taught to do by seven generations of tribal school teachers.

"Get in your damn seats," the soldiers shouted at us, the Indian children, though we were all sitting in our original seats.

"Let's get it together!" shouted the soldier-who-looked-like-me. His face was brightly lit by his anger. The long scar on his face was swollen and purple, as if he'd been injured just a few moments earlier rather than years before.

The bus rolled past isolated farmhouses where whole families stood on front lawns and watched us pass. One large white woman held a glass of lemonade in one hand and used her other to shade her eyes. She wore a white sundress and white pumps. She was beautiful. I wanted to climb out of the bus and call her mother. I wanted to lay my head down in her fleshy lap and listen to her stories.

"Talk to me," I whispered to her image and then to the memory of her image. I wanted to hear a story told by a woman who knew thousands of stories. Stories had always kept me safe before. I had always trusted stories. Frightened and tired, I wrapped my arms around myself and tried to tell myself a story. But I could think of nothing but the blood on that dead soldier's face. I could hear nothing but the monotonous hum of the bus. And I was still thinking of that blood when the bus rolled through the front gates of Steptoe Air Force Base.

At the gates, a few hundred protesters were being beaten by a few hundred soldiers with clubs. Smoke and tear gas. One large soldier raised his rifle into the air and fired at something only he could see. Another soldier walked up to an old-man protester, pressed a pistol against the old man's temple, and pulled the trigger. Blood fountained from the old man's head as he toppled to the ground. A third soldier, screaming something I could not hear, ran up to the murderous soldier. With their hands swinging wildly in obscene and obscure gestures, the two soldiers argued with each other. They argued until the murderous soldier pressed his pistol against the other soldier's chest and pulled the trigger again. And then both soldiers were swallowed up by the surging crowd.

Contamination.

As the bus pulled through the heavily fortified gates and drove deeper into the base, I saw plane after plane lifting off from runways. I didn't know then that those planes were carnivorous. I didn't know then that the bellies of those planes were filled with Indians.

I saw soldiers herding Indians into large buildings made of cold metal, steel and aluminum. I tasted steel and aluminum. The darkest Indians, the ones with black hair and brown skin, were herded into a red building. The Indians with brown hair and lighter eyes were herded into an orange building. The Indians with light hair and eyes, the Indians with white skin, were herded into a pale building.

I suddenly wondered if we were going to be slaughtered. I wondered if we were going to be eaten. I wondered if rich white men were going to turn the pages of books that were made with our skins.

On our bus, the soldiers pulled the Indian children to their feet. "Move, move, move!" shouted the soldier-who-looked-like-me.

Once we were off the bus, the soldiers divided us into three groups, each destined for a different building.

I was in the darkest group with two Juniors, a John, Kim and Arlene Cox, Billy the Retard, and the third Kateri. There were another dozen Indian kids I didn't recognize, but we had the same purple-black hair and brown skin. Randy Peone, the green-eyed Spokane, was in the second group with two Juniors, one James, two Kateris, Tyrone, the half-black kid who had dark skin, and many other half-breed kids. Sam the Indian, who was really white, was in the third group with two of the boys named James, two Johns, the girl named Junior, Teddy, the half-white kid with blond hair and gray eyes, and a hundred others. They were the largest group. When they were separated from each other, Tyrone and Teddy, the half-breed half brothers, wailed and beat their heads against the ground. The blood on their foreheads was impossibly bright.

"Pick them up! Pick them up!" shouted a tall white soldier with a crooked nose.

"No blood! No blood!" shouted another white soldier with large hands.

Strange aircraft hovered above us. I looked up and swore I could see tears on the face of one pilot. I wondered if he was Jesus.

There was so much gunfire in the distance that I thought it was birds singing. At that moment, the third Kateri rose up with the coiled metal spring she had pulled from her seat on the bus. She was beautiful. I could see in her face and form the woman she would have become. Screaming with rage, the third Kateri shoved that spring into the brown eye of a black soldier. She broke free and ran. Sam the Indian ran after her. Escape, and the thought of escape. I wanted to run with them, but my knees gave out, dropping me to the ground, and saved me. I watched Kateri and Sam the Indian run. I wanted to know how it felt to run.

"Stop them!" shouted the soldier-who-looked-like-me.

A white soldier, young and wide-eyed, raised his rifle and pulled the trigger twice. A chorus of screams. Sam and Kateri fell. They were now just two bags of blood.

"Goddamn it, who fired their weapon?" shouted a white officer. "Who fired their weapon?"

The wide-eyed white soldier raised his hand and the white officer stormed over to him. The officer snatched the soldier's rifle from his hands.

"Who gave you the order to fire?" shouted the officer.

"Nobody, sir!"

"I said, who gave you the order to fire?"

"Nobody, sir!"

"Then why in the hell did you fire?"

"They were escaping, sir!"

"We're in the middle of a goddamn Air Force base," shouted the officer. "Did you honestly believe those kids were going to escape?"

The wide-eyed soldier hesitated.

"I, I, I didn't think, sir," he said.

Furious, the officer smashed the barrel of the rifle down on the soldier's nose. The wide-eyed soldier crumpled to the pavement.

"Somebody get his dumb ass out of here!" shouted the officer.

Two other soldiers ran in and dragged the unconscious soldier away.

"Goddamn it!" shouted the officer. "This is a military operation and I want some discipline! I want some goddamn organization!"

The officer waded into the crowd of dark Indian children, scooped up a little brown girl, and marched toward the red building.

"Let's go, honey," the officer said to the little brown girl in his arms. "We've got work to do."

Silently and obediently, the rest of us in the red group followed the officer. I didn't know what happened to the other groups and would never know.

We walked into a bright light.

I walked into the bright light.

Inside the red building, beyond the bright light, I saw many more Indians than I had ever seen in one place in my entire life. There were so many Indians that I had to close my eyes against the magnitude of it. I wondered if every Indian in the world was inside that building.

We were forced into cattle chutes and led from station to station.

At the first station, we were shaved bald.

I was shaved bald by a white woman. I looked into her eyes as she took the last of my hair. She was beautiful. She was crying.

"What do you do with it?" I asked her.

"With what?" she asked.

"With the hair."

She looked down at her white uniform covered with the stray hairs of thousands of Indians. She looked down at all of the dark hair carpeting the floor.

Janitors were sweeping the hair into enormous piles, some of them taller than me.

"The hair," I asked her. "What happens to it?"

She opened her mouth to say something, but changed her mind, and then she was gone, moving to the next Indian in line.

I knew they must have burned the hair after we left.

I imagined the smoke and smell of burning hair filling the air.

At the next station, we were stripped of our clothes. Old men and old women, young boys and young girls, powerfully built fathers and beautiful mothers, all naked. I covered my genitals with my hands. Humiliated and defenseless, I kneeled down on the floor and tried to hide my body. Other Indians proudly stood still, their hands at their sides, and stared into the eyes of every soldier. At the third station, doctors and nurses huddled over our bodies and thrust tools and fingers into our ears, mouths, noses, vaginas, penises, and anuses. Sickly people were led away, through another door, and into what I was sure were the ovens.

Fire.

I tried not to breathe, because I knew I would be inhaling the ash those sickly Indians had become. We were then forced into red jump-suits and marched across a brightly lit tarmac into the belly of a plane. There were a thousand Indians inside that plane. I counted them, the sound of their screams and whimpers, the sound of their curses and whispers. We were made to crouch as the plane lifted up into the sky. That was the first time I had ever consciously thought about flight. I realized I had never flown before and laughed hysterically. A large hand reached out and touched my shoulder. It was too dark to see. That hand could have been my mother's or my father's. It had to be somebody's mother or father.

"Hush, hush," said a voice.

I moved away from that hand. I crawled through the dark, search-ing for something familiar. I smacked my face into another face.

"Billy," said the other face. I recognized it instantly, recognized the familiar lilt and upward inflections of my fellow tribal member.

"Billy," I repeated.

"Billy," he said again.

"Billy the Retard," I said.

"Billy the Retard," he repeated.

"Big Bill," I said.

"Big Bill," he repeated.

"What's happening?" I asked him.

He leaned in close to me. I could smell him. He smelled like the water and trees of home.

"They're going to take the tomorrow out of our bones," he said.

"The tomorrow?" I asked.

"The tomorrow," repeated Billy.

I could hear his heart and stomach working inside his body.

"I dreamed it," he said.

"I know it," I said. "I dreamed it too."

"They're going to take the tomorrow," Billy said again.

"I don't understand," I said.

"Big Bill," said Billy the Retard.

"I don't understand," I said again.

The plane rose higher and higher above the earth. At that height, I knew gravity was a story passed from one generation of undiscovered birds to the next. At that height, oxygen was a sacrament.

▲

The plane landed in a flat, anonymous desert. Other planes landed in the flat, anonymous desert.

A thousand Indians, beaten and exhausted, all dressed in red jump-suits, stepped carefully from the planes, onto the tarmac crowded with soldiers, and huddled together in the lonely desert. We moved as one unit, as if we were migrating birds.

The soldiers' faces were slack and anonymous, save for the brown face of the soldier-who-looked-like-me. We regarded each other. His eyes narrowed and he turned his head away with disdain or shame, or a combination of both, or perhaps with no emotion at all.

I recognized none of the other Indian prisoners, or perhaps I recognized all of them. In the haze and heat of the desert, we all looked alike, though I knew intuitively that we could not all look alike, especially given the vast tribal and geographic differences among us. But, as I scanned the faces around me, I saw that we all had the same brown skin, long noses, strong jawlines, and large cheekbones. We could all have been siblings. We could all have been the same person. We could all have been a thousand vestigial reproductions of a single organ, all of us struggling to find a purpose, a space to stand and breathe, enough room to function within the large body of a thing, a person, a crowd called Indian.

Like a newborn, I was losing my ability to tell the difference between my body and the body of the person next to me.

There, in the desert, the horizon was not a straight line stretched taut between the sky and earth. Instead, the horizon was a series of arcs that connected to form a circle of red sand that was a hundred miles wide at its diameter. I stood at the exact epicenter of that circle. I stood at the exact epicenter of seven different circles: circle of red sand, circle of Indians, circle of heat, circle of soldiers, circle of sun, circle of blood, circle of wind. Like a newborn, I turned my head and closed my eyes because it was all too much to comprehend. I listened and heard. Indians wept. I opened my eyes and witnessed. Children climbed into the arms of women strangers and reinvented their mothers. Men fainted and were held up only by the sheer weight of the people around them. The soldiers shouted at one another, then shouted at us. Soon, we were marched away from the plane and into the desert. We followed a path worn into the sand by thousands of recent footprints. Other Indians, other siblings. I knew that path would be swallowed up overnight by the sand and wind.

The soldiers marched us beyond the first horizon and through the one door carved into the desert floor. We carefully descended a long series of staircases. I counted steps. Fourteen steps to every flight of stairs. I counted flights. Ten, thirty, fifty, more. I counted and counted until the numbers grew too large for me to remember clearly. I counted until the numbers themselves held no meaning I could decipher. At the bottom of every flight of stairs, we paused on the landing. At every landing, another group of soldiers stood at the entrance of a long dark tunnel. At the mouth of every dark tunnel, more and more Indians were separated from the rest and marched into the darkness beyond. I wondered when it would be my turn to walk into the darkness. I was not afraid of it, the dark. I wanted to give it a name, so I called it Mother.

Finally, at the bottom of the last staircase, at the bottom of the world, I was marched into the darkness of the very last tunnel. Inside, it was cool, nearly cold, but dry. Beyond the walls, I could hear strange machinery working. I could hear voices in the distance. Screams, too. I walked with seven Indian strangers: two young girls who huddled together; a teenage boy whose eyes were twice as old as his face; two women, one of them pregnant; and two men, one of them large and imposing with a port-wine birthmark that covered half of his face and the other one smaller than me. With our shaved heads, in our red jumpsuits, we looked like we had been in a concentration camp for years, though we had been prisoners for only a matter of hours. Together, led by the soldiers, including the soldier-who-looked-like-me, we walked for miles, or for inches, I could no longer tell the difference. We marched through the darkness until we could see a bright light in the distance. The light grew larger and larger. I was afraid of it. I wanted to give it a name, so I called it Father.

Soon, the eight of us were marched out of the dark tunnel and into a long white hallway where white doors were evenly spaced along both

sides like God's teeth. We were marched through an open door at
the end of that hallway and into a circular room. In the room, eight
beds, each with clean sheets and thin blankets. In the room, an ex-
posed toilet. In the room, a water faucet, a large plastic bucket, and
eight small plastic cups. In the room, a surveillance camera.

No secrets in a circular room.

"Grab a bunk," said a soldier with a large nose. His voice shook
the floor of our room-cell and reverberated in the hollow bones of
my feet.

Each of us, the eight Indians, chose a bed. I could not tell north
from northwest. I only knew my position by the faces and shapes of
my neighbors. On my immediate left, the pregnant Indian woman,
then the two girls huddled together on one bed, then the small Indian
man, then the other Indian woman, then the boy with old eyes, and
then, to my immediate right, the large Indian man with the port-wine
birthmark.

"Okay, listen up," said the large-nose soldier. "I want to welcome
all of you here. Now, I know you've been through a rough journey
and the accommodations here are a bit spartan . . ."

"Why are we here?" shouted the large Indian man.

A nervous white soldier gently placed the muzzle of his rifle against
the large Indian man's forehead. The man was suddenly quiet. Though
he had never fired a gun, had never been threatened with a gun, had
never had the desire to use a gun, that Indian man understood the
meaning of a gun held in white hands and pointed at a brown face.
Genetic memory.

"Sir," the large-nose soldier said, nearly whispered, to the large
Indian man. "We don't really have the time to answer your questions.
We have quite a bit of work yet to do here."

The large Indian man said nothing. The large-nose soldier studied the Indian's garish red birthmark.

"Pity about your face," said the large-nose soldier.

"They want our blood," I said. "They're vampires."

Large nose turned away from the large Indian man, walked up close to my bed, and kneeled down in front of me.

"Son," he said. "What is your name?"

"Jonah."

"Ah, that's a good name. Very strong name, that Jonah." The large-nose soldier smiled. "Jonah, you can call me Ishmael. You see, we all have our whales."

Then he slapped my face so hard that I momentarily blacked out. In those seconds, I dreamed of my mother and father, though I dreamed only of their hands because I could not remember their faces. When I regained consciousness, Large nose was standing again in the middle of our room.

"First of all," he said, "we have a couple of basic rules here. Number one, you will not speak unless spoken to. Number two, you will follow our orders exactly. And by exactly, I mean you will not deviate in any form whatsoever. Any deviation will result in severe punishment. Continued rebellion will result in isolation and restraint."

Large nose looked around the room.

"As you can see," he said, "you have access to an unlimited amount of water for bathing and consumption. And you will receive six small meals a day. Three times a week, for one hour a day, you will be escorted into a recreation room where you will exercise your body. The lights will be dimmed for eight hours every night so that you may sleep."

I wanted to lie down on my strange bed and fall asleep forever.

"Citizens," said large nose, "you are here to perform a great patriotic service for your country. The sacrifices you have made and are going to make have been and will be greatly appreciated by your fellow Americans. And remember, please, that you are here for your own safety and we plan to take good care of you. Now, I wish you all a good night."

Without ceremony, large nose and all of the soldiers filed out of the room and locked the door behind them. I harbored a brief and dangerous hope that the soldier-who-looked-like-me would turn back, open the door, and release us, but the locked door stay locked. We, the eight Indians, waited together in the silence as thin and strong as our own skins. None of us said a word for minutes that slowly became hours. I looked down at my bare and dirty feet. I felt the rough cloth of my red jumpsuit. I studied the meager details of the room until I could close my eyes and see them, in exact reproduction, on the blank walls of my imagination. The two young girls, who had been strangers before and would never be more than a few feet apart for the rest of their lives, continued to huddle together and weep. The pregnant woman laid down on her bed with her back to us, with her face toward the curved wall, and pretended to sleep, or fell asleep and made all of us jealous with her ability to hide in plain sight. The other Indian woman drank cup after cup of water.

Two parts hydrogen, one part oxygen. Two parts hydrogen, one part oxygen. Two parts hydrogen, one part oxygen.

The large Indian man pounded on the closed door while the small Indian man softly sang a tribal song. The boy with old eyes stared at me and I stared back. His eyes were two abandoned houses standing together on a grassy plain burned brown by the sun. Wooden flesh fell away from those houses and left only two skeletal frames. Crows and owls perched on rotting timbers. Wild grass and prodigal weeds burst through the foundation.

Everything is reclaimed, everything is reclaimed.

The boy with old eyes stood and walked toward me. He leaned down so close to me I could see the old black woodstove still smoldering in the houses of his eyes.

"Jonah," he whispered.

"Yes," I whispered back.

"Everybody here is full-blood."

"I know."

"What happened to the others?" he asked, meaning the half-breeds, the mixed-bloods, the people with just a trace of Indian blood, and the white people who had lived among Indians for so long that they had nearly become Indians.

"I don't know," I said, but I assumed they had been shipped to prisons of their own.

"The soldiers want our blood," said the boy with old eyes.

"I know," I said. "I dreamed it."

"I dreamed it too."

"We all dreamed it," said the pregnant woman as she rose from sleep, or the illusion of sleep.

We all moved closer to one another, except for the small Indian man. He sat alone on his bed and continued to sing.

"We've got to escape," said the large Indian man. He looked strong enough to tear down the door.

"How?" said the Indian woman who was not pregnant. For the first time, I noticed her beauty. She was beautiful even with her head shaved bald. I could not imagine how beautiful she must have been before her hair had been taken. I imagined her hair had been a black river flowing down the landscape of her back.

"Tell us," she said. "Tell us how we're supposed to get out of here?"

There was no possible answer to her question. If we could have somehow crawled out of the belly of that underground prison, we would have found ourselves standing alone in the desert, without water, without shoes, without compass, without destination, without home.

"I don't want to die here," said the two Indian girls, together, as if they possessed only one voice. They were small and dark.

"If they were going to kill us," said the beautiful Indian woman, "they would have done it already. They need us for something."

"I told you," I said. "They want our blood."

"It has to be more than that," she said. "We must have some disease. The Black Plague or something."

"That couldn't be," said the large Indian man. "Those soldiers weren't wearing masks. They were breathing in some of the air we breathed out. They weren't afraid of us."

"But they kept talking about blood," said the boy with old eyes.

"Yes," I said. "I saw a soldier get beaten because he killed two Indians."

"No blood, no blood," said the two Indian girls together. "They kept saying that. No blood, no blood."

"You're right," said the pregnant woman. "It's our blood. There's something in our blood."

"You're all wrong," whispered the small Indian man. His voice sounded like a house fire.

We all turned toward him.

"You're all wrong," he said again.

"What do you think?" asked the beautiful woman.

"None of you," said the small man, pointing a finger at each of us. "None of you knows who you are anymore. None of you knows who we're going to be."

"You're talking riddles," said the large man.

"Listen to me," said the small man. "I'm talking truth. Don't you know what we are to them? What we have always been?"

"No," I whispered.

"You see," said the small man. "Right outside that door, those soldiers, those people are getting things ready. They've got their own ceremonies, you know?"

The small man stood. He was barely over five feet tall, though his hands were large, his fingers long and feminine. His skin was as dark as a black man's.

"Right outside that door," he continued, "they have big rooms. Big rooms filled with the dead. Filled with their dead. All the dead white people lined up in rows and rows and rows."

"What dead?" asked the large man.

"All of them. Every white person who has ever died. They've got them lying on beds, all clean and perfumed and naked."

"Naked?" I asked.

"Every man, woman, child. Naked. White skin everywhere. White skin so bright and shining it will blind you. And we will go blind down here, you know? Living down here like rodents, like worms."

"I'm no worm," said the pregnant woman.

"Yes, you are, you're a worm. You're less than a worm to them. You're an exile, you're a leper, you're a pariah, you're a peon, you're nothing to them. Nothing."

The short man stood on his bed. He was shouting, spittle flying from his mouth, and raising his arms like he was some kind of preacher. And maybe he was a preacher.

"Smell the air," he said. "Smell the air!"

I inhaled. I could smell nothing except the antiseptic walls and floors of our cell and the fear and fatigue of my fellow prisoners.

"Do you smell that?" asked the small man. "That's a feast you're smelling. That's roast beef you're smelling. Venison. Lamb. Veal. That's vegetables of every kind. That's fruits so sweet they'll make your mouth burn. That's bread from a hundred different countries."

My stomach rumbled with the thought of so much food. With a full belly, I believed I could begin to have some hope.

The short man ranted on. We were all entranced by him. He was our momentary savior and we were his temporary disciples.

"And do you know what they're doing with all of that food?" he asked us. "They're piling it on every one of those dead bodies. There's a feast on the chest of every one of those dead white people out there. And that food is soaking up all of the hate and envy and sloth in those white people. That food is soaking up all of the anger and murder and thievery. That food is soaking up all of the adultery and fornication and blasphemy. That food is soaking up all of the lies and greed and hatred."

We prayed; he preached.

Call and response, call and response.

He preached; we prayed.

Call and response, call and response.

"Children," he said. "There's a white body in there for each of us. There's a feast in there for each of us. There's a feast of sins shining on every one of those bodies. And tomorrow morning, those soldiers are going to lead us all, you hear me, lead us all into that room and they're going to force us to kneel at those bodies, and they're going to force us to devour those feasts, devour those sins."

The small man fell down on the floor and I fell facedown beside him because I believed.

▲

Early the next morning, or during what they wanted us to believe was morning, three soldiers, one black and two white, forced the large Indian man from our room, despite our cries and protests, and we wondered if we would ever see him again.

"He's gone forever," said the small Indian man, our prophet. His name was John, a Colville Indian. We all looked at one another and wondered who would be next. I closed my eyes and saw the room filled with the corpses of white people. I saw the feast piled on the chest of the white man I had been chosen to save. I opened my eyes and looked into the eyes of the Indians I would soon call my family.

"What are your names?" I asked.

The boy with old eyes said his name was Joseph. He said he was a Seminole Indian from Florida. He said he could run for days and days. The beautiful Indian woman said she was Navajo. She was a librarian, she said. I'll miss books, she said. The two girls who held each other and refused to let go were the same two girls who also refused to speak to us. They just cried and whimpered, so we left them nameless. The pregnant Indian woman lay on her bed with her back to us.

"What is your name?" I asked her.

"Leave me alone," she said.

"Please," I said. "We want to know who you are."

"I don't care," said the pregnant woman.

She stood, ran across the room, and smashed her big belly into the wall. She punched herself in the stomach again and again. Four of us, the prophet, the boy with old eyes, the beautiful woman, and I, all had to work together in order to hold her down.

"Let my baby die!" she screamed. "Let him die!"

We fought her. We wanted the baby to live, not because we loved him or loved the idea of life, but because we knew his death would take something else from us, and we had so little left to call our own.

Hours later, after the pregnant woman had passed out, after exhaustion had taken all of our energy, three other soldiers, including the soldier-who-looked-like-me, came into our room, and despite the cries and protests, which had grown considerably weaker, I was taken away.

I could hear the other Indians call my name as I was led away.

"Jonah," they said.

With two white soldiers walking a few steps behind me and the soldier-who-looked-like-me walking a few steps in front, I marched farther down the bright hallway, past those countless white doors. I knew there were Indian prisoners trapped behind every one of those doors. I wondered if they could hear us marching down the hallway, if they could hear the rhythmic stomp of the soldiers' boots and the soft shuffle of my bare feet. If I had pressed my ear to the cold metal of those white doors, I might have heard the stories, the rumors whispered so often that in just a few hours they had become myth. I might have heard the rumors about rescue attempts, about the half-breed Indian rebels who had broken out of their own prisons and who were now trekking across the desert to save us, or about the Indians who had avoided capture and who were now being secretly trained by sympathetic white soldiers, or about the multiethnic armies, formed by black, red, white, and brown soldiers, formed by men, women, and children, that were only awaiting a leader, a white man on a pale horse, to come along and lead them to victory.

I wondered if I was just a rumor as I walked down that hallway, between those white doors, with those soldiers marking time with each disciplined exhale, inhale, exhale, inhale. I wondered if I had been forgotten by the Indians still left in my room, in my cell. I wondered what had happened to the large Indian man after they had taken him from our room, and if they were now taking me to the same place where they had taken him.

I was young and small. I could have stepped inside the body of the soldier-who-looked-like-me and been lost forever.

I closed my eyes and easily marched in a straight line. All the while, I was convinced they were marching me toward a large room that was filled with the corpses of a million white people. The damp smell of disinfectant and indestructible mold could have been the smell of a terrible feast. I heard the hum of machinery and wondered if I was hearing a country of flies all speaking at once.

"Stop," said the soldier-who-looked-like-me.

I stopped.

"Open your eyes," he said.

I could not open my eyes. I was afraid of what I might see.

"Open your eyes," he said.

"I can't," I said.

"Open your eyes before I pry them open and staple your eyelids to your forehead."

I held my breath and opened my eyes. I was standing in a very small room with a stainless-steel table bolted to the floor. Black leather restraining straps were lying like sleeping snakes across that table. As with every other wall in our prison, the walls of that room were white and clean, clean, clean.

"Take off your jumpsuit," said the soldier-who-looked-like-me.

"Where's the large man?" I asked.

"I don't know who you're talking about," said the soldier-who-looked-like-me.

"The large Indian man," I said. "The one with the birthmark on his face."

"Strip," one of the white soldiers said as he pushed me to the floor. I looked up into the face of the soldier-who-looked-like-me. He pushed the muzzle of his rifle against my narrow chest.

"Stop looking at me," he said.

"Where's the large man?" I asked again.

"Get on your feet," he said as he looked down at me along the barrel of his rifle. I wondered if he was going to murder me. I dreamed of a hero's grave, a white cross, the proper flag.

I stood and stripped. It was cold, so cold that I could barely breathe, though it had absolutely nothing to do with the temperature of that room.

"Get on the table," said one of the white soldiers. I looked at him but could see only the blue of his eyes.

I tried to walk but my knees buckled. I sank to the floor.

"Get your ass up," said blue eyes.

I could feel the blood flooding through my veins. At that moment, I was convinced that most of my blood, the plasma, the red and white blood cells, was so close to the surface that it would take only a few moments to completely empty me.

"Stop," I said or thought I said. It did not matter.

The soldiers forced me onto the table and strapped me facedown with the black restraining belts. One belt on each ankle, one across the back of each knee, another across my lower back, another across my neck and shoulders, and one for each wrist. The only movement I could make was turning my head from side to side. I could see the silver belts circling the soldiers' waists. I could see their hands tightly gripping their rifles.

"Put the mask on," said blue eyes.

A black leather hood was pulled over my head. I was blind. I thrashed and struggled against the mask and the restraining belts, against the laughter of the soldiers.

"Please," I said. "Stop."

One of the soldiers slapped my bare behind and then all three of them walked out of the room. I heard the door click shut. I heard the lock turn. I heard the sound of their boots as they walked away. I heard everything.

When you are blind, there is no such thing as silence. In the dark and din, I waited. I waited. I whispered my name over and over, and whispered the names of my parents, and whispered the names of all of the trees and plants growing on my reservation, and whispered the color of my family's home and the color of the sky at three in the morning when I walked outside to use the outhouse, and whispered the date of my birth, and whispered the dates of my mother's birth and my father's birth, and the birth date of my twin brother, who died in the womb and was little more than a handful of flesh when he fell out of my mother's body. I was worried that my fear might take away all of my memories, as it had already eradicated the memory of my parents' faces, but as I listened to my own voice, as it traveled from one corner to the next, as it slid along the clean white walls and bounced off the clean white floors, I knew that place was being filled with my rumors, my myths, my stories. With my voice, I suddenly believed, I could explode the walls of that room and escape.

So I lifted my head and shouted my name.

My voice pushed against the walls.

The walls did not move.

I lifted my head and shouted my name.

My voice pushed against the walls.

The walls did not move.

Exhausted, I lay my head against the cold metal table and waited. I waited.

I waited until the door opened again and I heard the soft squeak of leather shoes, four shoes meaning two people, and the cacophonous rattle of four wheels. The two people pushed a cart, a table, something into the room until it bumped against my table.

"Excuse me, young Mr. Lot," said a male voice, accented, British perhaps or Australian, cultured, refined, as smooth as the clean white walls of the room.

"Don't hurt me," I said.

"I will certainly do my best not to," said the British or Australian man. I felt his cold hands touching my arms, my legs, pushing and prodding.

"Twelve years old, are you not?" he asked.

"Yes," I said.

"You're very big for your age, Mr. Lot."

"My family, we're all big."

"We don't need the local," the British or Australian man said to the other person in the room.

"No anesthetic?" asked the other person, a woman, a deep voice, no accent at all. "Are you sure?"

"Yes," said the British or Australian man as he flipped through a book. I could hear the turning of pages and wondered if he was reading the Bible.

"Are you priests?" I asked them.

Both of them laughed.

"No, Jonah," said the man. "We're doctors."

"Don't hurt me, " I said again. I begged. The male doctor placed his hand on my head. It was not a tender touch. His hand was heavy.

"Son," he said, though he was not my father. "We're going to do what we have to do, and we'll do it as quickly and as painlessly as possible. That's all I can promise. Now, you need to hush while we work."

I could hear the rattle of metal against metal. I did not know if I heard tools scraping against a metal tray or surgical instruments being sharpened. In my mind, I could see the needles and knives, the saws and hammers. I could see the cruel eyes of the doctors, the rest of their faces hidden by white surgical masks. Behind those masks, I knew there must be scars, open wounds, and jagged teeth. Behind those masks, I knew there must be more metal: aluminum staples holding the skin together, iron sockets containing the eyes, and steel blades substituting for teeth.

"This is going to be a little cold," said the female doctor.

I felt an icy liquid roll over my left hip, then my right hip. I was so frightened and cold that it could easily have been my own blood.

"What was that?" I asked, crying now.

"Disinfectant," said the male doctor. "Now, please, be quiet. I've told you once."

"What are you doing to me?" I asked. I lifted my head. I struggled against the restraining belts.

"Stop moving," said the woman doctor.

I felt a strong hand on the back of my neck as it pressed my head against the table. I could not move. The male doctor leaned down close to my ear.

"Jonah," he whispered. "That is your name, is it not? Jonah?"

"Yes," I said. The pressure on my neck was painful.

"Jonah," he said. "You're irritating me. And I am sure you're also irritating Dr. Clancy. Is he not, Dr. Clancy?"

"He certainly is," she said.

"Jonah," he said. "I know this is all very frightening for you. I wish there was something I could do about that. But there is simply nothing that can be done. Now, if you refuse to be quiet, we'll have to gag you. And you don't want that, do you now?"

"No," I whimpered.

"Then I suggest you keep your fucking mouth shut," he said. I heard the anger in his voice and something beyond that, a kind of resignation, a weary acceptance of his role in that prison.

"The ten-gauge?" asked Dr. Clancy, the female doctor.

"Yes," said the male doctor.

I wondered what kind of weapon the doctors were talking about. I felt two sets of hands on my body.

"You're going to feel some pressure here," said Dr. Clancy.

I felt a hot pain as a needle slid into my left hip, through the skin, through the muscle and into the hip socket, into the center of the bone. But more than that, I felt the pain deep in my stomach, and beyond that, in the very spirit of my stomach. I felt the needle bite into me, heard the impossibly loud hiss of the hypodermic syringe as it sucked out pieces of my body, sucked out the blood, sucked out fluid ounces of my soul, sucked out antibodies, sucked out pieces of all of my stories, sucked out marrow, and sucked out pieces of my vocabulary. I knew that certain words were being taken from me.

I cried out in surprise and pain, and my cries sounded like tiny prayers.

"Hush, hush, Jonah," said the male doctor as he pushed the needle deeper into my body, as Dr. Clancy pushed another needle deep into my other hip. "You're doing a brave thing. You're saving the world."

▲

I woke naked and alone in a bright room. I stood with much difficulty and stared into a wall of mirrors that were really windows. Beyond the glass, doctors and soldiers watched me. I was afraid. I was without words. I was small and would not grow again. Arrested. The door opened. Two soldiers pushed a naked Indian woman into the room. The door closed.

She stood there, tall and proud. Perfect brown skin. Large breasts. Shaved head. She threw obscene gestures against the mirrors that were really windows. Then she looked at me. She saw me.

"You're just a boy," she whispered. Then she shouted, "He's just a boy. Look at his penis."

She was right. I crouched low, trying to hide what I did not have.

"He's been tested," said a disembodied voice, filling the bright room. "He's fertile."

"I'm not going to do it," she said. "It's wrong. It's wrong."

There was no response.

She walked over to me, kneeled beside me. She lifted my face and looked into my eyes.

"What's your name?" she asked.

"I don't remember," I said. I would never remember.

She wiped the tears from my face with her fingers. She touched them to her lips.

"Why are they doing this?" I asked.

"I don't know," she said. "I've heard stories. But you know how Indians are."

"Yes, we just talk and talk."

We smiled together. She took my hand.

"Where are you from?" she asked.

"I'm Spokane," I said. "From the reservation."

"I'm Apache," she said. "I live, I used to live, in Los Angeles."

I closed my eyes and tried to see that city, with its large spaces between people.

"What is it like?" I asked. "That city?"

"It goes on forever," she said. "And there are earthquakes that shake you out of bed in the morning. And there are more Indians living there than in any city in the whole world."

"Wow," I said.

"Yes, wow," she confirmed.

"Please commence," said the disembodied voice.

"Shut the hell up," the Indian woman screamed at the walls. I startled, but she pulled me close, pressed my face against her naked breasts.

"I'm sorry, I'm sorry," she said. "But I hate them. I hate them."

"Please commence," said the disembodied voice again.

"No," said the Indian woman. She whispered it, more to herself than to me, or to the doctors and soldiers on the other side of the glass.

She spoke softly.

"This is five times today," she said.

"Five times what?" I asked.

She stood and took me with her. She marched up to the mirrors that were really windows.

"Look at him," she said as she pushed me closer to the glass. "Look at him. He's just a child."

"Please commence," said the disembodied voice.

"I've done it five times today," she shouted. "Five times. Isn't that enough? Isn't that enough?"

"Please commence. Or be punished."

"Fuck you," she shouted. "I'm not doing it, I'm not doing it."

Two soldiers rushed into the room. I could not see their faces behind their helmets, but I imagined their eyes were ivory-colored and fragile, as fragmented as eggshells. They carried electrical sticks. They jabbed one of the sticks into the Indian woman's belly and one into mine. The blue light rose from my belly, squeezed my heart, and stopped my brain for one breath.

The Indian woman screamed in pain as she fell to the floor. She kicked and punched at the soldiers. But I could only press my face against the cold floor and pray. I looked at my hands and remembered, briefly, so briefly, the feel of my father's hands when he touched my face, when he whispered secrets to me. And then it was gone, all gone.

"Fuck you, fuck you," shouted the Indian woman. She climbed to her feet and pushed against the soldiers.

"Please commence or punishment will continue," said the dis-embodied voice.

"What are you doing to me?" asked the Indian woman. She pointed at the soldiers. "Take off your masks. Let me look at you."

Like stained glass, the soldiers remained still and cold, all of their emotions created by the artificial light passing over their faces.

"Do you have mothers?" the Indian woman asked the stained-glass soldiers. "Do you have daughters? Look at me. I'm a woman. Would you do this to the women in your life? Would you?"

She pulled me to my feet. I retched, threw up what little food was in my stomach.

"Look at me," she shouted. "He's just a child. A boy. Look at him. Look at him."

The soldiers didn't move.

"Please commence or punishment will continue."

The Indian woman lifted her face toward the ceiling and screamed. I imagined that all of the Indians in the world—all of those who had survived the blood parade—turned their heads when they heard the sound of her voice. I would never again see most of those Indians. For the rest of my life, I would see only rooms with white walls and the brown skin of naked Indian women. For the rest of my life, they would come to my room and lie down with me. Most of them would not speak; a few of them would die in my arms. They would surren-der. I would survive and live on.

"He's just a boy," shouted the Indian woman and rushed the sol-diers. The larger one swung his electric stick and bloodied her mouth.

"Do not draw blood," said the disembodied voice. "Do not draw blood."

The Indian woman screamed through the red glow in her mouth.

"What's wrong with you?" she asked. "What is wrong with you?"

"Please commence or you will be eliminated."

She pulled me closer and whispered in my ear. I could hear the blood fall from her lips and felt it land on my shoulder.

"I'm sorry," she said. "But we have to do this. We have to do this."

She pushed me back to the floor. We lay there together as the two soldiers stood above us.

"What are we supposed to do?" I asked.

"We're supposed to make love, have sex," she said. "Do you know what that means?"

"Yes, " I said. I'd walked in on my mother and father when they were in bed. They'd explained it to me.

"They want me to get pregnant," she said. "I'm in my fertile time. I've already had sex with five men today. I don't know when they'll let me stop. I don't know when."

She cried then and pressed her face against me.

I touched her belly. I wondered if we would have a child together. I wondered if I would ever see my son or my daughter.

"Please commence or you will be eliminated."

She kissed my forehead.

"I'm sorry it has to be this way," she said. "This shouldn't be happening to you."

"I've never done it before," I said.

She smiled then—sadness—and kissed my lips—more sadness.

"Do you have children?" I asked. "I mean, did you have them before this?"

"Three," she said. "I'll never see them again."

She took my hand in hers and placed it on her breast.

"Rescue me," she said.

We made love.

"Close your eyes," she said. "Pretend we're alone. Pretend I'm not me. Pretend you're somebody else. Don't let them touch you. Don't let me touch you."

We made love.

I closed my eyes and saw my mother. I saw her bring a cup of water to my lips.

"Drink," my mother said. "Drink."

I touched my mother's hands. I held my face against her dark hair and breathed in all of her smells.

She smelled like smoke.

We made love.

"Keep your eyes closed," she said.

On the other side of the glass, they watched us. They were always watching us.

"Don't let them hurt you," she said.

My mother kissed my forehead. Her breath smelled of coffee and peppermint—the scent of forgiveness, of safety and warmth. She chased my nightmares out of the house with her mother's broom.

"Keep your eyes closed," she said. "And they can't see you."

We made love.

The two soldiers stood above us and prayed. They took deep breaths and smelled coffee and peppermint.

"Close your eyes," she said. "We're alone, we're alone."

I kept my eyes closed as I found my way inside of her, as I walked through the rooms of her, as I opened one door after another, as I found a bed where I could lie down and cover myself with thick quilts.

They wanted our blood. They would always want our blood.

"Hide," she said. "Don't let them see you."

Inside of her, I breathed in the dark. I was warm; I was safe.

"Are you my mother?" I said.

"Yes," she said. She said, "Yes."

"Mother," I whispered. "Mother, mother, mother."

INDIAN COUNTRY

▲▲

L ow Man Smith stepped off the airplane in Missoula, Montana, walked up the humid jetway, and entered the airconditioned terminal. He was excited that he was about to see her, Carlotta, the Navajo woman who lived on the Flathead Indian Reservation. All during the flight from Seattle, he'd been wondering what he would first say to her, this poet who taught English at the Flathead Indian College, and had carried on a fierce and exhausting internal debate on the matter. He'd finally decided, just as the plane touched down, to begin his new life with a simple declaration: "Thank you for inviting me."

He practiced those five words in his head—*thank you for inviting me*—and chastised himself for not learning to say them in her language, in Navajo, in Dine.

He was a Coeur d'Alene Indian, even though his mother was white. He'd been born and raised in Seattle, didn't speak his own tribal language, and had visited his home reservation only six times in his life. His mother had often tried to push Low Man toward the reservation, toward his cousins, aunts, and uncles—all of those who had survived one war or another—but Low Man just wasn't interested, especially after his Coeur d'Alene father died of a heart attack while welding together one of the last great ships in Elliott Bay. More accurately, Low Man's father had drowned after his heart attack had knocked him unconscious and then off the boat into the water.

Low Man believed the Coeur d'Alene Reservation to be a monotonous place—a wet kind of monotony that white tourists saw as spiritual and magic. Tourists snapped off dozens of photographs and tried to capture it—the wet, spiritual monotony—before they climbed back into their rental cars and drove away to the next reservation on their itineraries.

The tourists didn't know, and never would have guessed, that the reservation's monotony might last for months, sometimes years, before one man would eventually pull a pistol from a secret place and shoot another man in the face, or before a group of women would drag another woman out of her house and beat her left eye clean out of her skull. After that first act of violence, rival families would issue calls for revenge and organize the retaliatory beatings. Afterward, three or four people would wash the blood from their hands and hide in the hills, causing white men to write editorials, all of this news immediately followed by capture, trial, verdict, and bus ride to prison. And then, only then, would the long silence, the monotony, resume.

Walking through the Missoula airport, Low Man wondered if the Flathead Reservation was a dangerous place, if it was a small country where the king established a new set of laws with every sunrise.

Carrying a suitcase and computer bag, Low Man searched for Carlotta's face, her round, purple-dark face, in the crowd of people— most of them white men in cowboy hats—who waited at the gate. Instead, he saw an old Indian man holding a hardcover novel above his head.

"I wrote that book," Low Man said proudly to the old man, who stood with most of his weight balanced on his left hip.

"You're him, then," said the old man. "The mystery writer."

"I am, then," said Low Man.

"I'm Carlotta's boss, Raymond. She sent me."

"It's good to meet you, Ray. Where is she?"

"My name is Raymond. And she's gone."

"Gone?"

"Yeah, gone."

Low Man wondered if *gone* carried a whole different meaning in the state of Montana. Perhaps, under the Big Sky, being *gone* meant that you were having lunch, or that your car had run out of gas, or that you'd broken your leg in a fly-fishing accident and were stranded in a hospital bed, doped up on painkillers, eagerly awaiting the arrival of the man you loved more than anything else in the world.

"Where, exactly, is gone?" asked Low Man.

The old man's left eye was cloudy with glaucoma. Low Man wondered about the quality of Raymond's depth perception.

"She got married yesterday," said the old man. "She and Chuck woke up before sunrise and drove for Flagstaff."

"Flagstaff?" asked Low Man, desperately trying to remember when he had last talked to Carlotta. When? Three days ago, for just a minute, to confirm the details of his imminent arrival.

"Arizona?" Low Man asked.

"Yeah, that's where she and Chuck grew up."

"Who is Chuck?"

"That's her husband," said Raymond.

"Obviously."

Low Man needed a drink. He'd been sober for ten years, but he still needed a drink. Not of alcohol, no, but of something. He never worried about falling off the wagon, not anymore. He had spent many nights in hotel rooms where the mini-bars were filled with

booze, but had given in only to the temptations of the three-dollar
candy bars.

"Ray," said Low Man. "Can we, please, just put a hold on this conversation while I go find me a pop?"

"Carlotta's been sober for six years," said the old man.

"Yes, I know. That's one of the reasons I came here."

"She told me you drank a lot of soda pop. Said it was your substi-
tute addiction."

Shaking his head, Low Man found a snack bar, ordered a large soda,
finished it with three swallows, and then ordered another.

When he was working on a book, when he was writing, Low Man
would drink a six-pack of soda every hour or so, and then, hopped up
on the caffeine, he'd pound the keyboard, chapter after chapter, until
carpal tunnel syndrome fossilized the bones in his wrists. There it was,
the central dilemma of his warrior life: repetitive stress. In his day, Crazy
Horse had to worry about Custer and the patriotic sociopaths of the
Seventh Cavalry.

"Okay," said Low Man. "Now, tell me, please, Raymond, how long
has Carlotta been planning on getting married?"

"Oh, jeez," said Raymond. "She wasn't planning it at all. But
Chuck showed up a couple days back, they were honeyhearts way back
when, and just swept her off her feet. He's been sober for eleven years."

"One more than me."

"Oh, yeah, but I don't think that was the reason she married him."

"No, I imagine not."

"Well, I better get going. I got to pick up my grandchildren from
school."

"Ray?"

"It's Raymond."

Low Man wondered what had happened to the Indian men who
loved their nicknames, who earned their nicknames? His father had

run around with indigenous legends named Bug, Mouse, Stubby, and Stink-Head.

"You're an elder, right?" Low Man asked Raymond.

"Elder than some, not as elder as others."

"Elders know things, right?"

"I know one or two things."

"Then perhaps, just perhaps, you could tell me what, what, what *thing* I'm supposed to do now?"

Raymond scratched his head and pursed his lips.

"Maybe," said the elder. "You could sign my book for me?"

Distracted, Low Man signed the book, but with his true signature and not with the stylized flourish he'd practiced for years. He signed it: *Peace*.

"You're a pretty good writer," Raymond said. "You should keep doing it."

"I'll try," said Low Man as he watched the old Indian shuffle away.

Low Man began to laugh, softly at first, but then with a full-throated roar that echoed off the walls. He laughed until tears ran down his face, until his stomach cramped, until he retched and threw up in a water fountain. He could not stop laughing, not even after three security officers arrived to escort him out of the airport, and not even after he'd walked three miles into town and found himself standing in a phone booth outside a 7-Eleven.

"Shit," he said and suddenly grew serious. "Who am I supposed to call?"

Then he laughed a little more and wondered how he was going to tell this story in the future. He'd change the names of those involved, of course, and invent new personalities and characters—and brand-new desires as well—and then he would be forced to invert and subvert the chronology of events, and the tone of the story would certainly be tailored to fit the audience. Whites and Indians laughed at most of the same jokes, but they laughed for different reasons. Maybe Low Man would turn himself into a blue-collar Indian, a welder who'd quit a good job, who'd quit a loyal wife, to fly to Missoula in pursuit of a crazy white woman.

And because he was a mystery writer, Low Man would have to throw a dead body into the mix.

Whose body? Which weapon?

Pistol, knife, poison, Low Man thought, as he stood in the phone booth outside the Missoula 7-Eleven.

"Chuck?" he asked the telephone. "Who the fuck is Chuck?"

The telephone didn't answer.

Low Man's last book, *Red Rain,* had shipped 125,000 copies in hardcover, good enough to flirt with the *New York Times* best-seller list, before falling into the Kingdom of Remainders. He belonged to seven frequent-flier clubs, diligently tossed money into his SEP-IRA, and tried to ignore the ulcer just beginning to open a hole in his stomach.

"Okay," said Low Man as he stood in the telephone booth. "Crazy Horse didn't need Tums. Okay? Think."

He took a deep breath. He wondered if the world was a cruel place. He checked the contents of his wallet. He carried two hundred dollars in cash, three credit cards, and a valid driver's license, all the ingredients necessary for renting a car and driving back to Seattle.

He doubted they were going to let him back into the airport, a thought that made him break into more uncontrolled laughter.

Jesus, he'd always wanted to be the kind of Indian who *didn't* get kicked out of public places. He played golf, for God's sake, with a single-digit handicap.

Opening the phone book, Low Man looked for the local bookstores. He figured a small town like Missoula might have a Waldenbooks or a B. Dalton's, but he needed something more intimate and eccentric, even sacred. Low Man prayed for a used bookstore, a good one, a musty church filled with bibles written by thousands of disciples. There, in that kind of place, he knew that he could buy somebody's novel or book of poems, then sit down in a comfortable chair to read, and maybe drink a cup of good coffee or a tall glass of the local water.

He found the listing for a bookstore called Bread and Books. Beautiful. He tore the page out of the directory and walked into the 7-Eleven.

"Hey," said Low Man as he slapped the yellow page on the counter. "Where is this place?"

The cashier, a skinny white kid, smiled.

"You tore that out of the phone book, didn't you?"asked the kid.

"Yes, I did," said Low Man.

"You're going to have to pay for that."

Low Man knew the telephone directory was free because merchants paid to advertise in the damn things.

"Fine," said Low Man and set his suitcase on the counter. "I'll trade you this yellow page for everything inside this suitcase. Hell, you can have the suitcase, too, if you tell me where to find this place."

"Breads?"

A good sign. It was a place popular enough to have a diminutive.

"Yeah, do you read?" asked Low Man.

"Of course."

"What do you read?"

"Comic books."

"What kind of comics?"

"Not comics," said the kid. "Comic books."

"Okay," said Low Man. "What kind of comic books?"

"Good ones. *Daredevil*, *Preacher*, *Love and Rockets*, *Astro City*."

"Do you read mysteries?"

"You mean, like, murder mysteries?"

"That's exactly what I mean."

"No, not really."

"Well, I got a mystery for you anyway," said Low Man as he pushed the suitcase a few inches across the counter, closer to the cashier.

"This is a suitcase," said Low Man.

"I know it's a suitcase."

"I just want you to know," said Low Man as he patted the suitcase, as he tapped a slight rhythm against the lock. "I just need you to understand, understand this, understand that there are only two kinds of suitcase."

"Really?" asked the cashier. He was making only six bucks an hour, not enough to be speaking metaphysically with a total stranger, and an Indian stranger at that.

"There is the empty suitcase," said Low Man. "And there is the full suitcase. And what I have here is a full suitcase. And I want to give it to you."

"Mister," said the kid. "You don't have to give me your suitcase. I'll tell you where Breads is. Hell, Missoula is a small town. You could find it by accident."

"But the thing is, I need you to take me there."

"I'm working."

"I know you're working," said Low Man. "But I figure that car, that shit-bag Camaro out there is yours. So I figure you can close this place down for a few minutes and give me a ride. You give me a ride and I'll give you this suitcase and all of its contents."

There was a pistol, a revolver, sitting in a dark place beneath the cash register.

"I can't close," said the cashier. He believed in rules, in order. "This is 7-Eleven. We're supposed to be open, like, all the time.

Look outside, the sign says twenty-four hours. I mean, I had to work last Christmas."

"Sweetheart," said Low Man. "I'm older than you, so I remember when 7-Eleven used to be open from seven in the morning until eleven at night. That's why they called it 7-Eleven. Get it? Open from seven to eleven? So, why don't you and I get nostalgic, and pretend it's 1973, and close the store long enough for you to drive me to the bookstore?"

"Mister," said the kid. "Even if this was 1973, and even if this store was only open from seven to eleven, it would still be three in the afternoon, like it is right now, and I would still not close down."

"Son, son, son," said Low Man, losing his patience. "What if I told you there was a dead body inside this suitcase?"

The cashier blinked, but remained calm. He had once shot a deer in the heart at two hundred yards, and bragged about it, though he'd been aiming for the head, the trophy hunter's greatest sin.

"That suitcase is too small. You couldn't fit a body in there," said the kid.

"Fair enough," said Low Man. "What if there's just a head?"

The cashier ran through the 7-Eleven employee's handbook in his memory, searching for the proper way to deal with a crazy customer, a man who may or may not have a dead man—or pieces of a dead man—in his suitcase, but who most definitely had a thing for bookstores. The cashier had always been a good employee; his work ethic was quite advanced for somebody so young. But there was no official company policy, no corporate ethic, when it came to dealing with a man—an Indian man—who had so much pain illuminating both of his eyes.

"Mister," said the cashier, forced to improvise. "This is Montana.

Everybody's got a gun. Including me. And since you aren't from Montana, and I can tell that by looking at you, then you most likely don't have a gun."

"Your point being?"

"I'm going to shoot you in the ass if you don't exit the store immediately."

"Fine," said Low Man. "You can keep the damn bag anyway."

Leaving his suitcase behind, Low Man walked out of the store. He still carried his computer case and the yellow page with Bread and Books' address.

In the 7-Eleven, the cashier waited until the Indian was out of sight before he carefully opened the suitcase to find two pairs of shoes, a suit jacket, four shirts, two pairs of pants, and assorted socks and underwear. He also found a copy of *Red Rain* and discovered Low Man's photograph on the back of the book.

Away from that black-and-white image taken fifty pounds earlier, Low Man walked until he stumbled across the Barnes and Noble superstore filling up one corner of an ugly strip mall.

Fucking colonial clipper ships are everywhere, thought Low Man, *even in Missoula, Montana.* But he secretly loved the big green boats, mostly because they sold tons of his books.

Low Man stepped into the store, found the mystery section, gathered all the copies of his books, soft and hard, and carried them to the information desk.

"I want to sign these," he said to the woman working there.

"Why?"

"Because I wrote them."

"Oh," said the woman, immediately dropping into some highly trained and utterly pleasant demeanor. Perhaps everybody in Missoula, Montana, loved their jobs. "Please, let me get the manager. She'll be glad to help you."

"Hold on," said Low Man as he handed her the yellow page. "Do you know where this place is?"

"Breads?"

There it was again, the place with the nickname. Everybody must go there. At that moment, there could be dozens of people in Breads. Low Man wondered if there was a woman, a lovely woman in the bookstore, a lonely woman who would drag him back to her house and make love to him without removing any of her clothes.

"Is it a good store?" asked Low Man.

"I used to work there," she said. "It closed down a month ago."

Low Man wondered if her eyes changed color when she mourned.

"The kid at 7-Eleven didn't tell me that."

"Oh," said the woman, completely confused. She was young, just months out of some small Montana town like Wolf Point or Harlem or Ronan, soon to return. "Well, let me get the manager."

"Wait," said Low Man, handing her his computer case. "I found this over in the mystery section."

He'd purchased the computer case through a catalogue, and had regretted it ever since. The bag was bulky, heavy, poorly designed.

"Thank you. I'll put it in Lost and Found."

Low Man's computer was an outdated Apple, its hard drive stuffed to the brim with three unpublished mystery novels and hundreds of programs and applications that he'd never used after downloading them.

Free of his possessions, Low Man waited. He watched the men and women move through the bookstore.

He wondered what *Missoula* meant, if there'd been some cavalry soldier named Missoula who'd made this part of the world safe for white people. He wondered if he could kill somebody, an Indian or a white soldier, and what it would feel like. He wondered if he would cry when he had to wash blood from his hands.

He studied the faces of the white people in the store. He decided to choose the one that he would kill if he were forced to kill. Not the woman with the child, and certainly not the child, but maybe the man reading movie magazines, and, most likely, the old man asleep in the poetry-section chair.

Low Man stared at the gold band on the dead man's left hand. Low Man was still staring when the dead man woke up and walked out of the store.

Low Man had been married twice, to a Lummi woman and a Yakama woman, and had fathered three kids, one each with his ex-wives, the third the result of a one-night stand with a white woman in Santa Fe. He sent money and books to his Indian children, but he hadn't seen his white kid in ten years.

"Mr. Smith, Low Man Smith?" asked the Barnes and Noble manager upon her arrival in Low Man's world. She was blond, blue-eyed, plain.

"Please," he said. "Call me Chuck."

"My name is Eryn."

Low Man wondered if he was going to sleep with her, this Eryn. He'd spent many nights in hotel rooms with various bookstore employees and literary groupies. That was one of the unpublicized perks of the job. He always wondered what the women saw in him, why they wanted to have sex with a stranger simply based on his ability to create compelling metaphors, or even when he failed to create compelling metaphors. The women were interested in him no matter what *The New York Times Book Review* had to say about his latest novel. Low Man was bored with his own writing, with his books, and to be honest, he'd grown bored with his literary life and the sexual promiscuity that seemed to go with it. Last year, after meeting Carlotta at the Native American Children of Alcoholics convention in Albuquerque, after sharing a bed with her for five nights, he'd vowed to remain faithful to her—and had been faithful to her and the idea of her—even though they'd made no promises to each other, even though she'd talked openly of the three men who were actively pursuing her, of the one man that she still loved, who had never been named Chuck.

"Mr. Smith, Chuck?" asked Eryn, the Barnes and Noble manager. "Are you okay?"

"Yes, sorry," said Low Man. "I'm very tired."

"I wish we'd known you were going to be in town," she said. "We would have ordered more copies of your books."

She smiled. Low Man decided that she was the kind of woman who lost sleep so that she could finish reading a good novel. He wondered if he was going to wake up before her the next morning and pass the time by scanning the titles of the books stacked on her nightstand.

"I didn't know I was going to be in Missoula," he said. "I was supposed to be spending a week up on the Flathead Reservation."

"Oh, I thought you might be here to see Tracy."

"Who?"

"Tracy," said the manager, and when that elicited no response from Low Man, she added, "Tracy Johnson. You went to college together, right?"

"She lives here?"

"Actually, she works here at the bookstore."

"Really?"

"Well, she's here part-time while she's getting her MFA at the university."

"She's a writer?"

"Yes. Didn't you know that?"

"I haven't seen Tracy in ten years," said Low Man.

He closed his eyes and when he opened them again two uniformed police officers were standing in front of him. One of the officers, the tall one with blue eyes, carried Low Man's suitcase.

"Mr. Smith," said the tall cop. "Are you Mr. Smith?"

"No, no," said Low Man. "You must be mistaken. My name is Crazy Horse."

▲

Later, in the police station, Low Man paged through another telephone directory. He hoped that Tracy Johnson's number was listed.

He found her.

"This better be you," she said when she answered the phone, clearly expecting somebody else.

"Hi, Tracy, it's Low Man."

Low Man remembered, when it came to poetry, that a strategic pause was called a caesura.

"Bah," she said.

"No bah."

"Damn, Low, it's been forever. Are you still an Indian?"

"Yes, I am. Are you still a lesbian?"

They both remembered their secret language, their shared ceremonies.

"Definitely," she said. "In fact, I thought you were my partner. I'm supposed to pick her up after work. We've got a big date tonight."

"Well, you think maybe you could pick me up, too?"

"Are you in town?" she asked, her voice cracking with excitement. Low Man hoped it was excitement, though he feared it was something else. His chest ached with the memory of her. During college, when he was still drinking, he had once crawled through her apartment window and slept on her living room floor, though he'd made sure to wake up before dawn and leave before she'd ever known he was there. During the long walk home, he'd veered off the road into a shallow swamp, not because he was too drunk to properly navigate but because he wanted to do something self-flagellating and noble, or at least something that approximated nobility—a drunk twenty-year-old's idea of nobility. He'd wanted to be a drunk monk in love.

"Damn, Low," she said. "Why didn't you call me before? I would have gone out and bought a dress. I know how much you like me in dresses."

She remembered him so well. He liked that.

"I didn't know I was going to be here," he said. "And I didn't know you lived here."

"So, how'd you get my number?"

"Well, your manager at the bookstore told me you were getting an MFA."

"Eryn," she said. "I bet you were wondering if she was going to hop on you, right?"

Low Man couldn't answer.

"Damn, Low," she said, laughing loudly. Her laughter had always been too loud, impolite, and wonderful. "Eryn is a lesbian. You always fall for the lesbians."

Low Man had once kissed Tracy, though they each remembered it differently. She'd thought the kiss was a desperate attempt to change her mind about him in particular, and about men in general, but he believed that he'd kissed her only because he wanted to know how it felt, how she smelled and tasted, before he put his feelings into a strongbox and locked them away forever.

"Yeah, that's me," said Low. "The Dyke Mike. Now, can you pick me up?"

"Low, I can't, really," she said. "I mean, my partner's parents are coming over for dinner. They drove over here from Spokane Rez and, like, it's the first time I've met them, and they're not exactly happy their daughter has come roaring out of the closet on the motorcycle called Me."

"I really need you to pick me up."

"Low, I want to see you, I really do, but the time is so bad. How about tomorrow? Can't we do this tomorrow? Hell, we'll talk for three days straight, but I really need tonight, okay?"

"I'm in jail."

Low wondered if there was a word in Navajo that meant caesura.

"What did you do?"

"I broke my heart."

"I didn't realize that was illegal."

"Well," he said. "In Missoula, it seems to be a misdemeanor."

"Are you arrested?"

"No," said Low. "Not really. The police said they just don't want me to be alone tonight."

"Low, what happened?"

"I came here to see a woman. I was going to ask her to marry me."

"And she said no."

"Not exactly."

"What then?"

"She married Chuck yesterday and moved to Flagstaff."

"I hate Arizona."

She'd always known exactly what to say.

"Low, honey," she added. "I'll be right there."

▲

Tracy Johnson drove a 1972 half-ton Chevrolet pickup. Red with long streaks of gray primer paint. Four good tires and one bad alternator. Hay-bale molding in the bed.

"This truck," said Low as he climbed in. "What stereotype are you trying to maintain?

"There are no stereotypes in Missoula, Montana," she said, appraising his face and body. "You've gained weight. A lot of weight."

"So have you," he said. "I love all of your chins."

Forty pounds overweight, she was beautiful, wearing a loose T-shirt and tight blue jeans. Her translucent skin bled light into her dark hair.

On the radio, Hank Williams sang white man blues.

"You're lovely," said Low. "Just lovely."

"Yes, I know," she said. "But don't get your hopes up."

"My hopes have never been up," he said, though he knew he was lying. "Your partner, what's her name?"

"Sara Polatkin," said Tracy. "She's Indian."

"Indian dot-in-the-head or Indian arrow-in-the-heart?"

"She's Spokane. From the rez. Unlike your lame urban Indian ass."

"Yes," said Low Man. "And you can say that, given you've spent so much time on reservations."

Tracy dropped the truck into gear and drove down a narrow street.

"Yeah," she said. "I'm freaking out her parents. Completely. Not only am I a lesbian but I'm also white."

"The double whammy."

"She's in law school," said Tracy. "She's smart. Even smarter than you."

"Good for you."

"We're getting married."

"Really?"

"Yeah, that's why Sara's parents are coming over. They're going to try to talk her out of it."

"Jesus," said Low Man, wondering why he had bothered to get on the flight from Seattle.

"Jesus has nothing to do with it," said Tracy as she stared ahead and smiled.

Ahead, on the right side of the street, Sara Polatkin was waiting outside the coffee joint. She was short, thin, very pretty, even with her bad teeth and eccentric clothes—a black dress with red stockings, and Chuck Taylor basketball shoes with Cat in the Hat socks.

Low Man couldn't look Sara in the eye when she climbed into the truck. He remembered how Crazy Horse—that great Indian warrior, that savior, that Christ-figure—was shot in the face by his lover's husband.

Low Man sat on the bench seat between Tracy and Sara. He watched as the women leaned over him to kiss each other. He could smell their perfumes.

"So, you're Low," said Sara, her voice inflected with a heavy sing-song reservation accent. She probably had to work hard to keep that accent. Her black hair hung down past her waist.

"It's Low Man, both words, Low Man," he said. Only three people had ever been allowed to call him Low: his mother, his late father, and Tracy.

"Okay, Low Man, both words, Low Man," said Sara. "So, you're the one who is madly in love with my wife."

"Yes, I was," he said, careful with the tense. "And she's not your wife, yet."

"Details. Do you still love her?"

Low Man hesitated—*caesura*—and Tracy rushed to fill the silence.

"He just got his heart broken by an Indian woman," she said. "I don't think you want to be the second one today, huh, Sara?"

Sara's face went dark, darker.

"Did you ever fuck her?" Sara asked him, and Low Man heard the Spokane River in her voice, and heard the great Columbia as well, and felt the crash of their confluence.

"Sara, let it go," said Tracy, with some traces of laughter still in her voice.

"Do they talk like that in law school?" Low Man asked Sara.

"Yeah," she said. "Except it's in Latin."

Low Man could feel the Indian woman's eyes on him, but he didn't return the stare. He watched the road moving ahead of them.

"Sara, let it go," said Tracy, and there was something else in her voice then. "Remember, you're the one who used to sleep with guys."

Tracy put her hand on Low's knee.

"Sorry, Low," she said. "But these born-again dykes can be so righteous."

"Yeah, yeah, I'm sorry, Low Man," said Sara. "I'm just nervous about my ma and pa."

"So, you're a new lesbian, huh?" asked Low Man.

"I'm still in the wrapper," said Sara.

"She's still got that new-car smell," said Tracy.

"What made you change teams?" asked Low.

"I'm running away from the things of man," she said.

▲

At dinner, Low Man sat at the small table between Tracy and Sara. Directly across from him, Sid Polatkin, longtime husband, held the hand of Estelle Polatkin, longtime wife. All five of them had ordered the salmon special because it had just seemed easier.

"Do you think the salmon will be good?" asked Estelle, her voice thick with a reservation accent, much thicker than her daughter's.

"It's the Holiday Inn," said her husband. He was president of the Spokane Indian Reservation VFW. "The Holiday Inn is dependable."

Sid's hair was pulled back in a gray ponytail. So was Estelle's. Both of their faces told stories. Sid's: the recovering alcoholic; the wronged son of a wronged son; the Hamlet of his reservation. Estelle's: the tragic beauty; the woman who stopped drinking because her husband did; the woman who woke in the middle of the night to wash her hands ten times in a row.

Now they were Mormons.

"Do you believe in God?" Sid had asked Low Man before they sat down.

"Sure," said Low Man, and he meant it.

"Do you believe in Jesus?" asked Sid as he unrolled his napkin and set it on his substantial lap.

"How do you mean?" asked Low Man.

"Do you believe that Jesus was crucified and rose from the dead?"

"Come on, Daddy, leave him alone," said Sara. She knew how her father's theological conversations usually began and how they often ended. He'd always been a preacher.

"No, Sara," said Low Man. "It's okay."

"I think Mr. Smith can speak for himself," said Sid. He leaned across the table and jabbed the air with a sharp index finger, a twenty-first century Indian's idea of a bow and arrow.

"Low speaks too much," said Tracy. Sure, it was a lame joke, but she was trying to change the tone of the conversation. Hey, she thought, everybody should laugh. Ha, ha, ha, ha, ha! Let's all clap hands and sing!

"Hey, Mr. Smith, Low Man," continued Sid. "Why don't you and I pretend we're alone here. Let's pretend this is a country of men."

Low Man smiled and looked at the three women: Estelle, Sara, and Tracy; two strangers and his unrequited love; two Indians and one white. If asked, as a man, to rush to their defense, what would Low Man do? How far would he go? If asked, as an Indian, to defend Jesus, what could he say?

"Please, Low, tell me what you think about Jesus," said Sid, moving from question to command somewhere in the middle of that sentence.

"I don't think it matters what I think," said Low Man. "I'm not a Christian. Let them have their Jesus."

"How vague," said Sid. "Tell me, then, what do you think their Jesus would say about lesbian marriage?"

Tracy and Sara sighed and leaned back in their chairs. How often had men sat around dinner tables and discussed women's lives, their choices, and the reasons why one woman reached across the bed to touch another woman?

"Mr. Polatkin," said Tracy. "If you want to talk about our relationship, then you should talk to Sara and me. Otherwise, it's just cowardly."

"You think I'm a coward?" asked Sid.

"Daddy, let's just order dinner," said Sara. "Mom, tell him to order dinner."

Estelle closed her eyes.

"Hey," said Sid. "Maybe I should order chicken, huh? But that would be cannibalism, right? Am I right, Tracy, tell me, am I right?"

"Mr. Polatkin," said Tracy. "I don't know you. But I love your daughter, and she tells me you're a good man, so I'm willing to give you a chance. I'm hoping you'll extend the same courtesy to me."

"I don't have to give you anything," said Sid as he tossed his napkin onto his plate.

"No," said Estelle, her voice barely rising above a whisper.

"What?" asked Sid. "What did you say?"

"We came here with love," said Estelle. "We came here to forgive."

"Forgive?" asked Tracy. "Forgive what? We don't need your forgiveness."

Low Man recognized the anger in Tracy's eyes and in her voice. *Low,* she'd said to him in anger all those years ago, *I'm never going to love you that way. Never. Can you please understand that? I can't change who I am. I don't want to change who I am. And if you ever touch me again, I swear I will hate you forever.*

"Hey, hey, Sid, sit down," said Low. "You want to talk Jesus, I'll talk Jesus."

Sid hesitated a moment—asserting his independence—and then nodded his head.

"That's good," said Low. "Now, let me tell you. Jesus was a fag."

Everybody was surprised, except Tracy, who snorted loudly and laughed.

"No, no, no," continued Low. "Just think about it. I mean, there Jesus was, sticking up for the poor, the disadvantaged, the disabled. Who else but a fag would be that liberal, huh? And damn, Jesus hung out with twelve guys wearing great robes and great hair and never, ever talked about women. Tell me, Sidney, what kind of guys never talk about women?"

"Fags!" shouted Tracy.

"This isn't funny," said Sid.

"No, it's not," said Sara. "Tracy, let's just go home. Let's just go. And Low Man, you just shut up, you shut up."

"No, Sara," said Tracy. "Let them talk. Let them be men. And God said, let them be men."

"I don't like you this way," Sara said to Tracy. "You've been different ever since Low showed up. You're different with him."

Low Man wondered if that was true; he wondered what it meant; he knew what he wanted it to mean.

"Please," said Sara. "Let's just go, Tracy, let's go."

"Nobody's going anywhere," said Sid. "Not until this is over."

Estelle's eyes glowed with tears.

"I'm being dead serious here, Sid," said Low. "I mean, Jesus was an incredibly decent human being and they crucified him for it. He sounds like a fag to me."

"Jesus *was* a human being," said Sid. "At least, you've got that much right. He didn't rise from the dead. He wasn't the Son of God. He was just a man."

"No, Sid, you and me, we're just men. Simple, stupid men."

"Yes, yes, I'm simple," said Sid. "I'm a man who is simply afraid of God. And next to God, we're all stupid. That much we can agree on."

"Fine, fine, Sid, we agree."

Sid stared at Low Man. The question: How does any father prove how much he loves his child? One answer: the father must hate his child's enemies. Another answer: the father must protect his child from all harm.

"Listen to me," said Sid. "I'm being terrible. I'm not being good. Not good at all. We're all hungry and angry and tired. Why don't we eat and then figure out whether we're going to stay or go? How does that sound?"

Because they all loved one another, in one form or another, in one direction or another, they agreed.

All five of them ordered soda pop, except for Tracy, the white woman, who ordered red wine. Low Man wondered what would happen when every drunk Indian quit drinking—and he truly believed it would someday happen—when Indians quit giving white people something to worry about besides which wine went with fish and which wine went with Indians.

"So, you're a writer?" Sid asked Low Man.

"Yes."

"You make a living at it?"

"Sid," said Low Man, leaning close to the table. "I make shitloads of money. I make so much money that white people think I'm white." Nobody laughed.

"You're one of the funny Indians, enit?" Sid asked Low Man. "Always making the jokes, never taking it seriously."

"What is this *it* you're talking about?" asked Low Man.

"Everything. You think everything is funny."

Low knew for a fact that everything was funny. Homophobia? Funny! Genocide? Hilarious! Political assassination? Side-splitting! Love? Ha, Ha, Ha!

"Low, honey," said Tracy. "Maybe you should get some coffee. Maybe you should shut up, huh?"

Low Man looked at Tracy, at Sara. He wanted to separate them.

Sara looked at Low and wondered yet again why Indian men insisted on being warriors. *Put down your bows and arrows*, she wanted to scream at Low, at her father, at every hypermasculine Injun in the world. *Put down your fucking guns and pick up your kids*.

"Sid," said Low Man. "How many women have you had in your life?"

"What do you mean?"

"I mean, counting lovely Estelle here, how many women have you slept with, bedded down, screwed, humped, did the nasty with?"

Estelle gasped and slapped her hand over her mouth—a strangely mannered gesture for a reservation Indian woman.

"I think we made a mistake here," said Sid, rising with his wife. "I think we should just go home. Whatever treaties we signed here are broken now."

"No, no, no," said Sara. "Please, Mom, Dad, sit down."

Sid and Estelle might have left then, might never have returned to their daughter's life, but the salmon arrived at that moment.

"Eat, eat," said Sara, with tears in her eyes. She turned her attention to Low Man.

"I think you should leave," she said, understanding that Indian men wanted to own the world just as much as white men did. They just wanted it for different reasons.

Low Man looked to Tracy. He wanted her to choose.

"I think she's right, Low," said Tracy. "Why don't you take the truck and drive back to our place?"

Low Man stared into her eyes. He stepped through her pupils and searched for some sign, some indication, some clue of what he was supposed to do.

"Low, go, just go," said Tracy.

"Mom," said Sara, as she held her mother's hand. "Please, stay."

Tracy said, "Go, Low, just go for a ride. Sid and Estelle can give us a ride back to our place, right?"

Sid nodded his head. He sliced into his salmon and shoved a huge piece into his mouth.

"Please, Low," said Tracy. "Go."

"Sid," said Low Man. "I was wondering why you came here. I mean, if you don't approve of this, of them, then why the hell are you here?"

Sid chewed on his salmon. The great fish was gone from the Spokane River. Disappeared.

"I love my daughter," said Sid. "And I don't want her to go to hell."

Estelle started weeping. She stared down at the salmon on her plate.

"Mom," said Sara. "Please."

Sid finished his salmon with two huge bites. He washed it down with water and leaned back in his chair. He stared at Low Man.

"Come on, boys," said Tracy. "No need for the testicle show, okay?"

"You have a filthy mouth," Sid said.

"Yeah, I guess I fucking do," she said.

"Whore."

"Dad, stop it," said Sara. Her mother lowered her chin onto her chest and wept like she was thirty years older.

"I raised my daughter to be better than this," said Sid.

"Better than what?" asked Low.

"My daughter wasn't, wasn't a gay until she met this, this white woman."

"Maybe I should go," said Tracy.

"No," said Sara. "Nobody's going anywhere."

In Sara's voice, the others heard something new: an adulthood ceremony taking place between syllables.

"What's wrong with you?" Low asked Sid. "She's your daughter. You should love her no matter what."

Low Man wanted this father to take his daughter away.

"I don't think this is any of your business," said Sid. "You're not even supposed to be here."

"I'm not supposed to be anywhere," said Low. "But here I am."

Low Man smiled at himself. He sounded like a character out of film noir, like Lee Marvin or Robert Mitchum. Or maybe like Peter Lorre.

"What are you smiling at?" asked Sid.

"I'm going to the room," said Estelle as she stood up. Sara rose with her.

"Mom, Mom, I love you," said Sara as she hugged her.

Low Man wondered what would have happened if he had a pistol. He wondered if he would have shot Sid Polatkin in the face. No, of course not. Low Man probably would have raced out into the dark and tried to bring down one of the airplanes that kept passing over the motel.

"Do you know what I want?" Low asked Sid.

"No. Tell me."

"I want to take Tracy out of here. I want to take her back home with me. I want her to fall in love with me."

"Go ahead," said Sid. "And I'll take my daughter back home where she belongs."

"Sid," said Low. "These women don't belong to us. They live in whole separate worlds, man, don't you know that?"

Sid couldn't answer. His jaw worked furiously. When he was a young man, he used to fight Golden Gloves. Even at his advanced age, he could have beaten the crap out of Low Man. Both men knew this to be a fact.

Tracy stood up from the table. She took two steps away, then turned back.

"I'm leaving, Sara," she said. "Finally, I'm leaving."

Sara looked to her father and mother. Together, the three of them had buried dozens of loved ones. The three of them knew all of the same mourning songs. Two of them had loved each other enough to conceive the third. They'd invented her! She was their Monster; she was surely going to murder them. That's what children were supposed to do!

"Mom, Dad," she said. "I love you."

Sara stepped away from her mother, her father. She stepped away from the table, away from the salmon, and toward Tracy.

"If you leave now," said Sid. "Don't you ever call us. Don't you ever talk to us again."

Sara closed her eyes. She remembered the winter when her father fell from the roof of their house and disappeared into a snowbank. She remembered the dreadful silence after the impact, and then the wondrous noise, the joyful cacophony of his laughter.

Tracy took Sara's hand. They stood there in the silence.

"Sid," said Low Man. "These women don't need us. They never did."

"We're leaving," said Tracy and Sara together. Hand in hand, they walked away.

With surprising speed, Sid rose from the table and chased after them. He caught them just before they got to the restaurant exit. He pushed Tracy into a wall—pushed her into the plasterboard—and took his daughter by the elbow.

"You're coming with us," he said.

"No," said Sara.

Estelle couldn't move. "Help them," she said to Low Man. "Help them."

Low didn't know which "them" she was talking about. He rushed across the room just as Sid slapped his daughter once, then again. One Indian man raised his hand to slap an Indian woman, but a third Indian stepped between them.

"She's my daughter, she's mine," shouted Sid. He pushed against Low, as Sara fell back against a glass door, as she turned to hide her face.

Sid and Low grappled with each other. The old man was very strong.

At the table, Estelle covered her face with her hands.

"She's my daughter, she's my daughter," shouted Sid as he punched Low in the chest. Low staggered back and fell to one knee.

"She's my daughter," shouted Sid as he turned to attack Tracy. But she slapped him hard. Surprised, defeated, Sid dropped to the floor beside Low.

The two Indian men sat on the ground as the white woman stood above them.

Tracy turned away from the men and ran after Sara.

Sid climbed to his feet. He pointed an accusing finger at Low, who rose slowly to his feet. Sid turned and walked back toward his wife, back toward Estelle, who held her husband close and cried in his arms.

"What are you going to do?" Low called after him. "What are you going to do when she's gone?"

SAINT JUNIOR

▲▲▲▲▲▲▲▲▲▲▲▲▲▲▲▲▲▲▲▲▲▲▲▲▲▲▲▲▲▲▲▲▲▲▲▲▲▲

That winter, on a full-moon Monday on the Spokane Indian Reservation, the first snow fell sometime between midnight and dawn, when most of the reservation residents—Indian and white alike—were asleep, except for the Cold Springs Singers, those six Spokane Indian men who sat at a drum on top of Lookout Mountain and sang the indigenous blues:

> *Way, ya, hey, yi, hey, yo.*
> *On the road and on the street,*
> *They're just trying to keep the beat.*
> *Way, ya, hey, ya, ya.*
> *On the road and on the moon,*
> *They're just trying to keep the tune.*
> *Way, ya, hey, yi, hey, yo.*
> *Way, ya, hey, yi, hey, yo.*
> *On the road and on the run,*
> *Two little lovebirds having fun.*
> *Will their love survive the test?*
> *Romeo and Juliet.*
> *Way, ya, hey, yi, hey, yo.*

Wearing only T-shirts, blue jeans, and baseball caps, the Cold Springs Singers ignored howling winds and the impossibly white snow piling up on their shoulders. Three of the men wore their long black hair in careful braids, two wore crew cuts, and the last was chemotherapy bald. They'd all known one another since birth, since they'd spent their nine months in the wombs of six Indian mothers who'd sat together at their own drum—Big Mom's Daughters—and sung their own songs. Those mothers had taught their sons public and private songs and the most secret difference between the two. To show their devotion and love, those sons had kept their mothers' secrets safely hidden from the rest of the world.

From the age of three, those Indian boys sang and drummed together. Over the course of a twenty-year career, the Cold Springs Singers had traveled to one hundred different reservations and had fallen in love with three hundred and nineteen Indian women and sixteen Indian men. They'd fathered seven daughters and three sons. Three of them had married and two had divorced. They'd learned how to sing seven hundred and nine different songs:

> Ha, ya, ha, ya, ha, ya.
> Don't tell me you love me
> Unless you mean it.
> Ha, ya, ha, ya, ha, ya.
> Don't tell me you love me
> Unless you mean it.
> Ha, ya, ha, ya, ha, ya.
> I love you, I love you,
> I want to marry you.
> Ha, ya, ha, ya, ha, ya.
> Marry me once, marry me twice
> Marry me three times.
> Ha, ya, ha, ya, ha, ya.

But now, as they sang on top of Lookout Mountain, the Cold Springs Singers were in love with the drum and only the drum. They'd forgotten what it meant to love anything other than the feel of stick in hand and song in throat. Of course, the Cold Springs Singers were ghosts, having all been killed when their blue van collided with a logging truck on the S-curves of Little Falls Road, just a few feet away from the natural spring that provided the namesake for the group, but those Indian boys still sang and pounded the sticks better than any other drum alive or dead:

> *Hey, ya, hey, ya, ho, ya, ho.*
> *I don't have any money, honey.*
> *I don't have a nice car.*
> *Hey, ya, hey, ya, ho, ya, ho.*
> *I don't have a big house, mouse.*
> *I don't have a fast car.*
> *Hey, ya, hey, ya, ho, ya, ho.*
> *I don't have fancy shoes, Lou.*
> *I don't have a new car.*
> *Hey, ya, hey, ya, ho, ya, ho.*
> *Will you still love me?*
> *Will you still love me?*
> *Will you still love me*
> *When I'm old and broke?*
> *Hey, ya, hey, ya, ho, ya, ho.*

All night, they sang indigenous songs called "49s," though there's not an Indian alive who remembers exactly why they're called 49s. Some say those songs were invented after fifty Indian warriors went out to battle and only one came back alive. Distraught, the lone survivor mourned his friends by singing forty-nine songs, one for each of the dead. Others believe the 49s were invented when fifty warriors went out to battle and forty-nine came back alive. Distraught, they remembered the lost one by singing forty-nine songs, one by each of the living. Still others believe the 49s were invented by a woman who fell in love with forty-nine men and had her heart broken by each and every one of them. And still more believe the 49s were invented by forty-nine men who mourned the loss of one good woman. However they were invented, those songs have always been heavy with sadness and magic. However they were invented, the Cold Springs Singers knew all of the words and vocables, all the 4/4 signatures and atonal cries in the night.

On the Spokane Indian Reservation, with the coming of that first snow, the Cold Springs Singers sang 49s until every Indian was startled awake and sang along. They all sang because they understood what it meant to be Indian and dead and alive and still bright with faith and hope:

> *Basketball, basketball.*
> *Way, ya, hi, yo, way, ya, hi, yo.*
> *Give me the ball, give me the ball.*
> *Way, ya, hi, yo, way, ya, hi, yo.*
> *And let me shoot, and let me shoot.*
> *Way, ya, hi, yo, way, ya, hi, yo.*
> *And win the game, and win the game.*
> *Way, ya, hi, yo, way, ya, hi, yo.*
> *And then she'll love me, then she'll love me.*
> *Way, ya, hi, yo, way, ya, hi, yo.*
> *Forever and ever, forever and ever.*

First snow was a good time for most Indians, even the ghosts, and especially the Indians and ghosts of Indians who possessed a good sense of rhythm and irony. After all, it took a special kind of courage for an Indian to look out a window into the deep snow and see anything special in that vast whiteness.

On that night, in that reservation whiteness, the falsetto voices of the Cold Springs Singers drifted down from their mountain onto an outdoor basketball court covered with two feet of new snow. On that court, a Spokane Indian named Roman Gabriel Fury ran fast breaks with the ghosts of his mother and father, seven cousins, nine dead dogs, and his maternal and paternal grandparents. He was the best basketball player his reservation had ever known, though he was older now and no longer a magician. He was the only Fury left alive in the world, but he was not alone. He had his basketball, his ghosts, and an Indian woman named Grace Atwater asleep at home.

▲

Roman Gabriel Fury lived with Grace Atwater in a shotgun shack set down like a lighthouse in a small field about five miles north of Wellpinit, the only town on the Spokane Indian Reservation. Outside the shack, a mammoth satellite dish rose from the snow like the gray sail of a landlocked ship. Of course, unlike most others, that metal sail was covered with reservation bumper stickers and tribal graffiti:

> *Custer had it coming!*
> *Proud to be a Spokane Indian*
> $E = MC^2$
> *Fry bread power!*
> *American Indians for Nixon*

Roman had no idea who'd plastered the Nixon sticker on his dish—Indians were capable of the most self-destructive behavior— but Roman had never removed it because he believed wholeheartedly in free expression. Roman's entire political philosophy revolved around the basic tenet that a person, any person, had only enough energy at any given time to believe in three things.

"Choose your three," Roman was often fond of pontificating. "And stick with them."

Roman himself believed in free expression, Grace Atwater, and basketball. Neither a Republican nor a Democrat, Roman had always voted for the candidate who looked like he or she could hit a twenty-foot jump shot with three seconds left on the clock and the home team down by one. Therefore, he was very excited that Bill Bradley, former Princeton All-American and New York Knick, was running for President of the United States.

"Finally, a worthy candidate," Roman had said during Bradley's first press conference.

"Come on," Grace had said. "You can't vote for a guy with a jump shot that ugly. And besides, you grew up in a matriarchy. You should vote for a woman."

"If there's a woman out there with a jump shot," Roman had replied, "who believes in the socialization of medicine and education, then I will not only vote for her, but I will also devote my life to her administration."

"Well, then, I guess that means I'm running for president," she'd said.

"Now, wouldn't that surprise the hell out of them? I expect to see your announcement on television soon."

"I will begin my press conference by announcing that yes, I have smoked pot, and yes, I have had sex, lots of sex. In fact, I will introduce the seven men and one woman I have slept with and let them answer all the questions regarding my campaign and political philosophies."

"You will be a hero to all women and men."

"That's the power of television."

Roman had bought the satellite dish, spending most of the money he'd won by hitting a trifecta at Playfair Race Track in Spokane, because he'd wanted to enrich his life by partaking in the free expression of sitcom writers and shopping-channel salespeople, and because he wanted to provide Grace with a source of entertainment, education, and dozens of episodes of *Bonanza*, featuring the talents of her favorite actor, Dan "Hoss" Blocker, and because he wanted to watch every single college and professional basketball game ever played.

Though he rarely played seriously anymore, preferring to shoot baskets all by himself, he still loved the game and all of its details. For Roman, the beauty of a perfect pick-and-roll by the Utah Jazz's John Stockton and Karl Malone was matched only by the beauty of a perfect pick-and-roll by John and Michelle Sirois, the best brother and sister nine-year-old hoopsters on the Spokane Indian Reservation.

Roman knew that basketball was the most democratic sport. All you needed to play was something that resembled a ball and something else that approximated the shape of a basket.

These days, Roman himself resembled a basketball and hoop. But he didn't mind so much. Half of the Indians on the rez were fat and they all got laid by skinny and fat people alike. Standards of beauty were much more egalitarian on the rez, and Roman was an egalitarian man.

▲

On the morning after the first snow, Roman slept on the couch in the living room. Across the room, a twelve-inch black-and-white television was balanced on top of a twenty-seven-inch color television. The small television had a great picture but no sound, while the large one had great sound and terrible reception. Roman called his televisions the Lone Ranger and Tonto, though he never told anybody which television was which. That morning, as the first snow drifted against the door, both televisions replayed a classic press conference from a few years earlier:

> *Michael Jordan, wearing a custom-tailored*
> *Armani suit, stands at a podium in*
> *some beautiful hotel in downtown Chicago.*
> *His ebony skin reflects dozens of flashbulbs.*
> *He leans close to the porcupine of microphones*
> *rising from the podium. He smiles. Yesterday,*
> *he was playing minor league baseball,*
> *swinging at and missing curve balls by at least*
> *two feet. Today, the room is as silent as a*
> *Catholic Church on a Tuesday afternoon*
> *in July. Jordan licks his lips, takes a breath,*
> *drawing out the moment, ever the*
> *showman, ever the competitor, and says,*
> *"I'm back."*

Still asleep on the couch, holding a basketball like a lover in his arms, Roman was wrapped up like a two-hundred-and-eighty-pound butterfly in a Pendleton-blanket cocoon. He wore a huge white T-shirt and a pair of boxer shorts. He heard those words. He heard "I'm back," and he stirred in his sleep.

I'm back.

Still holding the basketball, Roman sat up with a bolt and stared at the television. For just a brief moment, he wondered if Jordan was coming back for the second time but then Roman came to his senses.

I'm back.

Roman remembered when Michael Jordan had announced he was returning to basketball. There had been joy, pure unadulterated joy, in Jordan's voice, in stark contrast to the grief and pain when he'd announced his retirement just a few short days after his father had been murdered by two teenage thugs. Roman recalled that one of those killers was a Lumbee Indian, a disturbing fact. But then again, it was Indian scouts who had helped white people kill Sitting Bull, Geronimo, and every other Indian warrior in the world.

I'm back.

After he'd returned to the NBA, Jordan had promptly led his Chicago Bulls to three more championships, the last coming on the final jump shot of Jordan's career, before he'd retired again and left Roman no options other than to take up coaching grade-school basketball at the Spokane Indian Tribal School.

I'm back.

Sitting in front of his two televisions, holding the basketball in one hand, Roman ran his other hand through his greasy black hair, always too thick to properly braid, and then swallowed the last drink out of a two-liter Diet Pepsi bottle sitting on the coffee table.

Roman was forty years old and forty pounds overweight. He pulled his thick, heavy body from the couch and shuffled from the living room into the bathroom. He tugged his underwear down to his ankles and sat on the toilet for a long morning piss. He'd always been a gentleman and knew that a stand-up piss made a terrible mess, no matter the accuracy of the shooter.

▲

Roman Gabriel Fury was named after an obscure professional football quarterback named Roman Gabriel—a man with his own kind of fury and the rumor of Indian blood—who'd toiled for the Los

Angeles Rams in the early seventies. Young Roman had never seen the elder Roman play, not in person, not on television, though one photograph of the dark-haired quarterback had been framed and nailed to the wall above the Fury fireplace.

"Was he your favorite player?" young Roman had once asked his father, Edgar Fury, in an effort to understand why he'd chosen such an ornate moniker for his only child.

"No," Edgar had said. "Just liked the name."

"I don't like it much."

"Well, just be glad your name ain't Namath Fury. Or Tarkenton Fury, for that matter. I could have named you after some old white boy quarterback."

Partly because of his name and partly because of his own stubborn nature, Roman Fury had never played football. Instead, he'd played basketball until his palms bled, and read books, hundreds of books, thereby saving himself from a lifetime of reservation poverty.

Oh, to this day, he still loved the reservation—he lived there, after all—but there was a time when he'd wanted to travel, when he'd known that he belonged elsewhere. From the very beginning of his life, he'd dreamed of leaving, not because he needed to escape—though his journey certainly could have been viewed as a form of flight—but because he'd always known that his true and real mission lay somewhere outside the boundaries of the reservation. There were Indians who belonged on the reservation and there were Indians who belonged in the city, and then there were those rare few who could live successfully in either place. But Roman had always felt like he didn't belong anywhere, like he couldn't belong to any one place or any series of places. Though his tribe had never been nomadic, he'd been born with the need to visit cities—every city!—where no Spokane Indian had ever been before.

He'd shaken hands with two different Popes, waded in the Mediterranean Sea, and walked one hundred miles atop the Great Wall of China. After a solid and unspectacular college basketball career— his name had never been mentioned on ESPN's *SportsCenter*—he'd played professionally in Norway, Italy, Japan, Des Moines, Russia, Hartford, Yugoslavia, Greece, Australia, Kamloops, British Columbia, Germany, France, Kalamazoo, and every other Spanish-speaking country in South America.

No habla Español. Indios de Norte Americanos.

Every autumn for ten years, Roman had attended NBA training camps—mostly for Eastern Conference teams because he had a great jump shot and slow feet—but he'd never even played in one exhibition game, let alone a regular-season contest, a feat that would have made him the first federally recognized Indian since Jim Thorpe to play professional basketball. But it had never happened, no matter how well he'd played in training camps. He'd been cut from fifteen different NBA teams in those ten years, and had always ended up as the second-best American player on third-rate international teams.

Then, one morning, after a particularly horrid game where he'd missed fifteen straight shots and turned the ball over seven times, he'd woken up in a Hilton Hotel in Madrid, Spain, with the sure knowledge that it was time to quit basketball for good and return to the reservation.

▲

On the morning after the first snow, Grace Atwater could hear the television playing out in the living room, could hear the replay of Michael Jordan's famous press conference.

I'm back.

Grace knew that her husband had fallen asleep out there again. He often fell asleep on the couch, leaving her alone in the bed. She didn't mind. He snored loudly and usually stole the covers. She smiled at the thought of her sloppy husband. He'd once been thin and beautiful.

She was a Mohawk Indian from the island of Manhattan—her father had been an iron worker who'd help build most of the New York skyline—but she'd lived on the Spokane Indian Reservation for so many years, and had spent so much time with the Spokanes, that she'd realized she was more Spokane than anything else. She'd always understood that an Indian could be assimilated and disappear into white culture, but she'd discovered, too, that an Indian of one tribe could be swallowed whole by another tribe. She was Jonah; the Spokanes were the stomach, ribs, and teeth of the whale.

I'm back.

She taught fourth grade at the Spokane Tribal School, and loved her job, though it had convinced her never to have her own children. Sometimes, she wondered what she was missing, if her life was somehow incomplete because she didn't see the reflection of her face in the face of a son or daughter. Maybe. That's what mothers told her: Oh, you don't know what you're missing; it's spiritual; I feel closer to the earth, to the creator of all things. Perhaps all of that was true—it must be true—but Grace also knew that mothering was work, was manual labor, and *unpaid* manual labor at that. She'd known too many women who'd vanished after childbirth; women whose hopes and fears had been pushed to the back of the family closet; women who'd magically been replaced by their children and their children's desires. But what about the maternal instinct? Well, for eight hours a day, over the last eight years, within the four walls of a fourth-grade classroom, she'd loved one hundred and thirty-six Spokane Indian boys and girls, had loved them well and kept them safe, and had often been the only adult in their lives who'd never actively or inactively broken their hearts. How many nights had one of her former students shown up at her house and asked to be sheltered?

Still, Grace had never thought of herself as any kind of saint. More likely, she was just a good teacher; nothing wrong with that, but nothing uncommon or special about it either. She'd often wondered if she was doing everything she could to ensure the survival of the Spokanes, the Mohawks, of all Indian people. Maybe she should have given birth to a dozen indestructible Indian children, part-Mohawk, part-Spokane, and part-Kevlar. Most of her fellow Mohawks, and most members of every other tribe, were marrying white partners and conceiving fragile children. Grace knew how fractions worked; Indians were disappearing by halves. But then again, she was only half-Mohawk herself and lived three thousand miles away from her people. Her people—what an arrogant concept! They didn't belong to her and she didn't belong to them. She was friendly with only twenty other Mohawks, having learned long ago that she preferred the company of these Spokanes, as bitter and sarcastic as they could be. Hell, these Spokanes started fistfighting one another in first grade and only stopped punching and kicking with the arrivals of their first Social Security checks. Then those former brawlers suddenly became respected elders and clucked their tongues at the young and violent. She was convinced the Spokanes survived out of spite. After a nuclear war, the only things left standing would be Spokane Indians, cockroaches, farmers, and Michael Jordan.

I'm back.

Inside their small house, Grace listened as Roman stood from the couch and walked into the bathroom. He sat down to piss. She thought that Roman's sit-down pisses were one of the most romantic and caring things that any man had ever done for any woman.

After the piss, Roman pulled up his underwear, climbed into a pair of sweatpants hanging from the shower rod, slipped his feet into Chuck Taylor basketball shoes, and stepped into the bedroom.

Grace pretended to be asleep in their big bed, warm and safe beneath seven generations of sheets, blankets, and quilts. She was a big woman with wide hips, thick legs, large breasts, and a soft stomach. She was deep brown and beautiful.

Still holding the basketball, Roman leaned close to Grace, his face just inches away from hers.

"There's a strange woman in my bed," said Roman.

"I know," said Grace, without opening her eyes.

"What should I do about her?"

"Let her sleep."

Roman touched the basketball to Grace's cheek.

"Michael Jordan is coming back again," he said.

"You can't fool me," said Grace. "I heard it. That was just a replay."

"Yeah, but I wish he was coming back again. He should always come back."

"Don't let it give you any crazy ideas."

Roman pulled the basketball away and leaned even closer to Grace. His lips were brushing against her ear.

"It snowed last night," he whispered.

"I can smell it," said Grace.

"What do you want for breakfast?"

"Make me some of your grandma's salmon mush."

Roman made the mush in the way he'd been taught to make it. Then he brought the mush, along with two slices of toast, a cup of coffee, and the morning newspaper, to Grace and watched her eat breakfast in bed.

▲

Up until her death, Grandmother Fury had been the very last Spokane Indian who knew how to make salmon mush in the way that Spokane Indians had been making salmon mush for the last hundred years or so. In terms of the entire tribal history, salmon mush was a recent addition to the traditional cuisine—just as human beings were among the most recent life-forms on the whole planet—but salmon mush was a singular and vitally important addition. After all, Grandmother Fury's own grandmother had served salmon mush to Chief Joseph just a few days before he led the Nez Perce on their heroic and ultimately failed thousand-mile flight from the Ninth Cavalry. Though he was captured and sent to the prison of some other tribe's reservation, Joseph praised the salmon mush he'd eaten and often hinted that the strange combination of fish, oats, and milk was the primary reason why he'd nearly led his people into the wild freedom of Canada.

Nine decades later, on the Spokane Indian Reservation, Grandmother Fury said a prayer for Joseph and stirred a few more slices of smoked salmon into the pot of oats boiling on her woodstove. At that point, many cooks would have poured in the milk and brought it all back to the boil. But Grandmother Fury was cousin to salmon and knew their secrets. She poured the ice-cold milk over the boiling salmon and oats just a few seconds before serving. In that collision between heat and cold, between mammal and fish, between liquid and solid, there was so much magic that Grandmother Fury trembled as she set a bowl in front of her grandson and watched him eat.

"It's good," said Roman. He was eighteen years old and lovely in his grandmother's eyes.

"*But you haven't even tasted it,*" she said, in Spokane, the tribal language.

"Don't have to," said Roman in English. "I believe in your mush more than I believe in God."

"*You liar*," she said in Spokane and laughed.

"Yes," he said in English. "But it's a good lie."

Grandmother and grandson sat in the small kitchen of her home—their home!—and found no need to speak to each other. Because they were Indians, they gave each other room to think, to invent the next lie, joke, story, compliment, or insult. He ate; she watched.

That afternoon, Roman was going to take the Colonial Aptitude Test, his college boards, and hoped to score high enough to get into college, any college. He was the first member of his extended family who'd even wanted to pursue higher education. In fact, there were only a couple of dozen Spokane Indians who'd ever graduated from any four-year university and only a few more than that who'd bothered to attend even the smallest community college.

A few small colleges had offered full basketball scholarships to Roman, but he'd turned them down. He wanted to attend the best school possible, whether he played basketball for them or not.

"You know," Grandmother Fury said in rough English, in careful and clumsy syllables, after Roman had finished one bowl of mush and started in on another. "Those college tests, they're not for Indians."

Roman nodded his head. He knew the Colonial Aptitude Test was culturally biased, but he also knew the CAT was *supposed* to be culturally biased. The CAT was designed to exclude from college as many poor people as statistically possible. Despite the rumors of democracy and fairness, Roman knew, when it came to the CAT, that meritocracy was to college as fish was to bicycle. He knew the CAT was an act of war. As a result, Roman wasn't approaching the test with intellect and imagination. He was going to attack it with all of the hatred and anger in his heart.

"I'm afraid," he said.

"*Yes, I know,*" she said in Spokane.

"I don't want to be afraid."

"Yes, I know," she said in English.

With tears in his eyes and a salty taste at the back of his throat, Roman finished another bowl of salmon mush and asked for another.

"Yes," said his grandmother. She said, "Yes."

Three months later, Roman Gabriel Fury sat in the waiting room of the Colonial Aptitude Testing Service office in Spokane, Washington. He held two letters in his hands. One letter congratulated him on his exceptional CAT performance. The other letter requested his presence for a special meeting with the president of the Colonial Aptitude Testing Service.

Nervous and proud, Roman wondered if he was going to be given a special commendation, a reward for such a high score, unusually high for anybody, let alone an Indian boy who'd attended a reservation high school without chemistry, geometry, or foreign-language classes.

Sitting in the CAT office, in that small city named after his tribe, Roman wore his best suit, his only suit, a JCPenney special that his father had purchased for him four years earlier. Roman's father was a poor and generous man who had given his son many things over the years, mostly inexpensive trinkets whose only value was emotional, but the JCPenney suit was expensive, perhaps the most expensive gift that Roman had ever received, certainly more valuable than being named after a professional quarterback who had some Indian blood, or the rumor of Indian blood. Young Roman had often wished his father had given him the name of the other professional Indian quarterback, Sonny Six Killer, the one who had demonstrable Indian blood. Roman Gabriel Fury often wished that his name was Sonny Six Killer Fury. With a name like that, Roman knew that he could have become a warrior.

"Mr. Furry," said the CAT secretary, mispronouncing his name for the third time, adding an extra r that changed Roman from an angry Indian into a cute rodent. She sat behind a small desk. She'd worked for CAT for ten years. She'd never taken any of their tests.

Roman sat in silence. He hated wooden chairs.

"Mr. Furry," she said.

"I'm not a hamster," said Roman.

"Excuse me?"

"My name is not Furry. It's not Hairy or Hirsute either. My name is Fury, as in righteous anger."

"You don't have to be so impolite."

"You don't have to mispronounce my name."

"Well, Mr. Fury," she said, feeling somehow smaller in the presence of a boy who was twenty years younger. "You can go in now. Mr. Williams will see you."

"Assuming that he has eyes, I'm sure that's an anatomical possibility."

Roman stepped into another office and sat in another wooden chair across a large oak desk from Mr. Williams, a white man who studied, or pretended to study, the contents of a file folder.

"Hmmm," said Mr. Williams, as if the guttural were an important part of his vocabulary.

"Yes," said Roman, because he wanted to be the first one to use a word actually found in *Webster's Dictionary*, Ninth Edition.

"Well," said Mr. Williams. "Let me see here. It says here in your file that you're eighteen years old, a member of the Spokane Tribe of Indians, valedictorian of Wellpinit High School on said reservation, captain of the chess, math, history, and basketball teams, accepted on full academic scholarship to St. Jerome the Second University here in Spokane."

"Yes," said Roman, with the same inflection as before.

"That's quite the all-American résumé, Mr. Fury."

"No, I think it's more of an all–Native American résumé."

Mr. Williams smiled. His teeth, skin, and pinstriped suit were all the same shade of gray. Roman couldn't tell where the three-season wool ended and where the man began.

"Roman Gabriel Fury," said Williams. "Quite an interesting name."

"Normally, I'd say thank you, sir, but I don't think that was a sincere compliment, was it?"

"Just an observation, young Mr. Fury. I am very good with observation. In fact, at this very moment, I am observing the fact that your parents are absent. A very distressing observation, to be sure, considering our specific request that your mother and father attend this meeting with you."

"Sir, my parents are dead. If you'd read my file in its entirety, you might have observed that."

Mr. Williams's eyes flashed with anger, the first display of any color. He flipped through the file, searching for the two words that would confirm the truth: *deceased, deceased.*

At that moment, if Roman had closed his eyes, he could have seen the yellow headlights of the red truck that smashed head-on into his father's blue Chevy out on Reservation Road. He could have remembered that his father was buried in a brown suit. At that moment, if Roman had closed his eyes, he could have seen his mother's red blood coughed into the folds of a white handkerchief. Roman was three years old when his mother was buried in a purple dress. He barely remembered her.

"Yes," said Mr. Williams. "I see now. Your grandmother has been your guardian for the last three years. Why didn't she come?"

"She doesn't speak much English, sir."

"And yet, you speak English so well, speak it well enough to score in the ninety-ninth percentile in the verbal section of our little test.

Quite an amazing feat for someone from, well, let' s call it a modest background."

"I've never been accused of modesty."

"No, I would guess not," said Williams, setting the file down on his desk. He picked up a Mont Blanc pen as if it were a weapon.

"But I guess you've been called arrogant," added Williams. "And, perhaps, calculating?"

"Calculating enough for a ninety-nine on the math section of your little test," Roman said. He really hated wooden chairs.

'Yes, indeed," said Williams. "A nearly perfect score. In fact, the second-highest score ever for a Native American. Congratulations."

"Normally, I'd say thank you, sir, but I don't think that was a sincere compliment, was it?"

Mr. Williams leaned across his desk, straightened his back, placed his hands flat on either side of his desk, took a deep breath, exhaled, and made himself larger. He owned all ten volumes of Harris Brubaker's *How to Use Body Language to Destroy Your Enemies*.

"Son," said Williams, using what Brubaker considered to be the second-most effective diminutive. "We've been informed there were certain irregularities in your test-taking process."

"Could you be more specific, sir?"

"You were twenty minutes late for the test."

"Yes, I was."

"I also understand that your test-taking apparel was, to say the least, quite distracting."

Roman smiled. He'd worn his red, yellow, white, and blue grass-dance outfit while taking the test—highly unusual, to say the least—but he had used two standard number-two pencils, as specified in the rule book.

"There's nothing in the rule book about a dress code," said Roman.

"No, no, there's not. But I certainly would enjoy an explanation."

"My grandmother told me your little test was culturally biased," said Roman. "And that I might need a little extra power to do my best. I was going to bring my favorite drum group and let them sing a few honor songs, but I thought the non-Indians in the room might get a little, as you say, distracted."

"Power?" asked Williams, using Harris Brubaker's favorite word.

Roman stood and leaned across the desk. He'd read Brubaker's first volume, had found it derivative and ambiguous, and never bothered to read any of the others.

"Well, you see, sir," said Roman. "The thing is, I was exhausted from having to walk seventy-five miles to get from my reservation to Spokane for the test, because my grandmother and I are too poor to afford a dependable car."

"You hitchhiked?" asked Williams.

"Oh, no, hitchhiking would mean that I actually got a ride. But people don't pick up Indians much, you know?"

"Do you expect me to believe you walked seventy-five miles?"

"Well, that's the way it is," said Roman. "Anyway, I get to the city, but then I have to run thirty blocks to get to the private high school where they're giving the test, because I had enough money for lunch or a bus, but not both, and sometimes you have to make hard choices.

"And then, once I got to the private high school, I had to convince the security guard, who looked suspiciously like a member of the Seventh Cavalry, that I was there to take the test, and not to vandalize the place. And hey, thank God I wasn't wearing my grass-dance outfit yet because he might have shot me down on the spot.

"Anyway, once I got past him, I was, as you observed, twenty minutes late. So I ran into a bathroom, changed into my grass-dance outfit, then sat down with your little test, realizing belatedly that I was definitely the only Injun in the room, and aside from the black kid in the front row and the ambiguously ethnic chick in the back, the only so-called minority in the room, and that frightened me more than you will ever know.

"But I crack open the test anyway, and launch into some three-dimensional calculus problem, which is written in French translated from the Latin translated from the Phoenician or some other God-awful language that only white people seem to find relevant or useful, and I'm thinking, I am Crazy Horse, I am Geronimo, I am Sitting Bull, and I'm thinking the required number-two pencil is a bow and arrow, that every math question is Columbus, that every essay question is Custer, and I'm going to kill them dead.

"So, anyway, I'm sure I flunk the damn test, because I'm an Indian from the reservation, and I can't be that smart, right? I mean, I'm the first person in my family to ever graduate from high school, so who the hell do I think I am, trying to go to college, right? So, I take the test and I did kill it. I killed it, I killed it, I killed it.

"And now, you want to take it away from me, a poor, disadvantaged, orphan minority who only wants to go to the best college possible and receive an excellent Catholic, liberal arts education, improve his life, and provide for his elderly, diabetic grandmother who has heroically taken care of him in Third World conditions.

"And, now, after all that, you want to take my score away from me? You want to change the rules after I learned them and beat them? Is that what you really want to do?"

Mr. Williams smiled, but none of his teeth showed.

"I didn't think so," said Roman as he turned away from the desk. He stepped through one door, walked past a woman who'd decided to hate him, and then ran.

▲

As a high school senior, Grace Atwater had also been accepted into St. Jerome the Second University, not because of her grades, which were only average, but because she'd obtained those average grades at the Pierpoint School, one of the most exclusive private high schools in the country. Grace was the only Native American to ever attend Pierpoint, but she'd always known her Indian blood had nothing to do with her admittance. Her mother, Ge Kuo, the Chinese-American daughter of parents who'd never left China, had been the music teacher for twenty-three years. Still, to her credit, Grace had worked hard, fought her way past an undiagnosed case of dyslexia, and surprised everybody with a perfect score on the CAT—the highest score ever for a Native American. She'd also submitted a personal essay that had surprised the St. Jerome admissions board.

To Whom It May Concern, began Grace' s essay. *This is the invocation I want to hear if I am accepted into your wonderful institution:*

Ladies and Gentlemen, welcome to St. Jerome the Second University, or as we affectionately call it, Saint Junior.

You are a very special group of students. In fact, the very best this great country has to offer. This year's incoming freshman class has an average high school grade point average of 3.81.

You have an average CAT score of 1280. Among you are forty-two American Merit Scholars.

One hundred and ten of you were president of your senior class. Seventy-five of you were president of your student body.

One hundred and sixty-two of you won varsity letters in various athletic endeavors. Sixty-three of you have received full athletic scholarships and will compete for St. Junior's in basketball, soccer, volleyball, tennis, and track.

You have excelled. You have triumphed. You have worked hard and been rewarded for your exemplary efforts. You have been admitted to one of the finest institutions of higher education in the world. Please, give yourself a hand.

Good, good. Now I want you to hold out your right hand, palm up.

Now, I want you to think hard about all that you have accomplished so far in your young lives. I want you to think about all the trophies on your mantels and imagine you're holding them in your right hand. I want you to think about all the news clippings in your scrapbooks and imagine you're holding them in your right hand. I want you to think about all the letters on your jackets and imagine you're holding them in your right hand. I want you to think about all of your accolades and rewards and imagine you're holding them in your right hand. Can you see them? Can you imagine them? Can you feel them?

Good, good. Now, I want you to crush all of that in your fist. I want you to grind it into dust and throw all of it away.

Because none of it means anything now. Today is your new birthday. Your new beginning. And I am here to tell you that twenty-five percent of you will not make it through your freshman year. I am here to tell you that more than forty percent of you will not graduate from this university. I am here to tell you that all of you will engage in some form of illicit activity or another. In premarital sex, in drug and alcohol abuse, in academic dishonesty and plagiarism. And you will tell lies. To yourselves, to each other, to your professors, to your confessors, to me. Most of you will fall in love and all of you will not be loved enough. And through all the pain and loneliness, through all the late hours and early mornings, you will learn.

Yes, you will grow from the frightened and confused teenagers you are now into the slightly less frightened and slightly less confused adults you will become.

I am Father Arnold, President of St. Jerome the Second University. May God bless you in all of your various journeys.

Three weeks before Grace left for St. Jerome, her mother died of breast cancer. Grace had never known her father—he'd fallen off a building and was buried in the foundation of the Rockefeller National Bank Building. When she was sixteen, Grace had opened up a savings account there and, without fail, had deposited one hundred dollars a month.

After they'd graduated together from St. Junior, Grace and Roman were married in a quick Reno, Nevada, ceremony and then flew to Greenland where Roman played shooting guard for a horrible team called the Whales. They won two and lost thirty-five that first season, despite Roman's twenty points and ten assists a game. The next year, the Whales won their first five games before the entire league went bankrupt. Grace and Roman then moved on to twelve other countries and nineteen other basketball teams in ten years before she'd woken up one bright morning in a Hilton Hotel in Madrid, Spain, with the sure knowledge that she wanted to return to the United States.

"Roman, are you awake?"

"I think it's time for us to go home."

"Why?"

"Because you've done all you can do over here."

She'd supported him, emotionally and spiritually, had traveled with him to more places than she cared to remember. She'd eaten great food and had been food-poisoned six different times—she couldn't look at a mushroom without retching—and she was reasonably fluent in five different languages. How many Indians could say that? She'd watched every minute of every one of his games—only God knows how many—and had held him equally tight after good and bad performances.

She had never loved him because he was a basketball player. In fact, she'd loved him despite the fact that he was a basketball player. She'd always understood that his need to prove and test his mascu-

linity was some genetic throwback. Given the choice, he'd rather
have been a buffalo hunter and soldier killer than the point guard
for the Lakers, but there was no such choice, of course. He couldn't
be an indigenous warrior or a Los Angeles Laker. He was an Indian
man who'd invented a new tradition for himself, a manhood ceremony that had usually provided him with equal amounts of joy and
pain, but his ceremony had slowly and surely become archaic. Though
she'd never tell him such a thing, she'd suspected his ceremony might
have been archaic from the beginning. After all, the root word for
warrior was war, and he'd always been a peaceful and kind man, a
man who'd refused to join anybody's army, most especially if they
were fighting and killing for something he believed in.

"You have lost the moment you pick up a gun," he'd always said.
"When you resort to violence to prove a point, you've just experienced a profound failure of imagination."

Lying together in that Madrid Hilton Hotel, with its tiny European bathroom and scratchy sheets, she'd realized how much she loved
her idealistic and pompous husband.

"Let's go home," she'd said to him again.

"Why?" he'd asked.

"Because I want to," she'd said to him again as he stood naked from
the bed and walked across the thin carpet.

No habla Español. Indios de Norte Americanos.

All during that time, during his domestic and foreign basketball
career, she'd been writing stories, poems, essays, and the first few
chapters of various failed novels. She'd never told Roman about her
writing because she'd wanted to keep something for herself; she'd
wanted to enjoy a secret, perhaps sacred, endeavor, and writing
seemed to be her best vocation and avocation. Under various pseudonyms, she'd published work in dozens of the various university literary
journals back in the United States, though she'd never bothered to

read any of her writing after it had been published. She didn't even bother to keep originals, preferring to start all over with the first word of each new poem, story, or essay.

"Let's go home," she'd said to him as he stood at the window of the Madrid Hilton. He was naked and thin and would never be that lovely again.

"I'm afraid," he'd said.

"Of what?"

"I'm afraid I won't know how to do anything else."

There, in Spain, he'd stood naked in the window and wept.

No habla Español. Indios de Norte Americanos.

"What if basketball is all I will ever be good at?"

"Hey," she'd said. "You're not even that good a basketball player."

"Ouch," he'd said and laughed. They'd laughed together, though both of them had a secret. His: he'd hated her, ever so briefly, for telling the truth about his failed dreams. Hers: she'd hated herself, ever so briefly, for devoting her life to his dreams.

Both of them had locked their secrets in dark boxes, never to be opened, and caught the next plane back to the United States.

▲

On the Spokane Indian Reservation, on the morning of that first snow, Roman sat down to piss. He could hear the television playing in the living room. He could hear Michael Jordan's voice.

I'm back.

Sure, Roman could have stood and pissed. That would have been easier, more convenient. Just pull it out and blast away. But he wanted to be polite, even kind to Grace. That was exactly what was missing in most marriages: politeness, courtesy, good manners. He was the kind of man who wrote thank-you notes to his wife for the smallest favors.

After years of marriage, Roman had learned one basic truth: It was easy to make another person happy.

To make Grace happy, Roman sat down to piss, did the dishes at least three times a week, vacuumed every day, and occasionally threw a load of laundry into the washer, though he'd often forgotten to transfer the wet clothes into the dryer. No matter. Grace didn't sweat the small stuff, and with each passing day she loved him more and more.

I'm back.

After his sit-down piss, Roman stood and pulled up his underwear, climbed into a pair of sweatpants hanging from the shower rod, slipped his feet into Chuck Taylor basketball shoes, and stepped into the bedroom.

Grace pretended to be asleep in their big bed. She loved this game. Still holding the basketball, Roman laid down next to her and pressed his body against hers.

"There's a strange woman in my bed," said Roman.

"I know," said Grace, without opening her eyes.

"What should I do about her?"

"Let her sleep."

Roman touched the basketball to Grace's cheek. He wondered if she wanted to make love. She usually did, and had approached him as often as he'd approached her, but he'd always liked to delay, to think about her—the taste, smell, and sound of her—for hours, or even days, before he'd make a pass.

"Michael Jordan is coming back again," he said.

"You can't fool me," said Grace. "I heard it. That was just a replay."

"Yeah, but I wish he was coming back again. He should always come back."

"Don't let it give you any crazy ideas."

Roman pulled the basketball away and leaned even closer to Grace. He loved her, of course, but better than that, he *chose* her, day after day. Choice: that was the thing. Other people claimed that you can't choose who you love—it just happens!—but Grace and Roman knew that was a bunch of happy horseshit. Of course you chose who you loved. If you didn't choose, you ended up with what was left—the drunks and abusers, the debtors and vacuums, the ones who ate their food too fast or had never read a novel. Damn, marriage was hard work, was manual labor, and *unpaid* manual labor at that. Yet, year after year, Grace and Roman had pressed their shoulders against the stone and rolled it up the hill together.

In their marriage bed, Roman chose Grace once more and brushed his lips against her ear.

"It snowed last night," he whispered.

"I can smell it," said Grace, choosing him.

"What do you want for breakfast?"

"Make me some of your grandma's salmon mush."

Grandmother Fury had died of cancer the previous winter. On her deathbed, she'd pulled Roman close to her. She'd kissed him full on the lips and cried in his arms.

"*I don't want to go,*" she'd said in Spokane.

"I know," he'd said and felt the heat leave her body.

"*I'm cold.*"

"I love you."

"*Listen,*" she'd said. "*You better keep making that salmon mush. You're the only one now. You have to keep it alive.*"

"I'll teach Grace."

"*She's a good woman, that one, a good person. You better hang on to her. She could live without you easily, but you'd be lost without her.*"

"She loves you as much as I do."

"*I am happy to hear that. But listen, the important thing is the salmon mush. You have to remember one thing, the big secret.*"

"I know, I know, pour the milk in just before serving."

"No, no, that's the most obvious secret. You don't know the biggest secret. You don't know it. Let me tell you."

Roman had leaned close to her ear and heard that secret. He'd listened to his grandmother's last words and then she'd died.

▲

On his first day at St. Jerome the Second University, Roman walked alone into the freshman dormitory. Everybody else carried new luggage, stereos, bicycles, books, but Roman carried all of his possessions in a Hefty garbage bag slung over his shoulder. He found his room, walked inside, and met his roommate.

"Hey," said the kid with blue eyes and blond hair. "You must be my roomie. I'm Alex Weber."

"Roman."

"I thought you were Indian."

"I am Indian. Roman is my name."

"First or last?"

"The first name is Roman, the middle name is Gabriel, the last name is Fury."

"A spectacular moniker."

"Thank you."

"Is that your luggage?"

Roman tossed his Hefty bag onto his bed. He was ashamed of it, his poverty, but pretended to be proud.

"Yeah," said Roman. "I got ninety-nine of them back home. The whole matching set."

"Scholarship student, huh?"

"Yeah. Do you have a problem with that?"

"No, not at all. I'm a legacy."

"A what?"

"My great-grandfather went to school here, as did my grandfather, my father, and now, I'm here. As long as there's been a St. Junior, there's been a Weber."

"Family tradition."

"My family is all about tradition. So, where you from? What's your major?"

Before Roman could answer, Alex pulled out a silver flask of whiskey.

"You want a drink?" asked the legacy.

"I'm undeclared," said Roman.

"About the drink or your major?"

"I don't drink."

"More for me."

Roman looked at Alex's side of the room. All of the white boy's possessions still carried price tags.

"Well," said Alex. "Get your stuff unpacked, that shouldn't take too long, and let's head upstairs where the lovely young women make their abodes."

"I'm not much for parties," said Roman. "I think I'm just going to hang around the room."

"Suit yourself. But I've got to get a little tonight, you know what I mean?"

"I assume you're referring to sexual intercourse."

"You make it sound so romantic. Listen. My great-grandfather had sexual intercourse on his first night at St. Junior. As did my grandfather, my father, and now, me."

"You're a legacy."

"Exactly. See you later, Chief."

With a nod of his head and a click of his tongue, Alex left the room. A little stunned and bewildered by his roommate—how had the personal-tastes questionnaire put them together?—Roman sat down on his bed. Then he noticed a box sitting on the desk. It was a "WELCOME TO ST. JUNIOR" care package.

He opened the box and discovered its contents.

"Donuts," said Roman.

▲

Six months into their freshman year at St. Junior, Roman and Grace made love for the first time. Afterward, squeezed together in his narrow dorm room bed, they'd nervously tried to fill the silence.

"So," he'd asked. "You must be the only Indian in New York City, enit?"

"There are lots of Indians in New York City. Lots of Mohawks."

"Are you full-blood?"

"No, I'm Mohawk and Chinese."

"Chinese? You're kidding."

"What? You have something against Chinese?"

"No, no. I just never heard of no Chinese Indians. I mean, I know black Indians and white Indians and Mexican Indians and a whole bunch of Indian Indians, but you're the first Chinese Indian I've ever met. Was it some kind of Bering Strait land bridge thing?"

"No. My mom was Chinese. She was playing piano in this bar in Brooklyn. That's where my mom and dad met."

"Where are they now?"

"Gone, all gone."

Over the next four years of college, they'd slept together maybe twenty more times without formal attachment, and each of them had

run through quick romances with a few other people, and each had
also experienced the requisite homoerotic one-night stand—both
with Hawaiians, coincidentally—before he'd run up to her after his
last college game, still in uniform and drenched in sweat, and hugged
her close.

"You're the best Indian I'm ever going to find," he'd said.
"Marry me."

Not the most romantic proposal in the world, to be sure, but a true
and good moment, demographically speaking.

"Okay," she'd said.

▲

In bed, on the Spokane Indian Reservation, eighteen years after their
graduation from St. Jerome the Second, Grace ate her salmon mush,
drank her coffee, and read the newspaper aloud. Roman laid back on
his pillow and listened to her. This was one of their ceremonies: she'd
read aloud every word of the newspaper, even the want ads, and then
quiz him about the details.

"Hey," she said. "What's the phone number of the guy who is sell-
ing the Ping-Pong table that has only been used once?"

"Harry."

"Uh, good remembering. That earns you a kiss, with tongue."

"A hand job would be better."

"God, you're so charming."

She smacked him with a pillow. He kissed her cheek, then walked
from the bedroom into the kitchen. Still holding the basketball,
he opened the refrigerator, pulled out another big bottle of Diet
Pepsi, and swallowed deeply. He breathed the sweet fluid in, as
if it were oxygen. He set the Pepsi back on the shelf, among a

dozen other bottles, and then pulled out a donut. A maple bar. He sniffed at it, took a bite, spit it back out, and threw the donut back into the fridge.

Roman slammed the fridge shut and walked outside into the backyard. Two feet of the first snow had covered the basketball half-court. Roman looked at the snow, at the hoop and backboard rising ten feet above the snow.

Smiling, Roman gave a head fake, took a step left, and dribbled the basketball, expecting it to bounce back up into his hand.

When the ball didn't return to his hand, Roman stared down to see the orange Rawlings embedded in the white snow. The contrast was gorgeous, like the difference between Heaven and Hell.

He had always been a religious man, had participated in all of the specific Spokane Indian ceremonies, most involving salmon, and in many of the general American Indian ceremonies like powwows and basketball tournaments. He'd also spent time in all three of the Spokane Reservation's Christian churches, singing Assembly of God hymns, praying Presbyterian prayers, and eating Catholic Communion wafers. Roman had always known that God was elusive. All his life, Roman had been chasing God and had never once caught sight of him, or her.

▲

During her first night at St. Junior, Grace was standing in the middle of a room full of drunken white kids when Alex Weber, the drunkest white kid, stepped up to her.

"Hey, sweetheart," he slurred.

"Hey," she said, a little nauseated by the whiskey smell of his breath. She'd never even sipped a glass of wine at dinner.

"Okay," he said. "Tell me. Have you enjoyed your St. Junior experience so far?"

"Yeah, I guess."

He kissed her then, a wet kiss that was meant for her lips but landed on her chin. She pushed him away.

"Hey, listen," she said, strangely polite. "You're drunk, man, and you're making a big mistake. Why don't you just leave before you do something really stupid? How does that sound?"

She didn't understand why she was negotiating. He wiped his mouth with the back of his hand.

"Can I ask you a personal question?" he asked.

"Yeah, you ask one question. I answer once. Then you leave. Deal?"

"Did you get in here because of affirmative action?"

"What?"

"Really. I want to know, did you get in here on account of some quota or something? Because you're Indian, right, excuse me, I mean, Native American?"

"I belong here. Just as much as you or anybody else."

"No, no, no, I'm not questioning your intelligence. Believe me, I'm not. Honestly. I just want to know if you got admitted because of affirmative action."

"If I tell you, will you leave?"

"Yeah."

"No, man, I got perfect scores on my CAT."

"Really?"

"Truth."

"I got in because of affirmative action."

"What do you man? You? You're white."

"Well, not because of affirmative action, not exactly. I got in here because I'm a legacy. Do you know what that is?"

"Yes, I do."

"My father went here. My father, my grandfather, and my great-grandfather. I'm a legacy."

"So what?"

"So, they let me in because of my family's money. Not because I deserve to be here. I don't have the grades. My test scores were, like, lower than football players'."

"Those tests don't mean anything. They're culturally biased."

"But they're biased for white guys, for me. And I flunked. I don't deserve to be here, man. I cheated my way in. I cheated."

Then he cried. Huge, sobbing, drunken tears.

She touched his face and then left him alone there with the rest of his tribe.

▲

Outside his house on the Spokane Indian Reservation, Roman stared down at the orange leather ball embedded in the white snow. Then he stomped through the snow to his storage shed, and carried back a gallon of kerosene. He poured the kerosene onto the snow covering the basketball court.

After the can was empty, Roman took a step back, lit a match, and dropped it onto the kerosene-soaked snow. The fire flared up wonderfully and began to melt the snow down to the frozen ground.

Even as the snow was still burning, Roman was dribbling the ball around the court, throwing up lazy shots. He was not playing very hard, just enjoying the mechanics of the game, the physical meditation. He was out of shape and breathing hard, his breath making small clouds in the air. He was missing many more shots than he was making.

Some of the snow was still burning.

Then Grace Atwater stepped out of the house. She wore a huge red parka and big black boots. She walked onto the court, stepped around her husband, and stood directly beneath the basket. Roman stood at the free-throw line. He shot and missed. Grace rebounded the ball and threw it back to him.

"Nice shot," she said.

"I used to be good," said Roman. "Back when it meant something."

"You're still good. But I'm better."

In the pocket of her coat, she carried a letter from a small press in Brooklyn, New York, that had agreed to publish a book of her poems. The press had consolidated all of the poems published under her various pseudonyms and would present them for the first time as her own, as her work, as her singular achievement.

Roman shot again, missed again. Grace rebounded the ball and threw it back to her spouse.

"Michael Jordan," she said.

Roman smiled, threw up a wild hook shot that missed everything, the rim, the backboard, everything, and landed with a thud in the snow behind the court. In fact, the ball disappeared in the deep white.

Grace and Roman stared out into the snow where the ball had disappeared.

"Help," said Roman.

"What?" asked Grace.

"Help me."

"Always."

Grace trotted out into the deep snow and searched for the basketball. Roman watched her with eyes stung red by the cold air. She had never been a skinny woman, not once, and was growing larger every year. She was beautiful, her long black hair dirty and uncombed.

Roman patted his own prodigious belly and closed his eyes against the sudden tears welling there.

"Brilliant," he whispered to himself. His love for his wife hit him like a strong wind and forced him to take a step or two back.

Grace found the basketball and carried it back onto the court. Holding the ball with both hands, she stood beneath the basket while Roman was now standing at least twenty feet away from the rim. In his youth, he had been a hungry and angry player, an exceptionally good shooter, as dependable as gravity, but age and weight and happiness had left him with slow hands and slower feet.

"Hey," said Grace.

Roman opened his eyes.

"You know," she said, "I'm not wearing anything under this coat."

"I suspected."

She threw the ball back to Roman, who caught it neatly.

"He's beautiful," she said.

"Who?"

"Michael Jordan."

"Yes, he is," said Roman.

Grace then opened her coat to flash her nudity at Roman. Flesh and folds of flesh. Brown skin and seventeen moles. He had counted them once when they were younger, and he hoped there were still seventeen moles now. New moles made Roman nervous, especially since the reservation skies still glowed down near the uranium mine.

Grace spun in a slow circle. Roman was shocked and pleased. Brown skin sharply contrasted with white snow. She was fat and gorgeous.

Still holding her coat open, Grace took a step toward her husband.

"You make the next shot and you can have all of this," she said.

"What if I miss?" he asked.

She closed the coat tightly around her body.

"Then," she said, "you'll have to dream about me all day."

He had dreamed about her often, had dreamed of lovemaking in rivers, in movie theaters, in sale beds in department stores, in pow-wow tents, but had never actually had the courage to make real love to her anywhere but a few hundred beds and the backseats of twelve different cars.

"Hey," he said, his throat suddenly dry, his stomach suddenly nervous. "We've got to be to work in fifteen minutes."

"Hey," she said. "It's never taken you that long before. I figure we can do it twice and you'll still be early."

Grace and Roman smiled.

"This is a good life," she said.

He stared at her, at the basket, at the ball in his hands. Then he lifted the ball over his head, the leather softly brushing against his fingers, and pushed it toward the rim.

The ball floated through the air, then, magically, it caught fire. The ball burned as it floated through the air.

Roman and Grace watched it burn and were not surprised.

Then the burning ball hit the backboard, rolled around the rim, and fell through. Grace stepped toward her husband. Still burning, the ball rolled to a stop on the frozen ground. Roman stepped toward his wife.

Ceremony.

DEAR JOHN WAYNE

▲▲▲

T he following transcript is adapted from an interview that took place in the visitor's lounge at the St. Tekawitha Retirement Community in Spokane, Washington, on February 28, 2052:

Q: Hello, I'm going to record this, that is, if that's okay with you? Is that okay?

A: Yes.

Q: Good, good. So, would you, could we begin, could you please begin by stating your name, your birth date, your age, where you were born, and that's it.

A: You first.

Q: Excuse me?

A: You should tell me who you are first. That's the polite way.

Q: Oh, okay, I suppose you're correct. I'm Spencer Cox, born July 7, 2007, in Old Los Angeles. I'm forty-five years old. Okay? Is that okay?

A: Yes, that's good. It's nice to meet you.

Q: Yes, it's my pleasure.

(ten seconds of silence)

Q: And?

A: And?

Q: Would you like to introduce yourself?

A: Yes.

(fifteen seconds of silence)

Q: Well, possibly you could do it now? If you please?

A: My name is Etta Joseph. I was born in Wellpinit, Washington, on the Spokane Indian Reservation on Christmas Day, 1934. I am one hundred and eighteen years old and I am the Last of the Spokane Indians.

Q: Really? I had no idea you were the last.

A: Well, actually, I'm not. There are thousands of us. But it sounds more romantic, enit?

Q: Yes, very amusing. Irony, a hallmark of the contemporary indigenous American. Good, good. Yes. So, perhaps we could officially begin by . . .

A: Spencer, what exactly is it you do?

Q: I'm a cultural anthropologist. An anthropologist is . . .

A: I know what an anthropologist is.

Q: Yes, yes, of course you do. As I was saying, I am a cultural anthropologist and the Owens Lecturer in Applied Indigenous Studies at Harvard University. I'm also the author of seventeen books, texts, focusing on mid- to late-twentieth-century Native American culture, most specifically the Interior Salish tribes of Washington State.

(twenty seconds of silence)

Q: So, Miss Joseph, can I call you Etta?

A: No.

Q: Oh, I see, okay. Formality. Yes, quite another hallmark of the indigenous. Ceremony and all. I understand. I'm honored to be included. So, Miss Joseph, perhaps we could begin, I mean, could I ask an introductory question? Yes. Well, let's see, you have been a traditional powwow dancer for the last eighty years. In that time, how has the powwow changed? Of course, the contemporary powwow is not a sacred ceremony, not as we have come to understand it, but rather a series of pan-Indian ceremonies whose influences include many tribal cultures and popular American culture as well, but I was wondering how you . . .

A: Why are you really here?

Q: Well, I was trying to get into that. I wanted to talk about dance and the Indian . . .

A: You're here about John Wayne, enit?

Q: Excuse me?

A: You came here to talk about John Wayne.

Q: Well, no, but the John Wayne mythology certainly plays an important role in the shaping of twentieth-century American and Native American culture, but . . .

A: Have you ever seen a John Wayne movie?

Q: Yes, yes, I have. Most of them, in fact. I was quite the little cowboy when I was a child. Had two Red Ryder six-shooter pistols. They shot these little silver pellets. I recall that I killed a squirrel. I was quite shocked. I had no idea the pellets were dangerous, but I suppose that's beside the point. Now, back to dance . . .

A: I used to be an actress.

Q: Really? Well, let's see here, I don't recall reading about that in your file.

A: What are you doing?

Q: Well, I'm reading through the file, your profile here, the pre-interview, some excellent books regarding your tribe, and a few texts transcribed directly from the Spokane Tribe oral tradition, which I must say, are quite . . .

A: Just put those papers away. And those books. What is it with you white people and your books?

Q: I'm afraid I don't understand.

A: How come you love books so much?

Q: As my mother used to say, they're the keys to the locked doors of the house of wisdom.

A: Did your mother really say that?

Q: Well, no.

A: So, then, it's a lie? You just told me a lie?

Q: Yes, yes, I suppose I did.

A: It's a good lie. Charming even. Attributing one of your faintly amusing and fairly poetic lines to your own mother. You must love her quite a bit.

Q: Oh. Well, I don't know how to respond to that.

A: Are you a liar?

Q: What do you mean?

A: Do you tell lies?

Q: Everybody tells lies. I mean, occasionally.

A: That's not what I asked you.

Q: Yes, I tell lies. But I hardly think of myself as a liar.

(twenty-seven seconds of silence)

Q: Okay, so perhaps I am a liar, but not all the time.

(thirty-two seconds of silence)

Q: Why exactly are you calling me a liar?

A: I haven't called you anything.

Q: But you've accused me of lying.

A: No, I asked you if you were lying and you said yes. So I think that means you accused yourself of being a liar. Good observation, by the way.

Q: What's the point of all this?

A: I'm having fun with you.

Q: Well, if you're not going to take this seriously, I'm afraid I might have to move on. My time is valuable.

A: Having fun is very serious.

Q: I hardly think a few jokes are serious. I am currently working on a serious and profound study on the effect of classical European ballroom dancing on the indigenous powwow—a revolutionary text, by the way—so I don't have time for a lonely woman's jests and insults.

A: You have a lot to learn. You should listen more and talk less.

Q: Pardon me. I think I'll leave now.

A: I'm not lonely. Have a good day.

(ten seconds of silence)

Q: Okay, wait, I think I understand. We were participating in a tribal dialogue, weren't we? That sort of confrontational banter which solidifies familial and tribal ties, weren't we? Oh, how fascinating, and I failed to recognize it.

A: What are you talking about?

Q: Well, confrontational banter has always been a cultural mainstay of indigenous cultures. In its African form, it becomes the tribal rite they call "doing the dozens." You know, momma jokes? Like, your mother is so fat, when she broke her leg gravy poured out. It's all part of the oral tradition. And here I was being insulted by you, and I didn't recognize it as an integral and quite lovely component of the oral tradition. Of course you had to insult me. It's your tradition.

A: Oh, stop it, just stop it. Don't give me that oral tradition garbage. It's so primitive. It makes it sound like Indians sit around naked and grunt stories at each other. Those books about Indians, those texts you love so much, where do you think they come from?

Q: Well, certainly, all written language has its roots in the oral tradition, but I fail . . .

A: No, no, no, those books started with somebody's lie. Then some more lies were piled on top of that, until you had a whole book filled with lies, and then somebody slapped an Edward Curtis photograph on the cover, and called it good.

Q: These books of lies, as you call them, are the definitive texts on the Interior Salish.

A: No, there's nothing definitive about them. They're just your oral tradition. And they're filled with the same lies, exaggerations, mistakes, and ignorance as our oral traditions.

Q: Have you even read these books?

A: I've read all of your books. You show me a book written by a white man about Indians and I've read it. You show me almost any book, any of your so-called Great Books, and I've read them. Hemingway, Faulkner, Conrad. Read them. Austen, Kakfa, James, read them. Whitman, Dickinson, Donne. Read them. We head over to this university or that college, to your Harvard, and grab their list of required reads, and I've read them. Hundreds of your books, your white-man books, thousands of them. I've read them all.

Q: And what is your point in telling me this?

A: I know so much more about you than you will ever know about me.

Q: Miss Joseph, I am a leading authority, no, I am the, the, the leading authority in the field . . .

A: Mr. Cox, Spencer. For the last one hundred and eighteen years, I have lived in your world, your white world. In order to survive, to thrive, I have to be white for fifty-seven minutes of every hour.

Q: How about the other three minutes?

A: That, sir, is when I get to be Indian, and you have no idea, no concept, no possible way of knowing what happens in those three minutes.

Q: Then tell me. That's what I'm here for.

A: Oh, no, no, no. Those three minutes belong to us. They are very secret. You've colonized Indian land but I am not about to let you colonize my heart and mind.

Q: Tell me then. Why are you here? Why did you consent to this interview? What do you have to tell me that could possibly help me with my work? You, you are speaking political nonsense. Colonialism. That's the tired mantra of liberals who've run out of intellectual imagination. I am here to engage in a free exchange of ideas, and you're here, you want to inject politics into this. I will have no part of it.

A: I lost my virginity to John Wayne.

(forty-nine seconds of silence)

Q: You're speaking metaphorically, of course.

A: Spencer, I am speaking of the vagina and the penis.

Q: As metaphors?

A: Do you know the movie *The Searchers*?

Q: The western? Directed by John Ford? Yes, yes, quite well, actually. Released in 1956, I believe.

A: 1952.

Q: No, no, I'm quite sure it was 1956.

A: You're quite sure of a lot of things and you're quite wrong about a lot of them, too.

(five seconds of silence)

Q: Well, I do know *The Searchers*. Wayne plays Ethan Edwards, the ex-Confederate soldier who sets out to find his niece, played by Natalie Wood. She's been captured by the Comanches who massacred Ethan's family. Along with Jeffrey Hunter, who plays a half-breed Cherokee, of all things! Wayne will not surrender to hunger, thirst, snow, heat, or loneliness in his quest, his search. A quite brilliant film.

A: Enough with that academic crap. Listen to me. Listen carefully. In 1952, in Kayenta, Arizona, while John Wayne was playing Ethan Edwards, and I was playing a Navajo extra, we fell in love. Him, for the first and only time with an Indian. Me, for the first time with anybody.

▲

"My real name is Marion," said John Wayne as he slid the condom over his erect penis. His hands were shaking, making it nearly impossible for him to properly fit the condom, so Etta Joseph reached down, smoothed the rubber with the palm of her left hand—she was touching John Wayne—and then guided him inside of her. He made love carefully, with an unintentional tantric rhythm: three shallow thrusts followed by one deep thrust, repeat as necessary.

"Does it hurt?" asked John Wayne, with genuine concern, and not because he was arrogant about being her first lover.

"It's okay," said Etta, but it did hurt. It hurt a lot. She wondered why people were so crazy about this act. But still, she was making love to John Wayne.

"Oh, oh, John Wayne," she moaned. She felt uncomfortable, silly, like a bad actress in a bad love scene.

"Call me Marion," he said between thrusts. "My real name is Marion. Call me Marion."

"Marion, Marion, Marion," she whispered.

They laid together on a Pendleton blanket on the red sand of Navajo Monument Valley. All around them, the impossible mesas. Above them, the most stars either of them had ever seen.

"I love you, I love you," he said as he kissed her face, neck, breasts. His lips were thin, his face rough with three days of beard.

"Oh," she said, surprised by his words, even frightened. How could he be in love with her? He didn't even know her. She was just an eighteen-year-old Spokane Indian woman—a girl—a thousand miles away from home, from her reservation. She was not in Navajo land by accident—she was an actress, after all—but she hadn't planned on lying beneath John Wayne—Marion!—as he confessed his love, his impossible love for her.

Three days earlier, she'd been an extra in the Navajo camp when John Wayne and Jeffrey Hunter traded blankets, hats, and secrets with the Navajo chief. Etta hadn't had any lines. She'd only been set dressing, a pretty girl in a purple dress. But she'd been proud and she was sure to be on camera because John Ford told her so.

"Girl," Ford had said. "You are as pretty as the mesa."

For just a moment, Etta had wondered if Ford might cast her then and there for a speaking role, perhaps even give her the role of Look, the chubby daughter of the Navajo chief, and send that other Indian woman packing. Of course not! But Etta had wished for it, however briefly, and had chided herself for her ambition. She'd wished ill will on another Indian woman just because a white man had called her pretty. Desperate and shallow, of course, but Etta had not been able to help herself.

This was John Ford! He was not handsome, no, but he was a Hollywood director. He made dreams come true. He was the one who filled the movie screens with the movies! He was a magician! He was a feature-film director and she knew they were the kindest and most decent men in the world.

"Stand here," Ford had directed Etta. "Right here, so the audience can see your lovely face in the background here. Right between Jeffrey and the Duke." She had not been able to contain her excitement. Five feet away, John Wayne was smoking a cigarette. John Wayne! But more than that, it had been Jeffrey Hunter who'd captured her imagination. He was a beautiful boy, with dark hair, brown skin, and those blue, blue eyes. John Wayne might have been a movie star—and a relatively homely one at that—but Jeffrey Hunter was simply the most gorgeous white man on the planet. But here he was playing an Indian, a half-breed Cherokee, so perhaps Jeffrey himself was part Indian. After all, Etta had thought, why would they cast a white man as an Indian if he didn't have some Indian blood himself? Otherwise, the movie would have been a lie, and John Wayne didn't lie. And judging by the kindness in his eyes, by the graceful turn of his spine, by the way he waved his sensuous hands when he talked, Jeffrey Hunter was no liar either.

Anyway, they'd filmed the scene, a funny one where Jeffrey Hunter had inadvertently traded a hat for a Navajo wife, for Look—how positively amusing!—and all the while, Etta had looked on and wished that Jeffrey Hunter had traded for her. Not Jeffrey Hunter the actor in the scene, but Jeffrey Hunter the blue-eyed man.

"Mr. Hunter, you were wonderful," she'd said when she'd approached him after the scene.

Without a word to her, he'd turned and walked away. She'd admired his silence, his commitment to his craft. He hadn't wanted to be distracted by the shallow attentions of some Indian girl other than Look. Still. Her feelings had been hurt and there might have been a tear in her eye when John Wayne sidled up close to her—yes, sidled—and shook his head.

"I don't understand actors," the Duke had said. "It's the audience that matters, and yet, so often, we shun them."

"What does shun mean?" she asked.

"Exactly. I mean, how can we, as actors, get close to the soul, to our hearts, if we don't look deeply into the souls and hearts of others? In the end, how can we fragile human beings possibly be sympathetic actors if we don't refuse to show sympathy for other people's emotions? How can we realistically project love, hope, and faith if we are not loving, hopeful, and faithful ourselves?"

"That's beautiful."

"Yes, yes. If we don't feel it in here, in our chest, then the audience will never feel it in their hearts."

"That's why I act," she said.

"Hello, my name is John Wayne."

"I'm Etta Joseph."

Now, three days after Jeffrey Hunter had walked away from her, Etta was naked with John Wayne.

"I love you, I love you," he whispered to her. He was gentle with her, of course, but he was strong as well. He rolled onto his back and lifted her, then lowered her down onto him. His penis was huge! It was a movie star's penis, for sure. Etta had never really thought about John Wayne's penis before. She'd never really thought about any man's or actor's penis before. Sure, she'd felt strong desires for men, sexual desires, but they'd always taken the form of vague shapes and sizes inside of her body. She'd never imagined what John Wayne would look like naked, but there he was! Strong arms, long legs, a pot belly. As he lay beneath her, as he closed his eyes, Etta wondered what she should do with her hands. Nobody had ever taught her how to do this, how to make love to a man. And it was John Wayne, so he must have made love to a thousand different women in his life. Other movie stars! He must have made love to Bette Davis, Vivien Leigh, Greta Garbo, Grace Kelly, maybe even Judy Garland. All those perfect women. Etta felt small and terrified in the presence of John Wayne.

"What's wrong?" he asked.

"I'm afraid."

"If you get pregnant, I'll take care of it."

In the rush, she'd never even thought about pregnancy. How stupid! She was only eighteen years old, unmarried, a thousand miles away from home. What would she do with a baby? And what did he mean by taking care of it? Did he want to marry her, be the husband of an Indian woman and the father of an Indian child, or did he want her to have an abortion? God, she'd heard about abortions, how they reached inside of you with a metal hook and scraped out all of your woman parts. In terror, she rolled away from John Wayne and ran naked through the desert, toward the lights of the distant set, where

John Ford and Jeffrey Hunter were sure to have the answers to all of
her questions.

"Wait, wait, wait," cried John Wayne as he chased after her. He
was not a young man. He wondered if he could possibly catch her.
But she was a child of the river and pine tree, of wild grass and mountain. She understood gravity in a different way and, therefore, tripped
in the rough sands of the desert. She fell face first into the red dirt
and waited for John Wayne to catch and hurt her. Isn't that what he
had always done? Wasn't he the man who killed Indians?

"Etta, Etta." He kneeled beside her. He stroked her long black hair.
She flinched and pushed him away.

"Go away, go away, John Wayne," she cried out.

"Oh, Etta, I'm not going to hurt you," he said. "I couldn't hurt you.
I love you."

"But you can't love me. You don't even know me."

John Wayne wept.

There, in Navajo Monument Valley, John Wayne wept. His tears
fell to the sand and flooded the desert.

"Nobody knows me," he cried. "Nobody knows me."

He was so afraid! Etta was shocked into silence. This was the great
John Wayne and he was afraid.

"But, but, but," Etta stammered. "But you're a star."

"John Wayne is the star. I'm Marion, I'm just Marion Morrison."
She held him for a good long time.

▲

Q: I can't believe this. Are you telling me the truth?

A: Yes, as far as I can remember it.

Q: This is not a lie, one of those good lies you were talking about?

A: Spencer, I was fooling you. There's no such thing as a good lie.

Q: Bad lies, good lies, whatever. Just tell me the truth. Did you really lose your virginity to John Wayne?

(seven seconds of silence)

A: He was afraid of horses, did you know that?

Q: John Wayne was afraid of horses? That's completely implausible. I mean, I'd sooner believe that you slept with him. We're talking about John Wayne here.

A: When he was seven years old, a horse kicked him in the head. He was in a coma for nearly three months. Everybody thought he was going to die. In the hospital, his mother brought in a Catholic priest to baptize him. His father brought in a Presbyterian priest for last rites. They thought he was going to die. They were sure he was going to die.

Q: I don't recall reading any of this about John Wayne. Kicked in the head by a horse? That must be urban legend.

A: He showed me the scar. Just behind his right ear. About five inches long. They hid it with makeup. The horse's name was Rooster. He liked me to kiss it whenever we made love.

Q: Wait, wait, wait, he liked you to kiss the horse?

A: Oh, no, no, no, silly. He liked me to kiss his scar. He said it was really sensitive, still, after all those years. He was really a sensitive man, you know? He knew how to cry. He cried every time we made love. Well, this is really embarrassing, but he cried every time he had, every time, he, well, you know, had an orgasm.

Q: Wait, wait, wait, what are you telling me? How many times did you make love?

A: Most every night during the filming of the movie. Except for those nights when his wife and kids came to visit.

Q: So, hold on here, let me get my head around this. Not only were you having sex with John Wayne, you were also having an affair with him?

A: I'm not proud of that particular nature of our relationship, but yes, John Wayne was a married man.

▲

In Navajo Monument Valley, during a long day of filming, John Wayne stepped into the makeup trailer for a touch-up and discovered his sons happily covering their faces with lipstick and mascara.

"Well, hello there," John Wayne said to his sons.

They were petrified, afraid of this large man, this male.

"Are you having fun?" the Duke asked his sons.

They didn't know how to answer. If they said no, they'd be lying, and their father always knew when they were lying. If they said yes, well, then, that could mean all sorts of things, and all of them were bad.

"Are you having fun?" he asked again. His face revealed nothing, his thin mouth was closed tight, his teeth were hidden behind that weathered face.

The eldest son cried, so the youngest son decided to join him.

"Wait, wait, wait," said John Wayne. "What's with all of the tears?"

"You hate us," cried the oldest boy.

"Don't hate me, don't hate me," cried the youngest boy.

John Wayne scooped up his boys. He set his big cowboy hat on the youngest boy's head.

"I don't hate you, I could never hate you," said John Wayne. "What makes you think I hate you?"

"Because we're girls," wailed the boys.

John Wayne held his sons and stroked their hair.

"Oh, there, there, you're not girls, you're not girls," said the father. "What makes you think you're girls?"

"Because we're putting on lipstick," said the youngest.

John Wayne laughed.

"Oh, sons, you're just engaging in some harmless gender play. Some sexual experimentation. Every boy does this kind of thing. Every man likes to pretend he's a woman now and again. It's very healthy."

"Daddy," said the oldest. "Do you dress up like a woman?"

"Well, I don't put on a dress or anything. But I often close my eyes and try to put myself into a woman's shoes. I try to think like a woman. I try to embrace the feminine in myself. Do you know what I mean?"

"No," said the boys.

"Well, sons, let me tell you the honest truth. There's really not that much difference between men and women. In all things, intelligence, passion, hope, dreams, strength, men and women are pretty much equals. I mean, gender is mostly a social construction. After all, males and females share about ninety-nine percent of the same genetic material. So, given that, how could we really be that much different? In fact, we're all so much alike that every woman must have some masculine inside of her and every man must have feminine inside of him. You just ain't a whole person otherwise."

"Daddy!" shouted the boys. They were shocked. "That's not what you said before when you were on the radio and television."

"Boys, I know. I know. I have a public image to maintain. But that's not who I really am. I may act like a cowboy, I might pretend to be a cowboy, but I am not a cowboy in real life, do you understand?"

"I think so," said the oldest son. "Is it like in school, when you're supposed to be listening to the teacher, but you're only pretending to listen so you don't get in trouble?"

John Wayne smiled.

"Yes, yes, it's something like that," he said to his sons. "Now, let me teach you a little something about the birds and bees. If you want to make a woman happy, really happy, there's only one thing you got to do."

"What, Daddy, what?"

"Listen to her stories."

▲

Q: So, what happened, I mean, what did you do when his wife and sons came to visit?

A: I felt bad, bad, bad. That John Wayne, he was a good father and a good husband, too. I mean, he was cheating on them, that's for sure, but he wasn't going to leave them. No way. All the time he and I were together, he just kept telling me the same thing. "I ain't leaving them," he'd say. "I ain't leaving them. I am a good man, and a good man ain't a good man without a good family."

Q: But how do you reconcile that? How did he reconcile that? How can a man claim to love his wife and children if he's sleeping, if he's in love with another woman?

A: Are you married, Spencer?

Q: No.

A: Kids?

Q: No.

A: Then you don't really understand why John Wayne fell in love with me or why he left me, do you?

▲

"We can't do this anymore," John Wayne said to Etta Joseph.

It was the last day of shooting. Natalie Wood had already gone home; John Wayne had already saved her from the Indians.

"I'm going back to Hollywood," he said.

Etta wept.

"I knew this day would come," she said. "And I understand. You're a family man."

"Yes, my family needs me," he said. "But more than that, my country needs me. They need me to be John Wayne."

He kissed her then, one last kiss, and gave her his cowboy hat. She never wore it, not once, and gave it to her next lover, a rodeo Indian who lost it somewhere at a powwow in Arlee, Montana.

▲

Q: I don't want to insult an elder. I know, within the indigenous cultures, that we're supposed to respect our elders . . .

A: Oh, no, no, you've got that all wrong. You're not required to respect elders. After all, most people are idiots, regardless of age. In tribal cultures, we just make sure that elders remain an active part of the culture, even if they're idiots. Especially if they're idiots. You can't just abandon your old people, even if they have nothing intelligent to say. Even if they're crazy.

Q: Are you crazy?

▲

On his deathbed in a Santa Monica hospital, over twenty years after he'd played Ethan Edwards in *The Searchers*, John Wayne picked up the telephone and dialed a number that had not changed since 1952.

"Hello," said Etta when she answered. "Hello, hello, hello."

John Wayne listened to her voice. He didn't know what to say. He hadn't talked to her since that last night in Monument Valley, when he'd climbed into the bed of a traveling pickup, and stood tall and proud—with the sun rising, of all things—and watched Etta get smaller and smaller on the horizon.

What was the last thing he'd said to her before he left her forever? He couldn't remember now—the painkiller, chemotherapy, and

exhaustion all played tricks with his memory—but he knew it was
something he should not have said. And what was he supposed to
say to her now, all these years later, as he lay dying? Should he apolo-
gize, confess, repent? He had lived a large and brilliant life with his
wife and sons—he'd loved them and been loved with tenderness—
but he had often thought of that tiny and lovely Spokane Indian
woman who was all alone and lost in the Navajo desert. He knew he
was going to die soon—and would, in fact, die later that night with
his wife and sons at his bedside—but he wanted to leave the world
without his earthly doubts and fears. But how could he tell Etta that?
How could he tell her the story of his last twenty years, how could
he listen to her story of the last twenty years, and how could either
of them find enough time and forgiveness for each other?

John Wayne held the telephone close to his mouth and eyes and
wept his way across all of the miles and years.

"Marion?" asked Etta. "Marion, is that you?"

▲

Q: Is that everything?

A: It's all I can remember. Quite an example of the oral tradition,
enit?

Q: Lovely. But I wonder, how much of it is true and how much of
it is lies?

A: Well, now, an Indian has to keep her secrets, or she's just not
Indian. But an Indian a lot smarter than me once said this: If it's fic-
tion, then it better be true.

Q: How oxymoronic.

A: Yeah, kind of like saying Native American. There's an oxy-
moron for you.

Q: Well, I better get going. I got to find a flight to California.

A: Good for you. But don't you want to talk about powwow dancing?

Q: Well, sure, what would you like to say?

A: I was the worst powwow dancer in the world. I'd start dancing at some powwow, and the Master of Ceremonies would shout out, "Hey, stop the powwow, stop the powwow, Etta is dancing, she's ruining ten thousand years of tribal traditions. If we don't stop the powwow now, she might start singing, and then we're really going to be in trouble."

Q: Well, I suppose that's not going to help my thesis.

A: No, I suppose not. But my sons were really good powwow dancers. They still like to dance now and again.

Q: Your sons? My God, how old are they?

A: One hundred years old today. They're twins. I have nine children, thirty-two grandchildren, sixty-seven great-grandchildren, one hundred and three great-great-grandchildren, and one great-great-great-grandchild. I've made my own damn tribe.

Q: I'd love to talk to your sons. Where are they, on the reservation?

A: Oh, no, they live up on the men's floor here. I baked them a cake. My whole family is coming.

Q: Your sons, what are their names?

A: Oh, look, here they come now. They're early. Boys, I'd like you to meet Dr. Spencer Cox, he's a good friend of the Indians. Dr. Cox, I'd like you to meet my sons, Marion and John.

▲

Sitting alone in his car outside of the retirement home, Spencer ejected the cassette tape from his recorder. He could destroy the tape or keep it; he could erase Etta's voice or transcribe it. It didn't matter what he chose to do with her story because the story would continue to exist with or without him. Was the story true or false? Was that the question Spencer needed to ask?

Inside, an old woman kneeled in a circle with her loved ones and led them in prayer.

Outside, a white man closed his eyes and prayed to the ghosts of John Wayne, Ethan Edwards, and Marion Morrison, that Holy Trinity.

Somebody said nothing and somebody said amen, amen, amen.

ONE GOOD MAN

▲▲▲▲▲▲▲▲▲▲▲▲▲▲▲▲▲▲▲▲▲▲▲▲▲▲▲▲▲▲▲▲▲▲▲▲▲▲

O utside the house, Sweetwater and Wonder Horse were building a wheelchair ramp for my father. They didn't need a blueprint, having built twenty-seven ramps on the Spokane Indian Reservation over the years, including five ramps that summer alone. They knew how to fix such things, and they knew how to work quietly, without needless conversation or interaction with their employers. Sweetwater was known to go whole weeks without uttering a single word, opting instead to communicate through monosyllabic grunts and hand gestures, as if he were a very bright infant. Consequently, on that day when my father's wheelchair ramp needed only a few more nails, a coat of paint, and a closing prayer, Wonder Horse was deeply surprised when Sweetwater broke his unofficial vow of silence.

"Jesus was a carpenter," said Sweetwater, trying to make it sound casual, as if he'd merely commented on the weather or the game (What game? Any game!) and then he said it again: "Jesus was a carpenter."

Wonder Horse heard it both times, looked up from his nail and hammer, and stared into Sweetwater's eyes. Though the two men had worked together for thirty years, building three or four generations of outhouses, picnic tables, and front and back porches, they'd never been much for looking at each other, for seeing. God forbid one of them ever turned up missing and the other became the only person who could provide a proper description to the authorities.

"*Jesus was a carpenter*," said Sweetwater, this time in the Spokane language, to make sure that Wonder Horse understood all the inflections and nuances (the aboriginal poetry) of such a bold statement.

"What?" asked Wonder Horse, as simple a question as could possibly be tendered, though he made it sound as if he'd asked *Where's the tumor?*

"Jesus was a carpenter," said Sweetwater. He would have said it in Spanish, Russian, and German if he could have.

Wonder Horse could think of no logical reply (in any language) to such a complicated statement, especially coming from a simple man like Sweetwater. The whole conversation reeked of theology, and Wonder Horse wanted no part of that. Confused, maybe even a little frightened, he turned back to his work and pounded a nail into the wood, then another, a third, a fourth. He was a middle-aged man made older by too much exposure to direct sunlight and one-and-a-half bad marriages. He knew the cost of wood (six bucks for one standard two-by-four, by God!). With dark hair, eyes, and skin, he was fifty or eighty, take your pick. A small man with large hands, he had to resist the daily urge to get in his pickup and drive away from the reservation, never to return. Sure, the people, the residents of the reservation, be they Indian or white or whatever, certainly needed him to build *things*, but he also believed the whole of the reservation—the streams, rivers, pine trees, topsoil, and stalks of wild wheat—needed him, even loved him. And so he remained because he was loyal and vain.

"What did you say?" Wonder Horse asked again, hoping that Sweetwater would change the subject, take back the complicated thing he had said, and make their lives simple again.

They were building a wheelchair ramp for my father, who was coming home from the hospital without his diabetic, gangrenous feet.

"Jesus was a carpenter," said Sweetwater for the fifth time. Surely, it had become a kind of spell, possibly a curse.

"I don't care," said Wonder Horse, though he cared very much about carpenters and carpentry, about those artists whose medium was wood, and about the art of woodworking itself. Wonder Horse respected wood. He touched it like good lovers touched the skin of their loved ones. He was a Casanova with the hammer, wrench, screwdriver, and circular saw. But now, he felt clumsy and desperate.

"Harrison Ford was a carpenter, too," said Wonder Horse. It was all that he could think to say.

"Who?" asked Sweetwater.

"Harrison Ford, the guy who played Han Solo, you know? In *Star Wars*, the movie?"

"Oh," said Sweetwater. "But Jesus was, you know, a *real* carpenter."

Wonder Horse stared into Sweetwater's eyes (Blue eyes! A halfbreed who had never considered himself white, or been considered white by other Spokanes!) and wondered why his best friend had decided to become a casual enemy. Wonder Horse hoped it was an impulsive and individual act and not part of a larger conspiracy.

"So, what are you saying?" asked Wonder Horse. "Are you telling me that Jesus was a good carpenter?"

"You'd think so," said Sweetwater. "Yeah, I bet he was."

"But does it say that, anywhere in the Bible, in those exact words, does it say Jesus was a good carpenter?"

"I don't know. I mean, maybe, yeah, of course. He had to be."

"Have you ever read the Bible?"

"No, not really, but I know all about it."

"Now you sound like a Christian."

"Hey, that's dirty."

"Yeah, you're right, I'm sorry," said Wonder Horse. He wanted to get back to work. He wanted to jump in his pickup and drive away. He swung his hammer again and again, missed the head of the nail once, twice, three times, and drove it sideways into the plywood floor, splitting the two-by-four that lay beneath.

"Damn," said Wonder Horse and punched the wood. He studied his bloody knuckles.

"Are you okay?" asked Sweetwater.

"Always," said Wonder Horse as he tugged at the wayward nail.

They were building a wheelchair ramp for my father, who was coming home from the hospital with no more than six months to live, according to most of his doctors, and as little as two weeks left, according to the others.

"I mean," said Wonder Horse. "What's with all this Bible talk?"

"Ain't Bible talk," said Sweetwater. "It's just something I learned. Jesus was a carpenter."

"Well, hell, anybody can call themselves a carpenter," said Wonder Horse. "I mean, those Tulee boys built themselves a tree house over yonder. I guess that makes them carpenters, but it sure don't make them good carpenters. That thing is going to roll out of that tree like a bowling ball."

"I suppose, but the thing is, Jesus was Jesus, enit? I mean, Jesus must have been a good carpenter. I mean, he was Jesus, enit? That's pretty powerful right there."

"You know," said Wonder Horse. "I have no idea what you're talking about. Why is that?"

"Come on," said Sweetwater, his voice cracking with one emotion or another. "He was Jesus. He could walk on water and, like, conjure up fish and bread and stuff."

"Is that it? Stuff? Stuff? Is that your whole proof on this thing? All that proves is that Jesus might have been a good magician. He might have been a good fisherman. He might have been a good baker. But it absolutely does not prove that he was a good carpenter. I mean, there Jesus was, running all over the place, trying to save the world. Do you really think he had time to study carpentry? Do you really think he had the time to study his tools, to memorize them, to understand them? Do you really think he had the time to devote himself to wood?"

"He was the Son of God. I think he could multitask."

"Multitask!" shouted Wonder Horse. "Multitask! Where do you learn that shit?"

"Television."

"Television? Television? Is that all you have to say to me?"

"I guess," said Sweetwater.

They were building a wheelchair ramp for my father, who was coming home because he didn't want to die in the hospital.

▲

Inside the house, I was looking for those things that could kill my father, for those things that had already killed him, or rather had already assigned to him an appointment with death, an appointment he would not and could not miss. Among the most dangerous or near-dangerous: two boxes of donuts buried beneath Pendleton blankets on the top shelf of his closet; a quart of chocolate milk lying flat in the refrigerator's vegetable drawer; a six-pack of soda pop submerged in the lukewarm water of the toilet tank; hard candy stuffed deeply into the pockets of every coat he owned; and then more hard candy stuffed into the pockets of my late mother's coats, my siblings' long-abandoned coats, and the coats I wore when I was a child, still hanging in the closet in the bedroom where I had not slept in ten years. Together, these items represented my father's first line of defense. He knew they would be found easily. He intended them to be found easily. Decoys. Camouflage. My father was smart. He'd sacrifice a few treasures in order to distract me from the large caches. In the garage, I poured out ten pounds of Hershey's chocolate kisses one by one from an aluminum gas can. In the attic, I wore gloves and long sleeves when I pulled seven Payday peanut bars from between layers of fiberglass insulation. I flipped through fifty-two westerns, twelve mysteries, and nine true-crime books, and discovered one hundred and twelve fruit wraps pressed tightly between the pages. Inside the doghouse, a Tupperware container filled with Oreo cookies was duct-taped to the ceiling. I gathered all of it, all of those things that my father stupidly loved, and filled seven shopping bags. Most people would have quit searching then, assured they'd emptied the house of its dangers, but I knew my father. I could see him. I could read his mind. I found three pounds of loose sugar waiting beneath three inches of flour in the flour sack. Carefully hidden beneath a layer of frost, popsicles were frozen to the freezer walls. How could my father accomplish such a thing? What were the mechanics? I had no idea, but I found my father's sweet treasures, proving once again that the result is more important than the process. In his bedroom, I lifted the northwest corner of the carpet and found more candy bars, moldy, apparently forgotten. But then, remembering my father's clever mind, I pulled the carpet back a few more inches, and discovered new chocolate bars carefully wrapped in aluminum foil. I filled more shopping bags (two, nine, thirteen bags) and carried them outside, past Wonder Horse and Sweetwater pounding the last few nails into place, and tossed the bags in a pile on the road. There, with the sky clear and blue, I doused those bags with kerosene and dropped a burning match on the pile.

▲

Later that day, I lifted my father from the passenger seat of my van, a Ford with more than two hundred thousand miles on the odometer. My father carried sixty-five years on his odometer and had lost forty pounds in the last few months. I carried him easily over to his electric wheelchair (purchased for five hundred dollars from a white woman whose paraplegic husband had died) and set him in the worn leather seat. He looked so frail that I wondered if he had the strength to move the joystick that powered the chair.

"Can you make it?" I asked.

Of course he could. He was a man who used to teach ballroom dancing, back when he was young and strong and financing his communications education at the University of Washington (he'd always meant to start his own radio station on the reservation). He was the man who had taught me how to waltz about fifteen minutes before I'd left to pick up my date for the high school prom. I'd always wondered how we looked: two tall Indian men, father and son, spinning around the living room of a reservation HUD house.

My father guided the wheelchair up the ramp. I wasn't nervous about its construction. I trusted Sweetwater and Wonder Horse. I knew the ramp would hold.

"Sweet and Wonder?" asked my father, using the nicknames only men of a certain generation were allowed to use.

"Yeah," I said. "But they got in a fight about Jesus. I don't think they're on speaking terms now."

"They're like an old married couple, enit?"

"They'll kiss and make up."

"They always do."

My mother had died ten years earlier from a brain tumor. She had been a librarian, a lover of books. By the end of her life, she could no longer speak, let alone read, so she had no last words from her death-bed, only the slow blinking of her eyes, and then the fading of the light behind them. It had been a quiet death for a woman with such a large vocabulary.

I followed my father and his chair into the house. He had not been here in some weeks and so was surprised to see the amount of home improvement I had done myself or had paid others to do. Or rather, he was surprised at the improvements he could see, since his vision was impaired by the blood that flowed from the broken veins in his eyes. The walls were painted a fresh white, a new carpet had replaced the twenty-five-year-old shag, and family photographs were fitted with new frames. Cosmetic changes, really, but my father acted as if I'd built him a mansion.

"You're good to me," he said. I didn't know if that was completely true, or if it had ever been true, even in part.

"You didn't have to do this," he said. "I'm not going to live long enough to get it ugly again."

"Hey," I said. "They always underestimate Indians. You're going to make it until next Christmas, at least. You eat better and you'll see Paul graduate high school."

Paul was my son. He lived with his Lummi Indian mother in Seattle, exactly two hundred and seventy-nine miles from my house in Spokane. She'd remarried a white man who made a lot more money than I did. He was a consultant for one thing or another—one of those jobs that only white guys seem to get. Consultant. He consulted. Others paid him to consult. They wanted to be consulted. He wanted to consult. All around me, white men were consulting other white men. My son lived with a consultor, or was it spelled differently? Did my son live with a consulter? The whole world could live in the space between that *o* and that *e*. My son lived in that space. My son asked another man for consultation. He was an Indian consultantee loved fiercely by a white consultant. Sure, my vocabulary was bitter (She'd chosen somebody over me!) but I was happy the white man, the step-father, was able to provide my son with a better life than I would have on my high school English teacher's salary. And I was happy that my son was living in Seattle, where twenty percent of the city was brown-skinned, instead of Spokane, where ninety-nine percent of the people were white. I'm not exactly racist. I like white people as a theory; I'm just not crazy about them in practice. But, all in all, ours was a good divorce. I still loved my ex-wife, without missing her or our marriage (I'm a liar), and spent every other weekend, all of the major holidays, and most of the minor ones, with the three of them in Seattle—all of us having decided to *make it work,* as the therapists had said. The nontraditional arrangement, this extended family, was strange when measured by white standards, but was very traditional by Indian standards. *What is an Indian?* Is it a child who can stroll unannounced through the front doors of seventeen different houses?

"How long before Paul graduates?" asked my father as we stood (I was the only one standing!) in our house. No, it wasn't my house anymore. Only my ghost lived there now.

"Nine months," I said. "In June."

"Six to five against me making it."

He always knew the odds. He'd always been a gambler and had lost more than one paycheck to the horses and the dogs and the Sonics and the Seahawks and the Mariners and the dice and the playing cards.

"I'll bet twenty bucks you make it," I said.

"I expect you to throw that Andrew Jackson in the coffin with me."

"I expect you to buy me lunch in July."

He wheeled himself into his bedroom at the back of the house. I hadn't changed anything about his personal space, knowing that he would have resented the invasion.

"What did you do in here?" he asked.

"Can't you tell?" I asked.

"Son, I'm mostly blind in one eye and I can't see much out of the other."

"Everything is the same, " I said (I lied) and wondered how long it would be before his vision left him forever.

His room had been the same for the last ten years, since my mother's death. (His wife! His wife! Of course, that's how he remembered her!) The same ratty chair, the same bookshelf overflowing with the same books, the same bed with the same two-by-fours holding it together. I'd been conceived in that bed, or so the legend goes. Of course, according to my father, I'd also been conceived in the front and/or backseat (and trunk!) of a 1965 Chevrolet Malibu; in a telephone booth in downtown Seattle; on the seventeenth floor of the Sheraton Hotel in Minneapolis; on the living room couch during halftime of a Duke–North Carolina basketball game; in a powwow tepee in Browning, Montana; and amid the broken eggs and expired milk of a 7-Eleven walk-in freezer in Phoenix, Arizona.

I missed my mother like crazy. During all of my childhood bedtimes, she'd read me books (Whitman! Dickinson!) I could not understand and would not understand until many years later.

What is an Indian? Is it a boy who can sing the body electric or a woman who could not stop for death?

My siblings, three brothers and two sisters, were scattered in the indigenous winds, all of them living on somebody else's reservation with lovers whose blood came from a dozen different tribes. I'd lost track of the number of nieces and nephews I had, but I didn't feel too guilty about that because I'm quite sure that my brothers had also lost track of the number of kids they'd helped conceive (the Fathers of our Country!).

Though I didn't see my siblings much, perhaps two or three times a year at family and tribal gatherings, we'd always been happy to see one another and had easily fallen back into our comfortable patterns: hugs, kisses, genial insults, then the stories about our mother, and finally the all-night games of Scrabble. None of us had ever found the need to chastise any of the others for our long absences from each other. We'd all pursued our very different versions of the American Dream (the Native American Dream!) and had all been successful to one degree or another. We were teacher, truck driver, logger, accountant, preacher, and guitar player. Our biggest success: we were all alive. Our biggest claim to fame: we were all sober.

In his bedroom, my father spun slow circles in his wheelchair. In his wallet, he kept photographs of all of his children, and pulled them out three or four times a day to examine them. He thought this small ceremony was a secret. Those photographs were wrinkled and faded with age and the touch of my father's hands.

"Look at me," he said as he spun in a figure eight. "I'm Mary Lou Retton."

"Ten, ten, ten, but the East German gives him a three," I said, reading the imaginary scores.

"Damn East Germans," said my father. He stopped spinning and tried to catch his breath.

"I'm an old man," he said.

"Hey, aren't you tired?" I asked.

"Yeah, I could sleep."

"You want to help me get you into bed?" I asked, carefully phrasing the question, setting down the pronouns in the most polite order. Of course, it was a rhetorical question. He couldn't have made it by himself but he didn't want to admit to his weakness by asking for help, and I didn't want to point out his weakness by helping him without asking first. The unasked question, the unspoken answer, and so we remained quiet men in a country of quiet men.

"I am tired," he said.

I picked him up, marveling again at how small he had become, and laid him down on his bed. I slid a pillow beneath his head and pulled a quilt over him. He looked up at me with his dark, Asian-shaped eyes. I'd inherited those eyes and their eccentric shapes. I wondered what else my father and I had constructed in our lives together. What skyscrapers, what houses, and what small rooms with uneven floors? I had never doubted his love for me, not once, and understood it to be enormous. I certainly loved him, but I didn't know what exact shapes our love took when we pulled it (tenderness, regret, anger, and hope) out of our bodies and offered it for public inspection, for careful forensics.

"Go to sleep," I whispered to my father. "I'll make you some soup when you wake up."

▲

I'd left the reservation when I was eighteen years old, leaving with the full intention of coming back after I'd finished college. I had never wanted to contribute to the brain drain, to be yet another of the best and brightest Indians to abandon his or her tribe to the Indian leaders who couldn't spell the word *sovereignty*. Yet no matter my idealistic notions, I have never again lived with my tribe. I left the reservation for the same reason a white kid leaves the cornfields of Iowa, or the coal mines of Pennsylvania, or the oil derricks of Texas: ambition. And I stayed away for the same reasons the white kids stayed away: more ambition. Don't get me wrong. I loved the reservation when I was a child and I suppose I love it now as an adult (I live only sixty-five miles away), but it's certainly a different sort of love. As an adult, I am fully conscious of the reservation's weaknesses, its inherent limitations (geographic, social, economic, and spiritual), but as a child I'd believed the reservation to be an endless, magical place.

When I was six years old, a bear came out of hibernation too early, climbed up on the roof of the Catholic Church, and promptly fell back asleep. In itself not an amazing thing, but what had amazed me then, and amazes me now, is that nobody, not one Spokane Indian, bothered that bear. Nobody called the police or the Forest Service. None of the Indian hunters took advantage of a defenseless animal, even those Indian hunters who'd always taken advantage of defenseless animals and humans. Hell, even the reservation dogs stopped barking whenever they strolled past the church. We all, dogs and Indians alike, just continued on with our lives, going to work or school, playing basketball and hide-and-seek, scratching at fleas, sleeping with other people's spouses, marking our territory, while that bear slept on.

During that brief and magical time, "How's the bear?" replaced "How are you doing?" as the standard greeting.

What is an Indian? Is it the lead actor in a miracle or the witness who remembers the miracle?

For three or four days, that bear (that Indian!) had slept, unmolested, dreaming his bear dreams, until the bright sun had disturbed him one sunrise. Bob May happened to be there with his camera and shot up a roll of film as the bear climbed down from the church, stretched his spine and legs, and then ambled off into the woods, never to be seen again.

But all of that was years ago, decades ago, long before I brought my father home from the hospital to die, before I left him alone in his bedroom where he dreamed his diabetic dreams.

What is an Indian? Is it a son who can stand in a doorway and watch his father sleep?

▲

Just after sundown, I woke my father from his nap, set him in his wheelchair, and rolled him into the kitchen.

"Do you remember that Catholic bear?" I asked him as we ate tomato soup at the table, which was really just a maple-wood door nailed to four two-by-sixes. The brass doorknob was still attached. The tomato soup was homemade, from my father's recipe. He'd once been the head chef at Ankeny's, the best restaurant in Spokane. I'd waited tables there one summer and made fifty bucks in tips every shift. Good money for an eighteen-year-old. Better yet, I'd lost my virginity on a cool July evening to a waitress named Carla, a white woman who was twenty years older. She'd always called me sweetheart and had let me sleep with her only once. Any more than that, she'd said, and you're going to fall in love with me, and then I'll just have to break your heart. I'd been grateful to her and told her so. I never saw her again after that summer, but I sent her Christmas cards for ten years, even though I'd never received a response, and only stopped when the last card had been returned with no forwarding address.

"The one that climbed on the church?" asked my father, remembering. His hand trembled as he lifted his spoon to his lips. He'd slept for three hours but he still looked exhausted.

"Yeah, what do you think happened to it?" I asked.

"It owns a small auto shop in beautiful Edmonton, British Columbia."

"Bear's Repairs?"

"Exactly."

We laughed together at our silly joke, until he coughed and gagged. My father, once a handsome man who'd worn string ties and fedoras, was now an old man, a tattered bathrobe on a stick.

"Excuse me," he said, strangely polite, as he spat into his cup.

We ate without further conversation. What was there to say? He slurped his soup, a culinary habit that had irritated me throughout our lives together, but I didn't mind it at all as we shared that particular meal.

"When are you heading back to Spokane?" he asked after he finished eating and pushed away his empty bowl.

"I'm not."

"Don't you have to teach?"

"I took a leave of absence. I think the Catholic teenagers of Spokane, Washington, can diagram sentences and misread *To Kill a Mockingbird* without me."

"Are you sure about that, Atticus?"

"Positive."

He picked at his teeth with his tongue. He was thinking hard.

"What are you going to do about money?" he asked.

"I've got some saved up," I said. Of course, in my economic dictionary, I'd discovered *some* meant *very little*. I had three thousand dollars in savings and maybe five hundred in checking. I'd been hoping it would last six months, or until my father died. By the light in his eyes, I knew he was guessing at exactly how much I'd saved and also wondering if it would last. He carried a tiny life insurance policy that would pay for the cost of his burial.

"It's you and me, then," he said.

"Yes."

He wouldn't look at me.

"What do you think they did with them?"

"With what?"

"My feet," he said. We both looked down at his legs, at the bandaged stumps where his feet used to be.

"I think they burn them," I said.

▲

What is an Indian?

That's what the professor wrote on the chalkboard three minutes into the first class of my freshman year at Washington State University.

What is an Indian?

The professor's name was Dr. Lawrence Crowell (don't forget the doctorate!) and he was, according to his vita, a Cherokee-Choctaw-Seminole-Irish-Russian Indian from Hot Springs, Kentucky, or some such place.

"What is an Indian?" asked Dr. Crowell. He paced around the small room—there were twenty of us terrified freshmen—and looked each of us in the eyes. He was a small man, barely over five feet tall, with gray eyes and grayer hair.

"What is an Indian?" he asked me as he stood above me. I suppose he might have been trying to *tower* over me, but I was nearly as tall as he was even while sitting down, so that bit of body language failed to translate in his favor.

"Are you an Indian?" he asked me.

Of course I was. (Jesus, my black hair hung down past my ass and I was dark as a pecan!) I'd grown up on my reservation with my tribe.

I understood most of the Spokane language, though I'd always spoken it like a Jesuit priest. Hell, I'd been in three car wrecks! And most important, every member of the Spokane Tribe of Indians could tell you the exact place and time where I'd lost my virginity. Why? Because I'd told each and every one of them. I mean, I knew the real names, nicknames, and secret names of every dog that had lived on my reservation during the last twenty years.

"Yeah, I'm Indian," I said.

"What kind?" asked Dr. Crowell.

"Spokane."

"And that's all you are?"

"Yeah."

"Your mother is Spokane?"

"Full-blood."

"And your father as well?"

"Full-blood."

"Really? Isn't that rare for your tribe? I thought the Spokanes were very mixed."

"Well, my dad once tried to make it with a Cherokee-Choctaw-Seminole-Irish-Russian, but poor guy, he just couldn't get it up."

My classmates laughed.

"You know," I added. "My momma always used to tell me, those mixed-blood Indians, they just ain't sexy enough."

My classmates laughed even louder.

"Get out of my classroom," Dr. Crowell said to me. "And don't come back until you can show me some respect. I am your elder."

"Yes, sir," I said and left the room.

Of course, my mother's opinion about the general desirability of mixed-blood Indians had been spoken mostly in jest. She had always been a funny woman.

"I mean, there's so many sexy white guys in the world," my mother had once told me. "There are white guys who like being white, and what's not to like? They own everything. So, if you get the chance to sleep with a real white guy, especially one of them with a British accent or something, or Paul Newman or Steve McQueen, then why are you going to waste your time on some white guy who says he's part Indian? Jeez, if I wanted to sleep with part-Indians, then I could do that at every powwow. Hell, I could get an orgy going with eight or nine of those Cherokees and maybe, just maybe, they would all add up to one real Indian."

"And besides all that, listen to me, son," she'd continued. "If your whole mission in life is to jump an Indian, then why not jump the Indian with the most Indian going on inside of him? And honey, believe me when I say that every last inch of your daddy is Indian."

She'd laughed then and hugged me close. She'd always loved to talk nasty. For her, the telling of a dirty joke had always been the most traditional and sacred portion of any conversation.

"If I'm going after a penis only because it's Indian," my mother had said, "then it better be a one-hundred-percent-guaranteed, American Indian, aboriginal, First Nations, indigenous penis. Hey, I don't want to get into some taste test, and realize one of these penises is Coke and the other one is Pepsi."

Tears had rolled down her face as she'd laughed. At that moment, I loved her so much that I could barely breathe. I was twelve years old and she was teaching me about sex and all of its complications.

Her best piece of sexual advice: "Son, if you're going to marry a white woman, then marry a rich one, because those white-trash women are just Indians with bad haircuts."

The last thing she ever said to me: "Don't take any shit from anybody."

Of course, my mother would have felt only contempt for a man like Dr. Lawrence Crowell, not because he was a white man who wanted to be Indian (God! When it came right down to it, Indian was the best thing to be!), but because he thought he was entitled to tell other Indians what it meant to be Indian.

What is an Indian? Is it a son who brings his father to school as show-and-tell?

"Excuse me, sir," Crowell said to my father as we both walked into the room. "Are you in my class?"

"Sweetheart," said my father. "You're in my class now."

After that, I didn't say a word. I didn't need to say a word. My father sat at a desk, pulled out his false teeth, tucked them into his pants pocket, and smiled his black-hole smile the whole time. My father also wore a U.S. Army T-shirt that said *Kill 'em all and let God sort 'em out.* Of course, my father had never actually served in the military (He was a pacifist!) but he knew how to wield the idea of a gun.

"What is an Indian?" Crowell asked as he stood in front of the class-room.

My father raised his left hand.

"Anybody?" asked the professor.

With his hand high above his head, my father stood from his chair.

"Anybody?"

My father dropped his hand, walked up to the front, and stood directly in front of Crowell.

"Sir," he said to my father. "I'm going to have to ask you to leave."

"Are you an Indian?"

"Are you?"

"Yes."

"So am I."

"I don't know," said my father. "Now, you may have some Indian blood. I can see a little bit of that aboriginal bone structure in your face, but you ain't Indian. No. You might even hang out with some Indians. Maybe even get a little of the ha-ha when one of the women is feeling sorry for you. But you ain't Indian. No. You might be a Native American but you sure as hell ain't Indian."

"Listen, I don't have to take this from you. Do you want me to call security?"

"By the time security arrived, I could carefully insert your right foot deep into your own rectum."

I hid my face and stifled my laughter. My father hadn't been in a fistfight since sixth grade and she'd beaten the crap out of him.

"Are you an Indian?" my father asked again.

"I was at Alcatraz during the occupation."

"That was, what, November '69?"

"Yeah, I was in charge of communications. How about you?"

"I took my wife and kids to the Pacific Ocean, just off Neah Bay. Most beautiful place in the world."

Though I'd been only three years old at the time, I remembered brief images of the water, the whales, and the Makah Indians who lived there in Neah Bay, or perhaps I had only stolen my memories, my images, from my father's stories. In hearing his stories a thousand times over the years, had I unconsciously memorized them, had I colonized them and pretended they were mine? One theory: we can fool ourselves into believing any sermon if we repeat it enough times. Proof of theory: the number of times in his life the average human whispers *Amen*. What I know: I'm a liar. What I remember or imagine I remember: we stayed in Neah Bay during the off-season, so there were very few tourists, though tourists had rarely visited Neah Bay before or since that time, not until the Makahs had decided to resume their tradition of hunting whales. The tourists came because they wanted to see the blood. Everybody, white and Indian alike, wanted to see the blood.

What is an Indian? Is it a man with a spear in his hands?

"What about Wounded Knee?" Crowell asked my father. "I was at Wounded Knee. Where were you?"

"I was teaching my son here how to ride his bike. Took forever. And when he finally did it, man, I cried like a baby, I was so proud."

"What kind of Indian are you? You weren't part of the revolution."

"I'm a man who keeps promises."

It was mostly true. My father had kept most of his promises, or had tried to keep all of his promises, except this one: he never stopped eating sugar.

▲

After we shared that dinner of homemade tomato soup, my father slept in his bed while I sat awake in the living room and watched the white noise of the television. My father's kidneys and liver were beginning to shut down. *Shut down.* So mechanical. At that moment, if I had closed my eyes, I could have heard the high-pitched whine of my father's engine (it was working too hard!) and the shudder of his chassis. In his sleep, he was climbing a hill (downshifting all the way!) and might not make it over the top.

At three that morning, I heard my father coughing, and then I heard him retching, gagging. I raced into his room, flipped on the light, and discovered him drenched in what I thought was blood.

"It's the soup, it's just the soup," he said and laughed at the fear in my face. "I threw up the soup. It's tomatoes, the tomatoes."

I undressed him and washed his naked body. His skin had once been dark and taut, but it had grown pale and loose.

"You know how to get rid of tomato stains?" he asked.

"With carbonated water," I said.

"Yeah, but how do you get rid of carbonated-water stains?"

I washed his belly, washed the skin that was blue with cold and a dozen tattoos. I washed his arms and hands. I washed his legs and penis.

"You shouldn't have to do this," he said, his voice cracking. "You're not a nurse."

What is an Indian? Is it a son who had always known where his father kept his clothes in neat military stacks?

I pulled a T-shirt over my father's head. I slipped a pair of boxer shorts over his bandaged legs and up around his waist.

"How's the bear?" I asked him, and he laughed until he gagged again, but there was nothing left in his stomach for him to lose. He was still laughing when I switched off the light, lay down beside him, and pulled the old quilt over us.

"You remember when I first made the tomato soup?" he asked me.

"Yeah, that summer at Ankeny's."

"The summer of Carla, as I recall."

"I didn't know you knew about her."

"Jeez, you told everybody. That's why she wouldn't do it with you anymore. You hurt her feelings. You should have kept your mouth shut."

"I had no idea."

I wondered what would happen if I saw her again. Would she remember me with fondness or with regret?

"Before I threw up my soup, I was dreaming," he said.

"About what?"

"I was dreaming there was a knock on the door and I got up and walked over there. I wasn't walking on my stumps or anything. I was just sort of floating. And the knocking on the door was getting louder and louder. And I was getting mad, you know?"

I knew.

"And then I open up the door," continued my father. "And I'm ready to yell, ready to shout, what the hell you want, right? But I don't see anybody right away, until I look down, and there they are."

"Your feet."

"My feet."

"Wow."

"Wow, enit? Exactly. Wow. There's my feet, my bare-ass feet just standing there on the porch."

"They talked, enit?"

"Damn right, they talked. These little mouths opened up on the big toes, like some crazy little duet, and sang in Spanish."

"Do you speak Spanish?"

"No, but they kept singing about Mexico."

"You ever been to Mexico?"

"No. Never even been to California."

I thought about my father's opportunities and his failures, about the man he should have been and the man he had become. *What is an Indian?* Is it a man with a good memory? I thought about the pieces of my father—his children and grandchildren, his old shoes and unfinished novels—scattered all over the country. He was a man orphaned at six by his father's soldierly death in Paris, France, and, three months later, by his mother's cancerous fall in Spokane, Washington. I thought about my mother's funeral and how my father had climbed into the coffin with her and how we, the stronger and weaker men of the family, had to pull him out screaming and kicking. I wondered if there was some kind of vestigial organ inside all of us that collected and stored our grief.

"Well, then, damn it," I said. "We're going to Mexico."

▲

Two hours later, my father and I sat (he couldn't do anything but sit!) in Wonder Horse's garage, which was really a converted old barn, while Wonder Horse and Sweetwater, reunited for this particular occasion, gave my battered van a quick tune-up.

"Hey," said Wonder Horse. "You've been treating this van like it was a white man. It's all messed up."

Sweetwater, having returned to his usual and accustomed silence, nodded his head in agreement.

"You see," continued Wonder Horse. "You have to treat your car with love. And I don't mean love of an object. You see, that's just wrong. That's materialism. You have to love your car like it's a sentient being, like it can love you back. Now, that's some deep-down agape love. And you want to know why you should love your car like it can love you back?"

"Why?" asked my father and I simultaneously.

"Because it shows faith," said Wonder Horse. "And that's the best thing we Indians have left."

Sweetwater pointed at Wonder Horse—a gesture of agreement, of affirmation, of *faith*.

I looked around Wonder Horse's garage, at the dozens of cars and pieces of cars strewn about. Most of them would never run again and served only as depositories for spare parts.

"What about all of these cars?" I asked. "They don't look so well loved."

"These selfless automobiles are organ donors," said Wonder Horse. "And there's no greater act of faith than that."

"I'm an organ donor," I said. "Says so right on my driver's license."

"That just means you're a potential organ donor," said Wonder

Horse. "Ain't nothing wrong with potential, but it ain't real until it's real."

"Well, you're potentially an asshole," I said. "With a whole lot of potential to get wider and wider."

The four of us, we all laughed; we were Indian men enjoying one another's company. It happens all the time.

"I mean," said Wonder Horse. "What would you be willing to give up to ensure somebody else's happiness?"

"That's a big question," said my father.

"Tell me a big answer," said Wonder Horse, and then he asked me this: "I mean, if you could give up your feet, would you give them to your father?"

"Oh, jeez," said my father before I could answer. "Now we're talking about potential. What kind of goofy operation would that be? I mean, if you could really do that, you wouldn't take away living people's feet, enit? You'd transplant dead people's feet."

"That's disgusting," said Sweetwater, then returned to his silence.

"Damn right, it's disgusting," said my father. "I mean, who's to guarantee I'd get Indian feet? What if I got white feet? I'd be an Indian guy walking around on some white guy's feet."

"Hey, Long John Silver," said Wonder Horse. "That would mean your feet would have a job, but you'd be unemployed."

We all laughed again. We could afford to laugh because all four of us carried money in our wallets.

"But, come on," Wonder Horse said to me. "Enough of the jokes. Would you give up your feet for your father?"

I looked at my father. He would be dead soon, maybe tomorrow, perhaps by the first snowfall, certainly by this time next year. I asked myself this: If I could take the days and years I had left to live, all of my remaining time, then divide that number by two, and give half of my life expectancy to my father, thereby extending his time on the planet, would I do it?

No, I thought. *No, no, of course not.*

"I tell you what I'd do," I said. "I'd give up one of my feet."

"Wouldn't you be the matching pair?" asked Wonder Horse and ducked his head into the engine of my van. I saw us: two Indian men holding each other up, trying to maintain their collective balance.

"No," I said. "We'd be opposites."

▲

Beginning in Wellpinit, Washington, my father and I traveled through Little Falls, Reardan, Davenport, Harrington, Downs, Ritzville, Lind, Connell, Pasco, Burbank, Attalia, Wallula, then across the border into Cold Springs, Oregon, and on through Hermiston, Stanfield, Pendleton, Pilot Rock, Nye, Battle Mountain, Dale, Long Creek, Fox, Beech Creek, Mt. Vernon, Canyon City, Seneca, Silvies, Burns, Riley, Wagonfire, Valley Falls, Lakeview, New Pine Creek, then across another border into Willow Ranch, California, and on through Davis Creek, Alturas, Likely, Madeline, Termo, Ravendale, Litchfield, Standish, Butingville, Milford, Doyle, Constantina, Hallelujah Junction, and then into Reno, Nevada.

From Reno, my father and I traveled to Carson City, Glenbrook, Zephyr Cove, Stateline, and then into Echo Summit, California, followed by Twin Bridges, Kyburz, Riverton, Pacific House, Diamond Springs, Plymouth, Drytown, 10 City, Jackson, San Andreas, Angels Camp, Tuttletown, Jamestown, Chinese Camp, Coulterville, Bear Valley, Mt. Bullion, Mariposa, Catheys Valley, Planada, Tuttle, Merced, El Nido, Red Top, Chowchill, Fairmead, Berenda, Madera, Herndon, Fresno, Easton, Hub, Armona, Stratford, Kettleman

City, Devils Den, Blackwells Corner, McKittrick, Derby Acres, Fellows, Taft, Maricopa, Venucopa, Frazier Park, Forman, Pear Blossom, Littlerock, San Bernardino, Redlands, Beaumont, San Jacinto, Aquanga, Warner Springs, Santa Ysabel, Julian, Guatay, Boulevard, Campo, Potrero, and finally, just after sunrise, we arrived in Tecate, California.

Of course this was just the itinerary I had planned before our departure. Did we truly follow it? Do you think we had enough time?

▲

Last Christmas, I woke up in my ex-wife's house (God! She might have screwed her husband while I was sleeping just a dozen feet away!) and wondered if my son understood his own life, if he realized how privileged he was. But Paul wasn't privileged because there were dozens of presents beneath the tree. (that was just evidence of his parents' materialism, and not of what Wonder Horse would call deep-down agape love!) No, my son was privileged because his stepfather was a good man. It pained me to know that; it pained me to wake up on the floor of that good man's house while he woke up with the woman who was the best part of my past tense.

I didn't love her anymore, not like I did (another lie), but I wondered what would happen if you let the archaeologists dig into my buried temples. What artifacts would they bring to the surface? What would those recovered cups and tools mean to me then? What would be redeemed, remembered, reborn?

That last Christmas, I walked into the kitchen and made coffee, a simple ceremony that white people perform just as well and as often as Indians. I poured three cups and carried them upstairs. *What is an Indian?* Is it a man with waiting experience, a man who can carry ten cups at the same time, one looped in the hook of each finger and both thumbs? I knocked on their door (the ex-wife and her new husband) and waited for them to open it. Of course, I was stepping across boundaries. What if they had been making love at that precise moment? What if my ex-wife had been forced to push her husband (and his penis!) away from her and rush to the door? What if she'd appeared to me with flushed cheeks, racing heart, and wild hair? What if she had smelled like sex?

Instead, he opened the door, saw the coffee in my hands, and smiled.

"Oh, how nice," he said and meant it. He took their coffees inside (I could hear the surprised murmur of her voice!) and then came back to me.

"We'll be down in a few minutes," he said. "I'm sure Paul is waiting for us."

"Oh, no, he's still asleep," I said. Since birth, Paul had been able to sleep twelve or thirteen hours at a stretch, refusing to wake early even at Christmas. In this way, I felt I knew my son better than anybody else.

"Paul will be asleep when Jesus comes back," said the stepfather. We both knew my son (our son?) and kept his secrets; we both loved him. *What is an Indian?* Is it a man who can share his son and his wife? I asked myself this: Would I take them back, would I break this good man's heart, destroy his life, if I could be married again to this woman, if I could wake up every morning in the same house with this child?

Of course, of course I would break this white man's heart. I would leave him alone in a cold house with an empty bank account and a one-bullet pistol in his hand.

"Merry Christmas," said the stepfather.

"Yes," I said and turned to leave, but the stepfather stopped me with a hand on my shoulder. Then he hugged me (Tightly! Chest to chest! Belly to belly!) and I hugged him back.

"Thank you for being kind to me," he said. "I know it could be otherwise."

I didn't know what to say.

The stepfather held me at arm's length. His eyes were blue.

"You're a good man," he said to me.

▲

South of Tecate, California, the van broke down. Then, five minutes later, north of Tecate, Mexico, my father's wheelchair broke down.

We stood (I was the only one standing!) on the hot pavement in the bright sun.

"We almost made it," said my father.

"Somebody will pick us up," I said.

"Would you pick us up?"

"Two brown guys, one in a wheelchair? I think the immigration cops might be picking us up."

"Well, then, maybe they'll think we're illegal aliens and deport us."

"That would be one hell of an ironic way to get into Mexico."

I wanted to ask my father about his regrets. I wanted to ask him what was the worst thing he'd ever done. His greatest sin. I wanted to ask him if there was any reason why the Catholic Church would consider him for sainthood. I wanted to open up his dictionary and find the definitions for faith, hope, goodness, sadness, tomato, son, mother, husband, virginity, Jesus, wood, sacrifice, pain, foot, wife, thumb, hand, bread, and sex.

"Do you believe in God?" I asked my father.

"God has lots of potential," he said.

"When you pray," I asked him. "What do you pray about?"

"That's none of your business," he said.

We laughed. We waited for hours for somebody to help us. *What is an Indian?* I lifted my father and carried him across every border.